A Shackleford Victory: A Romantic Comedy

The Dartmouth Diaries Book Six

Beverley Watts

BaR Publishing

Copyright © 2024 BaR Publishing

BaR Publishing Copyright © 2024 BaR Publishing. All rights reserved. No part of this publication may be reproduced, stored or transmitted in any form or by any means, electronic, mechanical, photocopying, recording, scanning or otherwise without written permission from the publisher.

It is illegal to copy this book, post it to a website, or distribute it by any other means without permission.

This novel is entirely a work of fiction. The names, characters and incidents portrayed in it are the work of the author's imagination. Any resemblance to actual persons, living or dead, events or localities is entirely coincidental.

BaR Publishing has no responsibility for the persistence or accuracy of URL's for external or third party Internet Websites referred to in this publication and does not guarantee that any content on such Websites is, or will remain, accurate or appropriate.

Designations used by companies to distinguish their products are often claimed as trademarks. All brand names and product names used in this book and on its cover are trade names, service marks, trademarks and registered trademarks of their respective owners. The publishers and the book are not associated with any product or vendor mentioned in this book. None of the companies referenced within the book have endorsed the book.

Cover design by Berni Stevens at bernistevenscoverdesign.com

Contents

Title Page
Copyright
Introduction
Prologue

Chapter One	1
Chapter Two	8
Chapter Three	16
Chapter Four	24
Chapter Five	33
Chapter Six	44
Chapter Seven	52
Chapter Eight	61
Chapter Nine	69
Chapter Ten	78
Chapter Eleven	86
Chapter Twelve	93
Chapter Thirteen	103
Chapter Fourteen	112
Chapter Fifteen	121
Chapter Sixteen	130

Chapter Seventeen	139
Chapter Eighteen	146
Chapter Nineteen	156
Chapter Twenty	165
Chapter Twenty-One	175
Chapter Twenty-Two	184
Chapter Twenty-Three	194
Chapter Twenty-Four	205
Chapter Twenty-Five	215
Author's Notes	219
Keeping in Touch	221
Grace	222
Books Available on Amazon	228
About The Author	231

Introduction

After much careful thought, I have included a Prologue to *A Shackleford Victory* which some of you may already have read. It was previously offered as a free short story entitled *A Potted Shackleford History*.

I decided to include it as it's actually quite important to the plot of *A Shackleford Victory*, and since the short story was only offered in eBook format, many of you may not have had the opportunity to read it.

If you have actually read *A Potted Shackleford History* and don't feel as though you need a refresher, then feel free to skip the Prologue and go straight to Chapter One.

Prologue

Tory

I really can't believe the only reason I discovered the existence of an uncle and a cousin was due to my father's lifelong passion for interfering. If he hadn't been sticking his nose where he shouldn't (again) I truly believe he would never actually have told me he had a brother.

To give him the benefit of the doubt, he might well have considered it inconsequential as they hadn't seen each other for so long. But to me, as an only child, it was anything but. I mean, I know just how lucky I am. Kit and Freddy have been my best friends since forever and now of course I have the two loves of my life – Noah and Isaac. Okay, three, if I count Dotty …

So, really, it shouldn't matter at all. But for some reason it does.

When I broached the subject to Noah, he came up with the eminently sensible advice of simply talking to my dad to see if there are any other skeletons lurking in our cupboard.

Not that my uncle and cousin are *skeletons* as such. But, knowing Admiral Charles Shackleford, master of all things slippery and evasive, it's perfectly possible that there are a whole pile of bones just waiting to be unearthed in our family history. It's getting my father to talk about them that's the challenge.

With Christmas less than a week away, Noah has splashed out on a limousine and gone up to Heathrow to meet his sister Kim and her family, taking Isaac with him. After our err… unique

Thanksgiving dinner this year, I have wisely decided to leave the cooking of the Christmas Day feast to Kim, who aside from being drop dead gorgeous, (she is Noah's sister after all) is also a first-rate cook. I'm not proud...

The house is decorated within in an inch of its life and tonight's supper will be the usual M&S picky bits as I'm sure they will have spent ten or so hours eating and drinking on the plane, so won't want to eat a large meal. That's my excuse and I'm sticking with it. In fairness, having tried absolutely everything in Marks and Spencer's deli counter, I am an expert at choosing which picky bits go together and which to avoid. You might not think so, but it's actually quite a challenge. In fact, I'm thinking of writing a book.

Anyway, I digress. The fact is that *everything* is ready for our guests' arrival. I am currently child free, so I finally decide to take the bull by the horns and head over to the Admiralty to ask my father what else I might be missing. Wisely I first pick up the phone to speak with Mabel to make sure that my father doesn't do a runner before I get there. As it's only ten in the morning, he can't use the excuse that he's meeting Jimmy at the *Ship*.

A mere fifteen minutes later, Dotty and I pull up outside the Admiralty. It's not actually raining for a change, and I was tempted to walk over, but doing so would cut down the amount of time I could keep my father cornered for. *And* as I may never get another chance...

With Dotty capering around my feet, clearly ecstatic at the thought of seeing Pickles, I press the buzzer at the gate.

'WHATEVER YOU'RE PEDDLING, I'M NOT BLOODY INTERESTED.'

I can't help but jump. Despite having had both the gate and the buzzer since *The Bridegroom* was filmed in his house, my father has never gotten the hang of the idea that he can actually speak normally through it. 'DAD, IT'S ME, TORY.' So why the bloody hell am I shouting back? Instinctive reaction. I suppose. I grit my teeth.

'VICTORY? WHAT THE BOLLOCKING HELL ARE YOU DOING HERE? IT'S NOT CHRISTMAS DAY FOR ANOTHER WEEK.'

'JUST OPEN THE GATE, DAD,' I yell in frustration. Good start.

Seconds later the gate clicks, and I push it open. Seriously, can a daughter not pay a visit to her father without an interrogation? Then I think about the grilling I'm about to put my cantankerous parent through and decide it might be wise to rein in my temper. Past experience tells me I'll need to tread carefully. And besides, I've never bested my father in a slanging match yet…

'Cup of tea, Tory?' Mabel asks when I'm cosily ensconced in the kitchen. 'I've made some shortbread from Aileen's recipe, so I'd like your opinion.'

'Mmm, lovely,' I enthuse. Kit and Jason's housekeeper, Aileen is a legend when it comes to shortbread. I take a large bite and wince. Mabel clearly is not. Still, I crunch determinedly, wondering if I've still got all my teeth and surreptitiously slip the last two bits to Dotty and Pickles who are clearly not quite so dentally challenged.

'So what's all this about, Victory?' my father hmphs, sitting down opposite me. He helps himself to a large piece of shortbread. From the sound of his vigorous chomping, his teeth are more at the Pickles end of the scale than mine.

Mabel comes to the table with a pot of tea while I gather my thoughts, wondering how best to broach the subject. There are some things my father will willingly talk about until his listener keels over. The Royal Navy for one. But getting him to talk about a subject he's either not interested in or being cagey about. Well, put it this way, waxing an orangutan would probably be easier.

And in this case, it could well be both.

I take a sip of my tea, wishing it was something stronger. 'Well,' I begin. 'The thing is ... I was wondering whether...'

'Spit it out Victory, you're acting like a fart in a bloody colander.' As I glare at my father's frowning face, I suddenly realise his irritable comment is actually covering up his apprehension. For some reason, this makes me feel much better about the whole thing. I'm ashamed to say I do enjoy the odd occasion I manage to make him uncomfortable. It makes up for all the times I've wanted to throw myself in the Dart after one of his priceless witticisms.

'I want you to tell me everything you know about our family history,' I declare, daring him to argue. 'And don't tell me you've got no idea. We both know that's complete bollocks.'

He stares at me in surprise. Whatever he was expecting me to say, it wasn't that. My stomach roils uncomfortably. Did I really think it was only our family history I was clueless about?

'Why, what else were you expecting me to ask about?' I challenge.

He takes another bite of his shortbread, his eyes now turning shifty. I've seen that look on him a thousand times. 'I never know what's about to come out of your mouth,' he responds with a calculated shrug. 'It was the same with your mother.'

I'm about to say, 'well, I know where I get it from,' but his comment about my mother takes the wind out of my sails. I wonder how on earth she put up with him.

'How come you never told me about Bill?' I ask instead.

He shrugs, this time in genuine bafflement. 'Never really thought about him. After the accident, Bill went to live with our grandparents on our mother's side in Nottingham, while I came here to live with Grandpa Shackleford. Your mother only met Bill once and that was at our wedding.' He squirms uncomfortably. 'Our second, *real* wedding.'

'How old were you when your parents died?' I ask, wondering if he's ever actually told me.

'Fourteen, give or take. Our Bill was nearly seventeen which is why he ended up in Nottingham I reckon. Back in the day, someone told him there were five women to every man up there.' He gives a small chuckle. 'He thought he'd have a better chance of finding someone to shack up with. Even then he was as boring as a wet weekend in bloody Wigan. He could take two bollocking hours to tell you he was a man of few words.'

'What exactly happened to your mother and father?' I ask, thinking I have to start somewhere.

He frowns and for a second I think he's not going to respond, but at length he gives a sigh and answers. 'My father was one of those damn pickle jar officers. He could tell you the square root of a pickle jar lid to three decimal places but could never get the bollocking thing off. He was on leave in Borneo. Sent for my mother and decided to take her for a romantic picnic on a secluded beach. You'd think, being an officer in the Navy that he'd at least know his bloody tides. But as I say, pickle jar. And to top it off, neither of them could swim.' He shrugs and I eye him carefully, wondering if losing his parents to such a tragedy could have contributed to his devil may care attitude to life. Likely, he doesn't even know himself.

'So what about my great grandparents then?' I ask instead. He looks at me irritably, then creases his brow thoughtfully. 'If you're not going to let the bloody matter drop,' he declares after a few seconds, 'there's a family bible in the attic. Not sure how far it goes back, but we can have a shufti if you want.'

'That would be brilliant, dad. I'd love to take a look.' He eyes me suspiciously as though suspecting an ulterior motive. Though what he thinks that could possibly be is beyond me. Maybe he thinks I'm hoping to discover we're not really related…

He climbs off his chair and goes to a large key rack in the corner of the kitchen. After a few seconds, he lifts a huge brass key from one of the hooks. 'Come on then,' he comments gruffly, heading out of the kitchen door.

I look down at Dotty. 'Stay with Aunty Mabel and Pickles,' I order. She wags her tail enthusiastically, clearly having no intention of moving more than a couple of feet from the concrete shortbread.

'Be careful dears,' calls Mabel after us. 'And don't bring any creepy crawlies back down with you.'

I follow my father into what looks like a large cupboard tucked away in a small inner hall next to what dad calls his boot room. I haven't been up into the attic for years and I'm really quite excited. I had no idea we were in possession of a family bible.

Even with the light on, the stairs are hard to negotiate, being both narrow and steep, and as my father puffs and pants up every step, I warn him to take his time. Some of my enthusiasm wears off as I envisage what would happen if he fell backwards. I've no idea what Noah would put in the obituary…

He reaches the attic door without incident however, and I hover halfway up as he fumbles to put the key in the lock. Seconds later, he pushes open the door with a grunt and steps inside. Hurriedly I climb after him and by the time I reach the main attic, he's turned on a light – a single bare bulb which floods the immediate area with a glaring light. The only other illumination comes from a dormer window set in the sloping roof.

I look around with interest. There is quite a lot of old furniture including a desk and a couple of ancient wingback chairs. I can't help but wonder how anyone got them up here. Beyond the bulb's reach, the shadows swallow other smaller items of furniture, which given Mabel's comment about creepy crawlies,

I'm in no hurry to investigate.

I look over at my father who is busy examining a pile of books on the old desk. With a muttered, 'Where the bollocking hell did I put it?' he steps to the side and bends down, searching through an even bigger pile. 'Here it is,' he mutters eventually, holding a large book to the light. Bloody hell, it's heavy,' he grumbles. 'Comes from the days when they took their God walloping seriously, I expect.'

Grunting, he sits down in one of the wingback chairs. Excitedly, I drag the second chair next to him. 'What does it say?' I ask eagerly. He doesn't answer, being busy brushing the cobwebs and dust from the front of the book, revealing a deep reddish-brown cover embossed with gold lettering. 'Have you ever looked inside before?' I query, trying to peer over his shoulder.

'Can't say that I have,' he frowns. 'Grandpa Shackleford told me it was here before he popped his clogs, but somehow I never got around to having a shufti.' Eyes creased in thought, he sits back, the huge bible resting unopened on his knee.

'Come to think of it, he did mention that he thought our family was named in old William's Doomsday Book. Reckoned we came over from Normandy with the Conqueror. Baron de Shackle, I think Grandpa said the bloke's name was. Don't know how the family ended up with the *ford* on the end. And, anyway how true it is, is anybody's guess.' He lays his hand down on the unopened book. 'And it's not likely to be in here, this bible's not that old'

'Hard to believe there might have been a Shackleford at the Battle of Hastings,' I breathe, impressed. Just wait until I tell Noah. I fight the urge to tell him to just open the bloody book, despite my eagerness to know what's inside. It isn't often I have any alone time with my father and for some bizarre reason I want to extend it as long as possible.

'You never know,' he comments jovially as he finally opens the

XIII

first page, 'we might have a title in the family.'

'Now, where did I put me specs,' he mutters, tapping round his pockets. 'Ah, here they are.' I tilt my head to look at the revealed page while he puts his glasses on, but all that appears to be written apart from the title is a name which I can't quite see from my seat.

'Reverend Augustus Shackleford,' he reads. 'Bollocking hell, I had no idea we had a God Botherer in the family. The bible must have belonged to him. I wonder when he was born?' He turns the page to reveal a long-handwritten list of names and dates. Bending his head, he frowns.

'What does it say?' I ask, unable to stay silent any longer.

'Well it seems our vicar was born in 1761. Let me see…' He pauses, tracing his finger down the page. 'Apparently he was the vicar of the parish of Blackmore in South Devonshire.'

'Where's that?' I frown, racking my brains. Geography is definitely not one of my strong points. My father shrugs.

'I reckon it might be Totnes way. Never been.' He looks back down at the book. 'It says here he married on … bloody hell, poor bugger had three wives. Glutton for punishment.' My father looks over at me, his face displaying a reluctant interest. 'Seems the first two ended up juggling halos.'

'Well, he must have had at least one son,' I comment, 'seeing as the name didn't die out with him.' My father looks back down.

'He did. He had one son by the name of Anthony.' He gives a short chuckle. 'Had a bit of a bloody cake and arse party before the lad was born though. Says here he had eight daughters. No wonder he got through three bollocking wives.'

'Does it give the daughters' names?' I breathe. He nods. 'The eldest was Grace, then came Temperance … and blimey … twins.

They were called Hope and Faith. After that there was Patience, and, hang on a minute, *another* set of twins called Charity and Chastity.' He looks over at me, eyebrows raised. 'Our Reverend was definitely looking for a free pass upstairs when he named 'em. Mind you, the youngest daughter was called Prudence. Bit like shutting the gate after the horse has bolted if you ask me.' He squints down at the dates. 'That's eight daughters in twenty years.' He shakes his head, grimacing in sympathy.

'So, when was Anthony born?' I question with a frown. 'The Reverend must have been getting on a bit.'

'Says Anthony Augustus Shackleford was born on the fifth day of December in the year of our Lord eighteen hundred and two.'

'I bet they brought out the Champagne,' I grin. 'Does it say who his mother was?'

'It just mentions her as Agnes Shackleford. Nothing about her maiden name. Hope she's got no connection to our Bill's Agnes, especially in the looks department. Still, likely our Reverend wasn't quite so fussy by the time he got to number three.'

'So, what about the eight daughters? Anything about who they married?'

My father shakes his head. 'They probably all ended up with farmers and the like. I doubt very much they'd have aspired any higher than that.' I nod in disappointment. Clearly the female side of the family wasn't deemed interesting enough to record. I couldn't help feeling sad for them all. They must have lived very dreary lives.

'What about Anthony then?' I ask, now thoroughly engrossed.

'Looks like he got married.' My father frowns. 'But I can't quite see the name of whoever it was he got hitched to. There's a splodge of ink covering it.'

'Does it mention what he did for a living? I thought eldest sons usually followed in their father's footsteps.'

'The splodge is covering that bit as well,' he grumbles. 'Looks like he definitely had more than one ankle biter with whoever he got leg shackled to though. There's no mention of another wife.'

I peer round his shoulder as he continues. 'He had two daughters. Charlotte, born in 1829 and Constance, born in 1832.'

'I don't suppose we know what happened to them?' I query with a sigh. My father shakes his head.

'Looks like he just had the one son. Henry Augustus, born in 1834.' He pauses. 'No, hang on a minute, I think he had another one.' It just says the second son was called Robert. He was born in 1837. He looks over at me in surprise. 'Says he emigrated to Australia.'

'So we could have relatives on the other side of the world? Do you think Robert might have been transported?'

He frowns. 'I doubt it. That bloody load of Horlicks ended well before then.'

There's a short silence as he goes back to the spidery writing, his next words sharing another revelation. 'Anthony's eldest son joined the police force. He narrows his eyes, staring pensively off into the shadows. 'I reckon Grandpa told me about this bloke, Victory. Henry Shackleford would have been my great, great grandfather.'

I wait with bated breath, not daring to interrupt in case he suddenly decides he's bored with the whole trip down memory lane.

'I do seem to remember Grandpa talking about his great grandfather being in the Old Bill. Exeter, I think.' He looks over at me. 'You might not believe this Victory, but there was a time when I considered becoming a copper myself.' I blink, resisting the urge to burst out laughing. The very thought of my irascible father joining the ranks of Britain's upholders of the law is… well, in all honesty it's not funny at all, it's bloody scary. Fortunately he doesn't appear to have cottoned on to my innermost thoughts as he continues. 'Grandpa told me old Henry came to a bit of a sticky end, or at least he was forced into early retirement. Not sure what happened to him after that.'

'Well, I assume he got married, and had at least one child before whatever his sticky end was,' I answer. 'Does it say anything about a wife?' My father returns to the register. 'It says he married someone called Emma in 1866. By the looks of it, they had two sons and … hang on a minute… bloody hell, *six* daughters.' He sits back before giving a ribald chuckle. 'Three sets of twins. It might be a good idea for you to give Noah a bit of a heads up. You could end up with half a dozen ankle snappers.'

'Well, it's hardly been a problem in recent years,' I point out.

'It can miss a couple of generations,' he insists with a wink.

'Does it give the children's names and when they were born?' I ask, definitely not in the mood to debate the possibility of multiple births with the man who sired me. And anyway I feel completely invested in these strangers who were part of my heritage.

My father looks down again and nods his head. 'They didn't hang around. Samuel was born in 1867 and Nicholas in 1869. As for the girls …' He peers down at the spidery writing. 'The first set of twins were called Alexandra and Arabella. Born in 1870.' He takes off his glasses and gives them a quick rub on his jacket. 'The next set popped out of the oven in 1872. Beatrix and Bernice, and finally Florence and Daisy in 1874.'

'Does it say what happened to the girls?' I ask, already guessing the answer, even before my father shakes his head.

I can't help but sigh. Another six women we know nothing

XVII

about. Clearly they weren't considered important. Perhaps I should think about joining *Ancestry.com*.

Focusing back on the book, I point at Henry Shackleford's first born.

'So that means Henry's eldest son - Samuel Shackleford was your great grandfather, which makes him your Grandpa's father,' I calculate. 'What did he do for a living?'

'I reckon he was the first matelot in the family, Victory. Joined the Navy when he was still a lad.'

I frown. 'What about his brother – what was his name… Nicholas?'

He peers down at the page. 'It doesn't say what happened to him. Strange that. Grandpa never mentioned he had an uncle.'

I can't help myself. 'Now there's a surprise,' I comment drily. 'Fancy not mentioning the existence of a close relative.'

My father looks over at me irritably but doesn't rise to the bait. Instead, he looks back down at the book. 'We're nearly at the end. It says that Samuel got hitched to a Miss Elizabeth Bailey, which I already knew. They had one son, Charles Edward. My Grandpa.'

'How about your father? Is he in there?' I ask.

He shakes his head. 'That's as far as it goes. Either Grandpa didn't hold with any of this writing stuff down or never got around to putting my parents in.' He frowned again. 'One thing I did notice, though. It doesn't say when any of 'em died apart from our God Walloper's first two efforts, Just when they were born and when they got hitched. Funny that.'

He shakes his head and closes the book decisively.

'Can I have a look?' I ask. Shrugging, he hands the heavy tome over.

'All these names,' I muse, tracing my finger down the page. 'It's hard to imagine they were living, breathing people. That some of their blood runs in our veins.'

He gives a rude snort. 'Our history might be a part of us girl,' he answers, 'but you can't let what your ancestors did rule your bollocking life.' I look over at him, knowing his soap box look of old.

'I mean, we might get some of our traits from those who came before us, but not all of 'em. Look at me,' he continues. 'Take for instance my dad. As long as his arse was pointing downwards, he'd always be a gopher. So how come I got to Admiral?' He shrugs again. 'Bill on the other hand, well, he was our dad through and through.'

I forbear to point out that my father's rise to such heady heights was mostly due to… well more than a few self-adjusting cock ups as he himself would say…

I look down at the list of family names. 'Perhaps you take after Anthony. We don't know what he did for a living. Or your great, great grandfather Henry. He could have gotten to the rank of Chief Inspector for all we know. And then there's your great grandfather Samuel. He could have risen to First Sea Lord…'

He gives another rude snort. 'I think Grandpa might have mentioned that.'

'Would he?' I shake my head. 'I don't really know anything about your grandfather. Just that you went to live with him after your parents died. What did he do in the Navy?'

'He ended up a pusser. Got to the rank of Captain before he retired.'

'Well, there you are then. That's pretty respectable.' I pause and frown, thinking about the dates. 'Did he fight in the First World War?'

Sighing, my father nods his head. 'He never really talked about it though. Grandpa was only fifteen when he joined up as an able seaman. Iron Duke was his first ship. She sailed straight up to the Orkneys and six months later Grandpa was at Jutland. Bit of a bloody baptism, especially as he should have been on Invincible. His draft was changed at the last minute.'

'Why, what happened to Invincible?' I probe.

'Bloody hell Victory, you need to swot up on your naval history. Battle of Jutland, biggest battle of the First World War. Fought just off the coast of Norway. We lost fourteen ships and over three thousand men. Invincible was hit five times by German shells and her ammunition magazine exploded, splitting the bloody ship in two. Only six survivors and doubt very much one of them would have been Grandpa had he been on board.'

I'm silent for a second, imagining what being in the middle of such a battle must have been like for a naïve fifteen-year-old boy. It must have been terrible.

'What happened to Grandpa after the battle?' I breathe, hardly daring to ask.

'He spent the rest of the War stationed in the Orkneys. Met my grandmother up there. She was Orcadian, born and bred.'

'I didn't know that,' I enthuse. 'It must have been hard following your Grandpa all the way down here. What happened to her?'

'Died when I was about eight,' he comments gruffly. 'Don't remember much about her apart from the perfume. For some reason, I remember her smelling like roses.' He sighs and climbs to his feet.

'So are you going to continue it?' I ask, standing up with the bible in my arms.

'Not much bloody point is there?' he answers, heading towards the door. 'There'll be no more Shacklefords after you.'

'Yes, but we don't know what happened to Robert, or to Nicholas. There could be Shacklefords all over the world.' I clutch the book to my chest. 'And, anyway, I'd like to be at least mentioned - and Noah, and especially Isaac.' I follow him to the door, still holding the book. 'And I think your brother should be in there, and Teddy.'

He gives an irritable hmph before starting carefully down the steep stairs. 'Make sure you turn off the light and lock the door,' he throws back over his shoulder.

Swearing under my breath, I juggle the heavy book and manage to turn off the light and shut the door. Locking it proves more difficult though, and in the end, I'm forced to put the book down on the top step. By this time my father has disappeared. Sighing, I turn the key and tuck it in my back pocket.

Walking down the almost vertical stairs carrying a heavy book definitely gives my calves and arms a bit of a workout. In fact I think it might be the most exercise I've had since running after that ice cream van last summer. Dad's abrupt departure might mean the whole thing is done and dusted in his mind, but not if I have anything to do with it.

My father's already helping himself to another piece of shortbread by the time I arrive back in the kitchen. Dotty of course greets me as if I've been away for six months, though it doesn't last long. Clearly the lure of Mabel's baking is too strong.

'I think you should put in the rest of the family,' I declare, plonking the heavy tome onto the table.

'Ooh, that looks interesting,' Mabel breathes. 'Can I have a look?' I push the book over to her and she opens it reverently. 'My goodness, Charlie, you've got more relatives than I ever imagined. To hear you speak, anybody would think you'd been left on a doorstep.'

'Yes, well, if you ever want your name in there, we're going to have to tie the bloody knot,' my father gripes. I look over at him wondering how much his desire to marry Mabel is because the merry widow is playing hard to get. I can't help but grin. It does him good not to get everything he wants.

'Let's get Kit and Jason's wedding out of the way first,' she responds blithely. 'Then we'll have a proper look for a ring.'

'Come on Dad,' I say. 'Let's write the rest of the family in. Even if I'm the last one. It's something I can give to Isaac when he grows up. And for all you know, I might have bought you a lifetime's membership to *Ancestry.com* for Christmas.'

'You'll be asking for a bloody refund if you have,' is his sour comment.

I shake my head at my father's griping. 'I know who you remind me off, Dad.' It comes to me suddenly. 'You're like Ebenezer Scrooge in *A Christmas Carol.*

He glares over at me in outrage and then over at Mabel who is trying very hard not to laugh.

'Where's your Christmas spirit?' I query with a grin.

'I'll have you know I've got plenty of spirit and not just at Christmas,' he protests indignantly. 'In fact I've always been the life and soul of the bloody party. You ask Jimmy.'

I think back to all the times my father has put his foot in it over the years. Clearly his view of what constitutes the life and soul of a party is very different to that of most people's.

'Then stop making a bloody meal of it and put our names into the family bible,' I repeat as Mabel pushes the large book towards him helpfully.

He gives a big heavy sigh, clearly designed to tell me and Mabel just how put upon he is. Fiddling around in his pocket, he finally unearths a pen.

Scooting round the table, I point to the last entry in the bible. 'Your Grandpa's the last name entered, so you need to put your Grandmother and your Father in next.'

'Any sharper, they'll stick a bloody tail on you and call you a fox,' he mutters sarcastically.

Contrary to his theatrically demonstrated reluctance, he takes great care entering his grandmother's name and the date of his grandparents' wedding. When I ask how he knows the date they got married, he pushes the book towards me. 11th November 1918. Armistice Day. I swallow, feeling an unexpected lump in my throat.

Next comes his father and mother, Jack and Mary, followed by his brother, William. 'I'll need to get some more intel before I stick Wonder Woman in there,' he frowns. 'What kind of a bloody name is Teddy anyway?'

'It's probably short for Theodora like Alex said,' I comment. 'But we can ask her on Christmas Day.'

There's a pause before he enters his own name. 'Makes me feel bloody old,' he mumbles, finally entering Charles Edward Shackleford, 'like I've already been put to bed with a bloody spade.'

'Well given your regular habit of upsetting everyone within shouting distance, I have to say I'm amazed you've made it this far,' I comment acidly. His response is a grunt.

'Well, the only bloody wife I'm putting down here is your mother,' he continues, glaring up at me, daring me to argue. I shrug. His first, very brief liaison with Kit's Aunt Flo wasn't really a marriage as such and I definitely can't see Flo losing any sleep over not being written into the Shackleford archives. And anyway, he's always declared that my mum was the love of his life, though I can't help but wonder whether part of the reason really was that she was the only one prepared to put up with him...

My father looks over at Mabel. 'I'll leave a space,' he mumbles in what is clearly meant to be a romantic gesture. I wince and look over at the elderly matron who looks back at me and winks. She might still be Dartmouth's reigning queen of malapropisms, but Mabel Pomfrey certainly knows how to handle my father.

Then it's my turn and suddenly I understand where my father is coming from. It feels almost bizarre joining a list of people who have been long dead and buried. Naturally, as I wasn't born on a date vital to world history, I have to remind him when I came into the world.

Noah comes next, and of course my father hasn't a clue when my husband was born. In fairness, he does manage to get the approximate date of our wedding but has to change the five to a nought. 'You *know* we didn't get married on Christmas Day, Dad,' I grumble in exasperation.

Lastly, it's time to enter Isaac's name. Strangely, my father needs no reminding of his grandson's date of birth and as I watch him carefully writing, I feel a sudden surge of love for my irascible parent, both unexpected and unaccustomed. It gets me through his next sentence...

'There you go then Victory, it's all yours. And given that you're unlikely to find another bloke daft enough to give you house room, I've not left any space for another husband. So make sure you look after the bloody one you've got...'

It's nearly six o'clock and Dotty and I are tucked up on the sofa with a glass of wine. Well, I've got the wine and Dotty's got a mini sausage. The family bible has pride of place on the coffee table so I can show it to Noah. All in all, I think it was a surprisingly successful morning. Naturally my father didn't hang about once Isaac's name had been entered for posterity. His lunchtime drink with Jimmy is practically sacred and we all know better than to put a spanner in the works.

I look down at my watch. I've heard from Noah. They've just come through Totnes, and he's promised he'll let me know when they arrive at the ferry. If the traffic's not too bad, they should be here within the hour.

I've already carefully arranged our picky feast in the kitchen and there's some bubbly chilling in the fridge. I might not be quite as good as Kit at the art of entertaining, but assembling food is my speciality. Especially when I haven't had to cook it first...

I'm sad Kit and Jason won't be with us this Christmas, but they have too much to do at Bloodstone Tower, especially with their wedding only weeks away. But at least Aunt Flo and Neil are heading north to keep them company.

It will be lovely to see Kim, Ben and the kids again, though. And of course, Isaac will be in seventh heaven with his cousins here. I chuckle. He's probably already causing mayhem in the limo, and I wonder whether Noah's regretting his decision to take our first born with him to meet his cousins. I should think Madison's grown. She's almost ten now and Joseph fourteen. Naturally we face-time regularly, but it's difficult to tell on a small screen. The one thing I do know though, is both Madison and Joseph take after Kim and Noah. Ben, bless him, is a wonderful man, but in all fairness... well, let's put it this way, he's the male equivalent of me...

Even without my bestie and her fiancé, there will be thirteen of us for Christmas dinner. Fourteen if you count Dotty – and the only thing she won't have is her own seat. In addition to Kim's family, my father and Mabel, Freddy and his new boyfriend Alex will be here. And I've invited my Uncle Bill and cousin Teddy. Second time lucky, since their Thanksgiving introduction to family dinners chez Westbrook was nothing if not an eye opener.

I wonder if they'll be interested in the bible.

Sighing, I take a sip of my wine and lean back. Dotty's warm little body is snuggled up close. She's long since finished the sausage and is now content to snooze until her next snack. Some things never change.

My thoughts go back to this morning. Unexpectedly, I'd felt closer to my father than I had since I was small enough to sit on his knee for a cuddle. It's strange really, remembering an affectionate version of my father, but he was. In between putting his foot in it of course. And I know my mother loved him. I think back to Mabel's face as she watched him stomp off with Pickles in tow. She loves him too and I wonder if my father realises just how lucky he is…

I give a small chuckle thinking back to his parting shot. 'What's for dinner Mabel,' he'd yelled as he wrestled with the large gate.

'Ravioli,' she shouted back, just as he managed to finally get the gate open. 'Bollocking hell Mabel, you know I hate them bloody Italian teabags…

No, I think I can safely say, hand on heart that my father has no idea…

Chapter One

Teddy

A box of mostly rubbish is not what I expected to leave with. A commendation, maybe, or even a nice carriage clock. I mean my services rendered might not have gone down well with the old school, but my methods definitely worked. Most of the time…

Unfortunately, when they didn't, they *really* didn't. No self-adjusting cock-up as my newly discovered uncle would say. No, this cock-up was a once in a career kind. The kind where you didn't get to pick up the pieces, or your job afterwards. Right royal. No doubt about it.

And given that said newly discovered uncle was at the root of the whole sorry business, I'm currently more than happy to place the whole bloody disaster at his door. Of course, my wallowing won't last forever, and sticking pins in an image of a relative is really not very British.

And neither does it help my situation. Jobless and fairly soon, penniless. I definitely can't afford to stay in London. But the idea of moving back in with my father…

I'm sitting in a café just off the Strand, sipping a macchiato and eating the biggest Danish pastry on the counter. As comfort foods go, it really sucks. It's dry, most of it actually ending up on the plate in front of me. Which pretty much sums up my life at the moment.

It's strange how one's so-called friends disappear into the woodwork when things go tits up, terrified of being tarred with the same brush. But then I suppose it just goes to show that having all one's friends in the same corporate basket is not a good idea. Not that the National Crime Agency would describe itself as corporate...

If I'm being brutally honest (and I'm rarely anything else which is actually part of the problem), the bigwigs were looking for an excuse to get rid of me almost as l got there. I didn't fit the mould. For a start, I could be described as a female equivalent of *Jack Reacher*. And when you look down on most of your superiors (literally), it doesn't go down well.

Sighing, I take a sip of my coffee. I really need to make a start on clearing my stuff out of the flat. But since I've got nowhere to put it... Oh bugger. Is it too early for a glass of wine?

Admiral Charles Shackleford (Retired) was sitting at his customary seat in the *Ship Inn*, sipping at his pint of real ale. He might have been sitting in his usual seat, but that was the only thing *customary* about it.

It wasn't his customary day of the week, or his customary time of day. Even stranger, he was without his customary drinking partners - both human and canine.

The Admiral, however, was completely oblivious to the furtive stares being cast his way as he was too busy staring down at the letter in his hands and wondering, not for the first time, how it was that trouble seemed to follow him around like a bad smell.

He had no idea why his niece Teddy Shackleford had lost her job. After all, the whole shenanigans with that bloody gangster had turned out all right in the end. But then, given she was the sort who only opened her mouth to exchange whatever foot was in there, it wasn't that surprising.

But it wasn't his fault she'd had no shit deflectors at the ready, and he had no idea what Mabel would think about her coming to stay at the Admiralty. In fact, it couldn't have come at a worse time since he was finally working up the courage to propose to his live-in partner having come to the realisation that Mabel Pomfrey wasn't going to accept anything less than the full monty. He only hoped that when he finally got down on one knee, he'd be able to get back up again.

He looked back down at the letter. Bill reckoned Teddy wouldn't come home, even though he'd begged her to. The Admiral grunted as he took another swallow of his pint. He wouldn't have rushed back to bloody Basingstoke either. But what made his brother think the damn woman would agree to come to Dartmouth? Even if it did boast a world-famous celebrity as one of its residents.

But apparently Teddy Shackleford was short on friends – why was he not surprised? And according to Bill, her only friend in the world was currently living in Dartmouth. But more than that. She had *family* here. Charles Shackleford sighed. This was precisely why he'd kept his head down all these years. Favours had a way of popping up to bite a body right where the sun doesn't shine – he only had to think back to Bible Basher Boris…

The Admiral shook his head sadly and ordered another pint. The old God walloper had finally cashed in his chips a couple of months ago. Apparently, the nursing home had advised a burial fearing that a cremation might end up taking the bloody roof off. Feeling a sudden, unexpected onset of tears, the Admiral lifted his pint in silent salute to the man who was closest he'd ever met to a saint on earth. The bloke might have had an arse that could give the atom bomb a run for its money, but Charles Shackleford had never met a more selfless, humble individual.

Sighing, he knew exactly why Boris had popped into his head. The old God botherer was telling him in no uncertain terms that Teddy Shackleford did actually have one shit deflector.

And that was her uncle.

∞∞∞

'When is she coming?' Victory Shackleford's voice was definitely on the shrill side. The Admiral winced. Even if he hadn't been informed that his only daughter was once again in the family way, he'd have guessed it from her less than sparkling personality. Sighing, he tried again.

'I told you, Victory, I'm not even sure she *is* coming. But I've got to offer her the bloody option. According to Bill, she won't go home, and she's got nowhere else. I was hoping you'd speak with Mabel to see what she thinks about the idea.'

'Why can't you speak with her?' Tory answered crossly before turning a peculiar shade of grey and grabbing a large bucket at her feet.

The Admiral grimaced, unaccustomed concern warring with distaste as she stuck her head in the bucket and made some disgusting retching noises. 'Where the devil is Noah?' he asked when she finally surfaced.

'He's taken Isaac and Dotty out for an hour. I'm supposed to be resting.' The last was said in an accusatory tone that was like water off a duck's back to her father.

'I thought it would be better coming from you,' he answered. 'I was hoping you could sound her out...'

Tory put the bucket back down and sighed. She was well aware she was being waspish and unkind, but her mouth sort of ran away with her. It had been the same when she was expecting Isaac – that and the almost continuous nausea. She did feel sympathy for Teddy, and her father was right for once. They were family, and her cousin needed their help.

The fact that it was actually her father offering assistance was bizarre to say the least, and fighting the instinct to ask him what he'd done with the Admiral, she agreed to speak with Mabel when she took Isaac round the next day.

Then, taking advantage of his uncommonly charitable mood, she asked if he'd empty the bucket and make her a cup of tea. Without waiting to witness his look of horror, she groaned and lay back on the sofa, ordering him not to be too long with the bucket.

Spooning a mouthful of cold baked beans directly from the tin, I sit down for the first time since waking and look down at the letter in my hand. I feel like I should recognise the handwriting on the envelope, but I can't actually place it. Clearly, my investigative instincts are fading already.

Grimacing, I tear it open and skim over the spidery handwriting until I get to the signature at the bottom. Why the hell is the Admiral sending me a letter? If he's writing to tell me how sorry he is, he can shove it. But then, I might not know my Uncle Charlie well, but in the few times I've been in his company, he's never given the impression he's the sensitive caring type.

Resisting the urge to simply throw the letter in the bin along with all my other crap, I take another spoonful of baked beans and look back down. Might as well see what the old reprobate has to say.

Five minutes later my incredulity is stretched to breaking point. He's actually offering me a place to stay. In Dartmouth. I've no doubt my father's put him up to it, but even so.

I've been in London for the last five years. How on earth would I cope, being buried away in the wilds of south Devon? To my amazement, my overactive brain hasn't actually dismissed the offer out of hand. Not in the way it did when my dad suggested returning to Basingstoke.

I shy away from the fact that Alex is in Dartmouth. My one and only friend – how bloody sad is that? He's the only one of my *colleagues* who's been in touch since my career went down the Swanee, which in itself is surprising since I'm fully aware of what a bitch I was to work for. I sigh and eat another spoonful of beans. Funny how I'd never considered him a friend until the shit hit the fan. But now there's no one else …

Forcing the thought away, I climb quickly to my feet and weave my way round the boxes to the fridge. Once there, I grab a bottle of rosé and pour myself a large glass. It's past midday and self-analysis without alcohol is too painful. Taking a large swallow, I fight a sudden onset of childish tears.

The simple *truth* is I've never *really* had any friends. Not in the Agency or out of it. In fact the last time I was out socially with a group of colleagues, I overheard one of them declare me so cold blooded, any mosquito unlucky enough to bite me would die of pneumonia. The resulting laughter was painful to listen to.

I take another swig and look at the chaos around me. Nearly everything I own is in boxes, but I have nowhere to put them. I'm running out of time, and so far, I've been offered the grand total of two options.

What the hell would I do in Dartmouth? My uncle's letter makes it clear that his offer of sanctuary is not long term, and I haven't seen him, Alex or my cousin since last Christmas. I think back to the chaotic but fun dinner my father and I were invited to six months ago. For all that she's married to the world's most famous movie star, there are no sides to Tory. She's modest, kind and funny. In fact, so is her superstar husband.

Would they welcome me with open arms? Would Alex and his new partner Freddy? With a sudden thought, I rummage for my mobile phone and search out the last text I had from my one and only buddy.

'Any time you want a break from the craziness of London, head down to Dartmouth. It's changed my life, Teddy. I love it here, and it might just be the one thing that gives you the peace you're searching for.'

I clearly remember dismissing his words as the corny ramblings of an idiot besotted by his latest boyfriend. Especially the bollocks about me searching for peace …

But maybe he wasn't so far off the mark after all. The truth is I'm exhausted. Even if the NCA hadn't binned me, I don't know how long I'd have been able to keep pretending I was in control of everything.

I finally acknowledge that they did me a favour. I was heading for a breakdown. Maybe Alex is right. I can finally stop chasing … whatever the hell has been driving me for the last few years and completely change my life. Though God knows where I'll get a bloody job.

Chapter Two

Sebastian Sinclair sat staring down at the letter informing him that his sham of a marriage was finally done. Swamped by sudden relief, he threw the letter on the table and climbed to his feet, walking over to stare out of the window. The wrangling was finally over.

It was raining outside, and the gardens were wreathed in a soft mist, creating an ethereal, almost otherworldly landscape. Normally, he loved mornings like this. As a boy he'd roamed the hills and valleys of the Blackmore estate in all weathers. He knew every stone, every tree.

And he'd come within an inch of losing it all – would have done if Carla had had her way.

Not that there was much left of the original estate. Most of the land had been sold to help with death duties over the years until finally Sebastian had been forced to turn the house itself into a very exclusive boutique hotel on the demise of his father. Fortunately the venture had proved hugely successful, and he'd been able to retain a penthouse suite in the former servants' quarters which suited him perfectly.

He'd actually met Carla as a guest in the hotel and been stupidly besotted from the onset. It was only after they married that he realised she was only interested in his money. His title had been an added bonus – in fact she'd used it more than he did. How could he have been such a bloody idiot not to see through her wiles to the gold digger she really was?

A few seconds later, he was dragged back to the present by a small whine coming from his feet. Lifting his head away from the glass, he looked down. Coco wagged her tail in response. He couldn't help but smile. In theory, she was a collie, but truthfully, her legs were too long and her nose too short. And the icing on the cake? Sheep scared her shitless. But she'd been his faithful companion since he'd found her as a tiny pup shivering on the side of the road.

She'd never liked Carla. He should have taken note.

'Come on girl, let's go for a walk,' he murmured, bending down to give her a quick fuss. In answer, she did an excited twirl, her tail wagging so fast it was almost invisible.

He had about two hours before he had to be on a train to London for a meeting with his solicitors to sign over the house in Mallorca to his money grabbing ex-wife before the decree was absolute. Calling Coco to him, he strode to the door, suppressing a small grin at the thought that Carla would no longer be able to use the title of Duchess. It was a small victory but nonetheless sweet. The greedy bitch would hate it.

'I think it was very generous of you to offer Teddy somewhere to stay, Sir.' Jimmy Noon, the Admiral's oldest (and possibly only) friend, risked giving his former commanding officer an approving pat on the back.

The Admiral gave a loud sigh before muttering, 'Can't say I'm particularly looking forward to it, but what's a man to do. I'm too compassionate for me own good, Jimmy lad – it's my biggest failing.'

In fairness, Jimmy could have listed enough of the Admiral's failings to fill a book, but he contented himself with a nod and another swallow of his pint.

'I've given Freddy and Alex a heads up that she's coming so I'm hoping they'll help with getting her set up somewhere of her own fairly sharpish.'

'What did Tory have to say about it?' Jimmy asked curiously.

'Not quite as sympathetic as I'd hoped, if I'm honest. But she's expecting and Kit said she turned into a bit of a bloody harpy when she was carrying Isaac. Can't say I noticed any difference to be honest.'

'Oh I'm certain it won't last,' Jimmy chuckled. 'I remember Emily being very difficult when she was carrying our eldest.'

'How come she never got any better then?' Charles Shackleford grunted. 'Right then, fish and chips is it?'

Alex stared down at the text from Teddy. It was the first time he'd heard from her since her career had gone up in flames. He'd tried calling, but she never picked up. In the end, he'd sent her a message. Oh he'd known his words wouldn't go down well, and her complete lack of response had confirmed it. He thought back to the last time he'd seen her at Christmas. She'd been white-faced and strained – clearly well aware that her career was about to take a nosedive.

And now, wonder of wonders, she was about to take him up on his suggestion. But more than that, Tory's old man had offered her a bed. He shook his head in disbelief before clicking on the reply box. Before he had a chance to write anything, the door to his office opened and his other half burst in.

'You are absolutely not going to believe what I've got to tell you,' Freddy declared, posing dramatically against the filing cabinet. Alex grinned at the love of his life.

'Teddy Shackleford is coming down to Dartmouth and staying at the Admiralty,' he responded.

Freddy's dismay at being pipped at the post was so comical, Alex found himself laughing out loud. He held out his phone. 'I've just had a text from Teddy. Where did you get the juicy gossip from?'

'Horse's mouth,' Freddy responded, throwing himself petulantly into a chair. 'The Admiral himself called me just as we were about to go into rehearsals for *Showboat*. I got away as soon as I could.' He sniffed before adding, 'Clearly not soon enough.'

'I was just about to respond to Teddy when you arrived,' Alex answered, soothing ruffled feathers. 'Now you're here, you can help me compose it.'

Freddy's face lit up. 'What did she say exactly?' he asked, holding out his hand for the phone. Alex handed it over.

'Curt and to the point – typical Teddy really.'

'Bloody hell, she's as bad as the Admiral.' Freddy shook his head before reading the text out loud.

'You know what's happened so no point in going over old news. I'm coming to stay with Uncle Charlie. Pick me up from Totnes station? Monday 17.30.'

'So how do you think I should phrase the reply?'

Freddy pursed his lips for a second, then sighed. 'I think *ok* should just about cover it…'

∞∞∞

In the end, I left most of the stuff in my flat to the landlord who was more than happy to take it off my hands. Since I rarely did much of anything but sleep within its four walls, most of the furniture was practically brand new, and he even magnanimously gave me back my deposit without a fight – score one for me.

That left me three boxes of personal stuff – rubbish mostly, but sentimental rubbish for all that. I had them sent by courier to my uncle's – keeping my fingers crossed that I'd arrive before they did.

So now I'm sitting in Paddington Station waiting for the 1335 to Totnes. It's hard to believe I've actually given up my flat, making me effectively homeless. With a sudden thought, I take a surreptitious glance down at myself to check I don't look too much like a bag lady. Unfortunately my fashion sense is not up to the minute. Truthfully, it's not really up to the decade – but then you try finding women's trousers to fit an inside leg of thirty-three inches.

Fortunately I've never had much of an interest in fashion and generally relied on men's suits during my heady days in the NCA. Nondescript in the police force was good.

But now? Frowning, I stand up and head over to the nearest ladies to have a quick look in the mirror.

Once there, all I can do is stare in horror. Except for the length, I look like I'm wearing my dad's clothes. My grey suit is hanging off me – clearly I haven't been eating properly. At least, I hope that's why I look so bloody awful. Surely I didn't look like this when I was working? When was the last time I actually bothered to look in a full-length mirror? *Shit*. I'm going to have to use some of my savings to get a new set of clothes. Or at the very least some jeans. But then maybe I'd be better looking for something a bit more nautical to fit in with all the yachty types in Dartmouth.

Sighing, I turn away from the depressing sight. I don't know why I'm worrying – it's not like I'm going to be there long anyway. I push open the door to begin the long walk back to the concourse. As I step out into the corridor, I register that someone even taller than me is striding swiftly in my direction. He's looking down at his phone, and I abruptly realise he hasn't actually clocked my presence.

I step hurriedly to the right, just as he looks up. Unfortunately, he chooses that moment to step the same way, and seconds later we crash into each other. He's carrying a briefcase which falls to the floor, spilling documents everywhere. My overnight bag slides across the corridor spilling my very serviceable underwear, including half a dozen Marks and Spencer's white high waisted full briefs that from this angle look as though they should just about fit a sumo wrestler (and given that sumo wrestling was my absent mother's profession, I don't say that lightly).

Muttering in embarrassment, I scrabble to pick up my errant knickers, not daring to look to see what the man I collided with is doing - even though it was his bloody fault. Once I've shoved everything back into my bag, I realise the stranger is still picking the contents of his briefcase up off the floor. With an exasperated grimace, I plonk my bag down and bend down to help him. At this rate I'll miss my damn train.

I manage to retrieve a small bundle of papers that are now obviously all mixed up and can't help but notice that the one on the top has the words DECREE ABSOLUTE stamped in big letters across the top. I finally look over at the man. Whatever possesses me to say my next words, I can't even begin to imagine. 'Sorry about your marriage.'

Unsurprisingly, he doesn't answer immediately, and I have the chance to note that he's probably one of the handsomest men I've ever met – including Noah Westbrook.

As I previously discerned, he's tall – approaching six foot four or five. His hair is almost completely burnished silver, styled in a cut that likely cost him as much as mine would for a whole year. He has a close-cropped beard, equally silver. The colour belies his age which I would put at around mid to late thirties. But his eyes … oh, his eyes are almost the colour of a fine aged brandy.

His words, when I finally register them, bring me back down to earth with a resounding bump.

'Do you make a habit of reading strangers' documents?' His voice is deep but wintery cold.

Swallowing uncomfortably, I hurriedly hold out my hand, and he takes the papers without further comment, sliding them quickly into his briefcase. For some reason, his complete lack of remorse at almost knocking me on my backside suddenly rankles.

'Do you make a habit of wandering around without looking where you're going?' I return coolly.

His beautiful eyes narrow, but at length he bends his head slightly. 'My apologies for my distraction. I trust you weren't hurt at all?'

By this point, I'm beginning to feel like a complete philistine. I instinctively recognise that this man is far above me socially. I almost have to fight the urge to offer a curtsy. In the end, I just want to get me and my baggy suit away from his penetrating gaze.

Hitching my bag onto my shoulder, I hold my chin up and say, 'I am uninjured, thank you.'

I am uninjured …? Bloody hell, just let the floor swallow me now. With my face the colour of a ripe tomato, I give a small self-conscious cough and step round him to march determinedly back towards the concourse.

I don't look back.

Chapter Three

'So are you going to tell me exactly what happened?' We've been in the car all of ten minutes before Alex asks the question. I glance over at him, stifling the temptation to tell him to mind his own bloody business. But after a lengthy silence, I give him the bare bones.

'The long and the short of it is I knowingly risked the lives of civilians. Apparently it makes no difference if they're family.' I give a shrug. 'I have no defence *milord*. They're right, I did.'

'But for all the right reasons,' Alex offers.

I give a bark of laughter and shake my head. 'The road to hell and all that.

'And anyway, it's all water under the bridge now. We both know the powers that be were looking for an excuse to get rid of me. They saw you off first, and then it was my turn.'

'You weren't the one who left a bloody gun where a hostage could get her hands on it. That was my bad,' Alex protests.

'Oh, I know that, and so do they. But when you *resigned*, it left me completely without allies…' I stop and shake my head again, giving a mirthless chuckle. 'What the hell am I saying … I mean, ally. You were the only one who had my back.'

'Why didn't you call me?' I wince from the sympathy in his gaze.

'Pride,' I mutter, finally letting go of my *I don't give a shit* routine.

I look back out of the car window, effectively putting an end to the conversation. Contrary to my mood, the late afternoon is warm and sunny which feels like an affront to my little pity party. Then I find myself noticing the profusion of primroses and bluebells poking through the hedgerows and inevitably my eyes lift to the picture-perfect rolling hills and woodlands beyond, and I feel a sudden catch in my throat. When was the last time I actually stopped and simply looked for looking's sake?

Surprisingly, I feel my spirits begin to lift. Casting a furtive glance over at Alex, I wonder for the first time what he's actually doing instead of chasing bad guys.

He catches me looking. 'What?' he asks mildly.

'Do you miss it at all?' I ask, suddenly curious. Alex shakes his head.

'I've never been so happy,' he responds simply. Unable to help myself, I scoff softly.

'Pooh-pooh all you want,' he shrugs. 'I know how I feel.'

'You don't miss the thrill of the chase?' I insist. To my surprise, he laughs.

'I still get to chase things, but they're not usually carrying a firearm.' He glances over at me before adding, 'I work for The Dartmouth Herald.'

I raise my eyebrows.' A newspaper?'

'More like a pamphlet,' he chuckles. 'It goes out once a month.'

'So what do you do exactly? Interview little old ladies who've lost their cats?' I can't help it, my voice is both sarcastic and contemptuous. I can't believe he's sunk so low.

'You'd be surprised how interesting some little old ladies can be,' he retorts without rancour. 'But the owner patently has a similar opinion. She wants me to spice it up a bit. Expand the readership.'

'Ah, so you'll be going undercover to expose private wife swapping groups in the future then?'

'Not really. I was hoping that would be your job...'

∞∞∞

Although I've visited Dartmouth twice, this is the first time I've been in the Admiralty. I remember having a private snigger when my uncle first told me the name of his house. But now, seeing it for the first time, I realise just how well the name fits. The house is apparently Edwardian - all very King and Country, and even with its slightly shabby air, it's impressive. I can see why they wanted to use it for *The Bridegroom*. It's a far cry from the standard 1950s three bedroom semi I grew up in after we came back from Japan.

Mabel shows me into a charming room that was apparently Tory's. It's large enough to contain a small sofa as well as a bed, has a small ensuite bathroom and a delightful view over the River Dart. All in all, much better than I expected.

Standing at the window watching the Higher Ferry make its way across the river, I think back to the conversation with Alex. A job offer was the last thing I expected. Evidently my name came up up in conversation with the paper's owner and the lady is very keen to meet with me. According to Alex, she's as mad as a box of frogs and will undoubtedly love me – although what the connection is between her being barking and thinking I'm the best thing since sliced bread, he kept to himself. I didn't ask how she can afford to pay two employees for what is essentially a monthly leaflet. Could be she's an eccentric millionaire.

By the time he dropped me off, he'd convinced me to at least meet with this Mrs. Sinclair, though I could see he was already having second thoughts. I think it was when I asked how many cats she'd got. His parting shot of *beggars can't be choosers* was definitely un-Alex-like, even if he was right.

∞∞∞

'*Twins?*' Tory gasped, her panicked eyes flying to her delighted husband. 'This is all my bloody father's fault.'

Noah raised his eyebrows. 'I'm pretty sure it isn't,' was his grinning response.

'He predicted this. He said it can miss a couple of generations.' Tory turned back to the doctor. 'You're sure there aren't any more in there?'

'As sure as I can be Mrs. Westbrook.' The paediatrician's voice was soothing.

'Oh my God, I'm going to get like the size of a house.'

'A sensible diet, light exercise combined with plenty of rest and I'm certain you'll sail through your pregnancy.'

The doctor's reassurance fell on deaf ears. All Tory could think about were the frequent sets of twins in her family tree. Until this moment, she'd never really given any thought to the possibility that she might follow suit, despite her father's flippant warning. But what if history was about to repeat itself? What if this was the first of many? She was never having sex again…

'Can you tell the sex of the babies?' Noah was asking, the smile evident in his voice. Clearly, he was up for fathering a bloody dynasty.

'They're girls,' Tory responded flatly.

'At this stage, it's impossible to tell,' countered the doctor. 'In another month we should be able to give you an answer if you still want to know.'

'Trust me, they're girls,' Tory insisted. 'There have been female twins in my family for at least the last two hundred years and likely before that.' Her voice had taken on a resigned tone, and Noah laughed out loud.

'Just think, twin girls, honey. Dotty will hate it.'

∞∞∞

'So are you going to take that job with Alex then? I reckon you won't have too much of a problem dragging information out of people - especially if you take after your mother. But then again, you might find it a bit tricky finding a patch of greenery large enough to hide behind when you're staking 'em out.'

My uncle's version of small talk clearly hasn't improved since I saw him last and why am I not surprised he's aware I've been offered a job as a hack with Dartmouth's answer to the *Private Eye?*

I'm saved from replying as Mabel glares at him over her casserole.

'What?' he frowns. 'The woman's got to earn a living, and all that digging around in other people's business should make ferreting out where Harold Parkinson buried his mother up at the Naval College a doddle.

'In fact,' he went on enthusiastically, 'I'm certain me and Jimmy would be a definite asset to your investigations seeing as how we're experts at undercover operations. Not to mention digging up the dirt in the first place.'

I stare at the Admiral's animated face, for once at a loss for words. It's clear he's deadly serious.

'Don't be so ridiculous Charlie,' Mabel butts in, though my relief is short lived. 'Everyone knows that that Harold Parkinson's mother was buried in Sandquay Woods, not the College grounds.'

They both turn to look at me expectantly.

'Err…' I manage at length, my customary sangfroid disappearing quicker than you can say woosah, 'I'm not actually sure whether I'm going to take the job with Alex. To be honest, I'm not … err … I'm not even sure it will amount to anything.' I pause, searching for the right words, finally adding, 'What I mean is, I might not be here that long…' I finish the last sentence in a rush and let my words hang in the air.

'Oh, that's a shame,' Mabel sighs. 'I've put you down for the Ladies Afloat annual quiz night. We could do with someone under sixty.'

∞∞∞

'Darling, how are you?'

'Tired!' Sebastian's blunt response went completely over his mother's head like always. Why she always chose to phone him in the early hours was a mystery he'd never managed to fathom.

'I wanted to tell you I'm interviewing someone for the paper.'

'Couldn't the news have waited until morning?' At the silence on the other end of the line, he finally sighed and sat up. 'I thought you employed somebody back in January. Have you got rid of them already?'

'No, of course not darling. Alex is doing a wonderful job.'

'Then why are you interviewing someone else?'

'I need someone in the field, Sebastian. Someone with a bit of grit, who's not afraid of upsetting a few people in her relentless pursuit of the truth.'

'It's a woman?'

'Yes dear.' His mother's voice had taken on a fervent tone which made his heart sink. 'She was very high up in the National Crime Agency in London. I'm certain she won't balk at bashing a few heads together if the occasion demands it.'

'Firstly, I can't imagine a situation likely to involve any head bashing in Dartmouth, and secondly, if there was, I assume she's familiar enough with the law to know that indulging in violence of any kind will likely land her on the wrong side of a cell.'

'Have they got any cells in Dartmouth?'

Sebastian gritted his teeth. 'I think you're missing the point, Mother. I know the Dartmouth Herald is important to you. But you haven't got an infinite allowance and if you want to maintain your comfortable lifestyle, you can't afford to throw money away sending people on fools' errands that may or may not end with someone in bloody hospital.'

'Or jail,' his mother added cheerfully. 'Don't you worry sweetheart; I have everything in hand. I'll let you know what our ex-cop turns out like.'

And with that, the phone went dead. Did his mother just say ex-cop? Groaning, he put his phone back on the bedside table and lay back against his pillows. Three o'clock in the bloody morning. Sometimes he doubted his mother ever slept at all.

There was the sound of movement from the corner of the room and seconds later, Coco jumped onto the bed. 'She woke you up too, did she girl?' In answer, the dog nudged his hand and settled down next to him with a contented sigh. Stroking her soft fur, Seb gave a dark chuckle. 'You wouldn't have been doing this a year ago. Carla would have been screaming for her inhaler and dousing herself in Chanel No 5 just about now.'

A sudden wave of sadness swamped him. Not for his marriage – he was beyond relieved the nightmare was over. He glanced over at the empty side of the bed. But he finally realised that there would never be someone curled up on the other side of Coco. In all honesty, he couldn't even imagine it. One spectacularly failed marriage was enough. There wouldn't be a second.

Chapter Four

In contrast to yesterday, this morning is wet and dismal. Pulling open the curtains, I peer through the mist and pouring rain and can just see the other side of the river. This is the first time I can remember actually waking up with no idea at all of what I'm going to do with my day.

Fighting an unexpected panic attack, I determinedly make my bed and hang up the remainder of my paltry wardrobe, firmly telling myself to get a grip. 'I still have choices,' I say out loud to the walls. 'I don't have to stay here. I have no commitments. I'm footloose and fancy free. I can do whatever I want with my life.'

Unfortunately, a voice in my head sounding suspiciously like the Admiral mutters, *'Bollocks,'* in response to my little Ted Talk, and I sink down on the bed.

I need a job. That's the long and the short of it. My savings will last me about three months if I'm careful, and don't have to find somewhere to rent.

I'm certain my uncle won't kick me out, but he won't be expecting me to loaf around on my arse doing nothing either. I might have told him I wasn't sure if I'd be staying, but the truth is, I have nowhere else to go.

So, the wallowing has got to stop. First things first. I might as well try and get some more information from Alex about my probable employer. Then, clearly I need to spend some of my savings on some new clothes. Gritting my teeth, I climb to my feet and go back to the window. The Higher Ferry is just about to leave for the other side. If I get my skates on, I can make it down to the road before it comes back.

Although it's early June and the weather is foul, the town is actually heaving. I can't help but wonder what it'll be like in the height of summer. I've arranged to have lunch with Alex in a pub called *The Seven Stars*, and since I've spent the last hour and a half checking out the charity shops, I'm more than ready for a sandwich – especially since I missed breakfast. A glass of wine wouldn't go amiss either. As the Admiral says, *the sun's over the yardarm somewhere in the world.*

I manage to find the pub relatively easily, and once through the door, I stand for a second, letting my eyes become accustomed to the dimness. Looking around, I hope Alex has booked a table, because the place is packed with people undoubtedly trying to get out of the weather.

'Don't look now, Wonder Woman's just walked through the door.' I barely register the comment to my right having been on the receiving end of much, much worse. In fact I'm more than happy to be compared to either *Linda Carter* or *Gal Gadot*, though I'm pretty certain the bloke who spoke needs glasses.

Momentarily elevated by my superhero status, I sweep through the thick of bodies, looking for Alex. Seconds later, I'm brought back down to earth with a bump. 'Bloody hell, it's the jolly green giant.' Without acknowledging the comment, I make a quick mental note to dispose of my khaki anorak in the nearest bin.

'I happen to be very partial to canned peas.' The voice sort of coming to my defence is definitely not Alex's. I peer in the direction it came from and suddenly recognise Freddy sitting at a table in the corner, a glass of fizz in his hand. Knowing it's unlikely to be a coincidence, I make my way towards my friend's partner.

'I was expecting to meet with Alex alone,' I comment brusquely. Then I bite my lip. Alienating people from the outset is something I'm particularly good at.

'Alex is on his way,' Freddy declares with a pained sigh. 'Believe me, it wasn't my choice to spend my lunchtime with such *ill will'd and frampled waspishness*.' I stare at him for a second.

'I *think* I probably deserved that.'

'Yes you did, but pay him no attention, he's just showing off.' Alex appears at my elbow. 'Drink?'

I nod my head, and try for a small smile, reminding myself I can ill afford to piss people off just for the hell of it. Those days are long gone. His slightly alarmed response doesn't bode well for the new and improved cheerful me.

'OMG, is that sparkling? Just let me sniff it.' Another voice. This time female and one I do recognise.

'Tory!' I'm happy to see her and my smile really is genuine, but … well, so much for our business meeting…

'Hello, Teddy.' She reaches up and enfolds me in a hug. 'Freddy happened to mention you'd be here. So I came straight over as soon as I'd dropped Isaac at nursery.' She sits down, picks up her furry baby and waves at Alex to bring her a sparkling water.

'Hello, Dotty,' I smile at the little dog who for some reason appears delighted to see me. She promptly jumps from Tory's lap to mine, tail wagging furiously. 'I haven't got any treats,' I laugh, stroking her head. Disgruntled, she nevertheless circles a few times and makes herself comfortable on my knee, clearly willing to wait. I look down at Tory's slight bump. 'Congratulations, by the way.'

'That's one of the reasons I'm here.' She gives a slightly morose sigh, and pulls off her raincoat.

'Don't tell me it's another boy,' Freddy commiserates.

She shakes her head before giving a small rueful smile. 'Oh no, I'm certain they're both girls.'

'OMG, you're having twins.' Freddy's squeal turns the heads of everyone around us. Tory glares at him.

'Why don't you tell the whole world,' she snaps.

'You want to keep it a secret?' I ask curiously.

'From my dad, definitely. I can't deal with his smug *I told you so* look at the moment. Not until this dratted morning sickness has passed.'

'Why, what's he told you?'

She looks at me and suddenly breaks out in a grin. 'I forgot, you're a Shackleford too.' She laughs harder at my frown. 'Perhaps I should be breaking it to you a little more gently, but twins are in our family. Specifically female twins. Lots and lots and lots …'

'How do you know?' I counter. 'I mean neither of our parents had twins.'

'Apparently, it can miss two or three generations.' She points to her swollen stomach. 'And it seems our generation is the one it's resurfacing in.'

I force back the disquiet. I mean I'd like children and all that – I think. But twins? 'That doesn't mean anything,' I scoff, a little too vehemently. 'Just because you're having twins doesn't mean I'll follow suit.'

'You keep telling yourself that,' Tory responds smugly. 'And once we've had one set…' She lets her voice trail off. I can see the thought of me knee deep in nappies with a baby on each hip has cheered her up no end.

'Well, I think it's wonderful,' Freddy enthuses, before I get the chance to argue further. 'Mind you, it's a bloody good job we've set our wedding for next summer instead of this. I don't want all the attention on you when I walk down the aisle.'

'With me and Kit walking behind you, I'm afraid you'll pale into insignificance, bump or no bump,' Tory retorts.

'I wasn't aware you're intending to make it official,' I smile, genuinely pleased for them both. Freddy holds out his right hand, wiggling his ring finger to draw attention to the ebony and white gold band he's wearing.

'You know Alex, doesn't like to make a song and dance about anything.' He leans forward to add conspiratorially, 'Don't tell him I told you, but I think he's planning on asking you to be his best man.' I stare at him, lost for words. It's so ... *unexpected*. Freddy taps his nose and winks, turning back to Tory.

'Have you got any names?'

Tory shakes her head as Alex returns with our drinks.

'What about, Chloe and Zoe?' Freddy grins after quickly bringing Alex up to speed.

'Or Poppy and Penelope?' I suggest, getting into the spirit.

'Daisy and Maisy?' Alex offers.

'Lilly and Millie?' proposes a complete stranger who's clearly been earwigging on our conversation. I give him one of my trademark *looks* which always worked so well in the NCA. What do you know, they work just as well in Dartmouth.

'What does Noah think about being on the minority side?' Freddy asks.

'Oh he's over the moon.' Tory smiles softly, and I feel an unaccountable pang at the look in her eyes, but then she gives a wicked laugh. 'I'm pretty certain he won't be so happy when he realises the hourly rinse and repeat in the wee small hours will involve both of us.'

'You're certain you're carrying girls?' Alex chimes in. 'I mean, there's always Eric and Derek.'

'Well, for the last two hundred years, every set of twins appear to have been girls – at least the ones in the family bible. And each time there was more than one set.'

'You have a family bible?' Freddy asks, clearly intrigued. Tory nods.

'Noah's convinced there's a story in there somewhere. He's joined *Ancestry.com* – I think he fancies the idea of writing and directing his own movie.'

'You've never mentioned it before,' Freddy accuses, evidently peeved at the thought of not knowing everything.

'My father gave it to me just before Christmas,' Tory answers. 'I updated the family tree and originally put it on the coffee table for everyone to see, but with Isaac's curiosity and sticky fingers, I had to move it. I'll show you next time you come over.' She turns back to me before adding quietly, 'I put you and your dad in there. I wasn't sure if you'd want me to put in your mum's name.'

The warm fuzzy feeling I get at being included scares the pants off me, and I give a good imitation of a nonchalant shrug. 'I haven't seen my mother since I was about seven, so it's not as if she's played a big part in my life.'

To my horror, Tory reaches out and squeezes my hand. 'I really hope you'll stay in Dartmouth,' she murmurs.

'Have you told Kit yet?' I blurt, fighting a sudden ridiculous urge to cry.

She grins. 'Yep. Her reaction was even louder than Freddy's. She's been texting me girl's names ever since.'

'How's the hotel doing?' I ask, genuinely curious.

'According to Kit, she and Jason are up to their ears in it, so I think that means it's going very well. Jason's talking about taking on a manager in the autumn. Hopefully, Noah and I will get the chance to visit post morning sickness but pre imminent labour.'

'That's great,' I smile, privately wondering if I'd be up to managing an exclusive boutique hotel in the middle of nowhere …

I'm still musing as Tory picks up a menu. 'So, what are we going to eat?' she quips. 'As Dad is so fond of saying, *I could eat a scabby donkey between two mattresses.*'

∞∞∞

'I understand congratulations are in order.'

We're finally alone since Freddy's had to get back to work and Tory's gone to pick up Isaac. Before dashing off, she invited me round for dinner tomorrow night and there they were again – the warm fuzzies. I'm doomed.

Alex looks at me and grins. 'I knew Freddy wouldn't be able to keep it to himself.'

'Is it a secret?'

He shakes his head and laughs. 'Freddy couldn't keep a secret to save his life.'

'Well, he seems to think you're planning on asking me to be best man, which is patently ridiculous.'

He frowns and my stomach does an uncomfortable flip. 'Why is it ridiculous?'

I stare at him for a second, not quite knowing what to say. 'Well, you have lots of friends to choose from. Why would you want me to do it – I'd be awful.'

'That's irrelevant,' he retorts, though I can't help but notice he doesn't disagree with me. 'Will you do it?'

'So Freddy wasn't bullshitting then?' I stall. He raises his eyebrows, waiting. I stare back at him, feeling a warmth creep up my body. 'I'd be honoured,' I manage at length. Bloody hell, I really *am* doomed.

When he looks as though, he's going to get up and hug me, I cough and hurriedly change the subject. 'So, who exactly *is* your boss?'

Alex takes a sip of his cider. 'Her name is Daphne Sinclair. She told me all her friends call her Daphers and that I was to do the same.'

'And do you?' I ask doubtfully. He shakes his head.

'Can you imagine calling anyone *Daphers*? No, prefer Mrs. Sinclair, though I think her husband was a lord or something. She's lived in Dartmouth for about ten years give or take – ever since he cashed in his chips.'

'And she owns this ... Dartmouth Herald?'

Alex grins. 'There's not really much to own. Just a name and the rent on a small office on Anzac Street.'

'So what exactly is it you do?'

'It's not what *I* do,' Alex counters, 'it's what she wants *you* to do.'

'And exactly what *does* she want me to do?' I frown before

adding, 'It all sounds a bit dodgy to me. How can she afford to pay two people to work on a monthly pamphlet? Is she money laundering?'

'Well, she's not exactly paying me Fleet Street rates. And I doubt it will be any different for you – though you might get paid extra danger money. You know for rescuing cats up trees and stuff.'

'How the hell did you go from chasing career criminals to interviewing old ladies? I'll be out of my mind with boredom within a month.'

'Very likely,' agreed Alex. 'And you haven't got the same reason to be here as I do.' He gave a shrug. 'But there's no harm in meeting her. And there are worse places than Dartmouth to spend the summer.' He looks at me, with a boyish grin. 'If you bugger off though, I'll expect you back this time next year.'

Chapter Five

'I admit I offered Teddy Shackleford a place to bunk up since she was heading for the scrap heap, but this could actually work out in our favour, Jimmy lad.'

'What do you mean, Sir? What could work out in our favour?'

The Admiral sighed. 'I know you've never had any ambition in life apart from breathing, Jimmy, but even you've got to admit things have been a bit bloody boring since we solved *Operation Lighthouse*.'

'Why, has someone been murdered in Dartmouth?'

Muttering, '*Not yet,*' under his breath, Charles Shackleford gave an irritated shake of his head. 'I was thinking about Teddy. You know, if she starts that job for Dippy Daphers.'

'You said she just wanted Teddy to do a bit of reporting for that leaflet of hers.'

'Well, I've been giving it a bit of thought. I reckon she's looking for someone to do a spot of undercover snooping. The kind we're good at Jimmy.'

Jimmy's heart did a familiar double skip. 'I'm certain if she was looking for someone to investigate something specific, Sir, she'd have gone to a private detective agency … or the police.'

Charles Shackleford took a sip of his pint. He didn't normally meet Jimmy in the *Ship* on a Thursday teatime, but since Teddy had let it slip she was meeting the owner of the Dartmouth Herald the very next morning, he decided there was no time to lose.

'But what if she's looking to keep it under wraps? What better way to do it than under the guise of a newspaper.'

'It's hardly a newspaper,' Jimmy chuckled.

'That's exactly it, Jimmy my boy. 'Why the bloody hell does she need another reporter?' He tapped his nose. 'I smell a big bollocking rodent.'

'Well seeing as she's known locally as Dippy Daphers,' Jimmy declared, 'she's likely just bored. I've heard she's loaded. Old money.' He paused thoughtfully. 'I've never actually met her. Is she as eccentric as they say?'

'Used to be president of Ladies Afloat. According to Mabel, she never wears the same pair of shoes.'

'Well, that's nothing unusual, Sir, most women wear lots of different shoes.'

'But not at the same time. Last week Mabel reckoned she was wearing one red one and one green one.'

Jimmy frowned and dipped into the packet of crisps in front of him, making sure to drop one for Pickles since the springer's soulful eyes indicated he was about to collapse from starvation. 'So what kind of business could she be investigating?'

The Admiral shrugged. 'Who knows. These wealthy eccentric types have all sorts of skeletons in their cupboards.' He helped himself to one of Jimmy's crisps. 'Teddy's having a chat with her tomorrow, so I thought we needed to come up with a plan.'

Jimmy looked at him in bewilderment. 'A plan for what, Sir?'

The Admiral sighed. 'Seriously, Jimmy, I sometimes think you've got the instincts of a bloody doorknob.' He looked around to check no one was listening to their conversation, before adding in a whisper loud enough to be heard within a hundred-yard radius, '*We need to know what they talk about.*'

'Well, why don't you just ask Teddy?'

'I can't just ask her. I only met her a few months ago. And she's a cagey sort. Not a gatling gob like our Victory.'

Jimmy took a long sip of his pint to give him time to think. As he placed the glass back on the bar, he realised there was no way he was going to avoid having to ask the question. He gave a long-suffering sigh and tipped the crisp crumbs on Pickles's delighted head.

'So how are you going to find out then, Sir?'

∞∞∞

Sebastian was up at dawn the following morning to take Coco out for her daily walk. Friday was one of his busiest days in the hotel, especially since the restaurant had gained a Michelin star a year earlier.

But that wasn't the only reason. Every Friday the restaurant advertised *Dinner with the Duke*. Yep, unbelievably tacky, but despite his misgivings, the concept had proved hugely popular. The hotel was booked up every weekend months in advance. Seb had often wondered what would happen if he happened to pop his clogs. Simon, the hotel manager would probably get him stuffed and prop him up in the corner. Or failing that, a cardboard cut-out.

Chuckling, Sebastian called Coco to him and made his way down the hall into the private lift linking his personal quarters with the main hotel. A couple of minutes later he was stepping out into a secluded corner of the reception area. His personal lift was tucked out of sight, away from prying eyes, and to anyone nosing around, it looked like another locked door.

The night manager hadn't yet been replaced by the day staff and Coco dashed ahead of him, skidding on the marble tiles in her eagerness to reach the elderly employee seated at the front desk.

'You spoil her, Tom,' Sebastian declared as Coco wolfed down her morning treat.

'She's a good girl, Sir, and deserves a bit of coddling.' He looked up and smiled. 'Ready for the fray this evening?'

'Tiara polished and ready,' Sebastian chuckled. 'Come on, Coco, leave the man alone. You've had your treat.' He started to walk towards the front door, then stopped and turned back. 'Before you leave, Tom, would you mind getting the *Defender* out of the garage and leaving it next to the Rose Garden? I have to go out this morning and would rather keep a low profile. I'll save my witty repartee for this evening.'

'Very well, Sir. I'll leave the keys on the wheel.'

Waving his thanks, Sebastian walked out into the early morning mist. He wasn't a morning person, or even an afternoon one, if he was being honest. His small talk was a finely honed instrument that functioned best after five p.m. – usually about the time he had a gin and tonic.

Striding after Coco who'd gone dashing down the steps and was already halfway to the orchard, Seb's thoughts turned to his ex-wife. He wasn't entirely convinced he'd heard the last of her. The look in her eyes as they'd parted had been one of vindictive malice.

Perhaps he shouldn't have prevented her using the title of Duchess. Looking back, it seemed a little petty. But then, the last thing he wanted was for her to drag the Sinclair name through the mud she seemed determined to wallow in. The sooner her connection to Blackmore was forgotten, the better.

∞∞∞

In the end, I abandon my overlarge suit in favour of a new pair of jeans and a shirt. It's hardly an interview – not the kind I've been used to anyway. Just a chat over coffee. I stare at myself in the mirror imagining the kind of questions she'll be asking. What are my tree climbing skills like? Can I tackle a rabid chihuahua?

How the hell have I come to this? Once the - well, not exactly the darling of the NCA - to… All of a sudden I find myself chuckling. It's all so ridiculous. Grabbing my bag, I hang it across my shoulders in a perfect Sloaney imitation. There, any eccentric worth her salt is bound to be impressed.

I head downstairs to the kitchen intending to grab some toast before catching the ferry over. To my surprise, the Admiral is sitting at the table. His loud, jovial, 'Good morning,' immediately makes me suspicious. Blimey, I've only been here a few days, and already I'm questioning every move he makes. I can't help but wonder if it's Tory's distrust of her father's motives that's rubbing off.

'Sleep well?' he booms, making me jump as I fiddle with the toaster. Pickles starts barking. Clearly he's not accustomed to his master being polite either.

'Very well, thank you,' I confirm, equally politely.

'Where are you meeting old Daphers then?'

I turn round surprised. 'You know her?'

'I reckon most Dartmothians have at least heard of her. She lives up near the Castle. Big old place above Warfleet Creek.'

I frown, buttering my toast. Basingstoke is actually beginning to look tempting. Sitting down at the table, I give a calculated shrug. 'We're just having a chat over coffee – in the ... err ... paper's headquarters I think. It'll probably come to nothing.'

'Oh I'm certain she'll be falling over herself to take you on,' the Admiral disagrees, climbing to his feet. 'I can't imagine there are many six-foot-three Miss Marples knocking around Dartmouth.'

With the Admiral's version of a pep talk still ringing in my ears, I head over the river. Just before eleven, I make my way to the Dartmouth Herald's head office (okay, its only office) on Anzac Street. It's next door to a tiny boutique called *Bohemian Bliss*. Looking at the eclectic selection of clothes and artifacts in the window, I wonder if Daphers owns that too.

The door to the office is on the side, a little way up a narrow alley. There's a small but tasteful plaque together with a small brass bell. It's all very *noir detective*. Pulling self-consciously at my shirt, I have a sudden image of *Jessica Rabbit* in my head. The thought of me sashaying through the door on five-inch heels wearing a sprayed-on dress makes me chuckle as I press the doorbell and push open the door – half expecting the bell to punch me in the nose in true *Toontown* fashion.

The lady sitting with Alex is bizarrely wearing one blue and one pink shoe. Her dress in contrast is a bilious green colour reminiscent of a public toilet circa nineteen seventy.

I blink, and for a second, the silence is absolute. Then Alex jumps to his feet. I can tell he's trying hard not to laugh.

'How good of you to join us, Ms. Shackleford.' If I had any doubt that here was one of England's great eccentrics born with a silver spoon in her mouth and condemned to be forever caricatured, her next words rid me of it. 'One lump or two in your Darjeeling, my dear?'

∞∞∞

'Right then, she's gone in. Jimmy, how much money have you got on you?'

'Err …,' the small man paused, rummaging around in his pockets. 'I think I might have about six pounds in change.'

'You won't be able to buy a bollocking toe ring with that.'

'I don't need a toe ring,' Jimmy protested in bewilderment.

'Well, we've got to have some excuse to go into the damn shop.' Jimmy frowned, his eyes following the direction of the Admiral's finger.

'*Bohemian Bliss*,' he read. 'Are you looking for something for Mabel, Sir? I can't imagine you'll find a toe ring big enough to get over her bunion. You might be better looking in Marks and Spencer's.'

Charles Shackleford gave an exasperated sigh and spoke slowly. 'The shop's next to the Dartmouth Herald's office. I've brought an empty glass with me.' He held up the large bag he'd been carrying. 'If I put it against the wall, I'll be able to earwig on their conversation.' He gave a frown. 'Mind you, I'll have to do it in the changing room.' He peered through the window at the fringed tasselled harem trousers laid out on the display.

'Come on, Jimmy they'll do. It says one size on the label, and I only need to try 'em on.'

∞∞∞

'So, tell me, dear girl. What was it you actually got up to in the NCA?'

'I'm afraid I'm not actually at liberty to discuss that,' I respond firmly. 'Perhaps we could talk about what it is you're looking for. Do you have a copy of the terms of reference for the post of ... err ...?' I pause, looking helplessly at Alex.

'Investigative journalist,' he interjects smoothly.

'Oh, I don't think we need to worry about all that.' Mrs. Sinclair waves her hand in dismissal before leaning forward, eyes narrowing. 'I just need to know whether your investigative skills are up to the job.'

'And what job is that precisely?' I keep my voice polite and my face impassive. Any minute now she's going to ask me to infiltrate a drug ring…

'This year is my son's fortieth birthday,' she declares. 'I'm supposed to be holding a surprise birthday party for him at his home in Blackmore, but before then I need you to look into our family tree rather urgently.'

I raise my eyebrows and shoot a quick glance over to Alex who looks as surprised me. 'You're willing to pay me just to look into your family archives? Is it a birthday present?'

'I'm very much hoping so, but it's not quite as simple as perhaps it sounds. If you'll allow me to explain. The family seat in Blackmore is rather old. We have records of a chimney fire in 1867. It did little damage to the overall structure of the building, but it practically gutted the library, and all records before that date were destroyed. The Duke of the time was the ninth…'

'Your son is a duke?' I butt in incredulously. Mrs. Sinclair gives a disapproving frown. Clearly interrupting is extremely bad manners.

'Why yes, dear. Sebastian is the Fourteenth Duke of Blackmore.' She gives a sad sigh. 'And very likely the last in the direct line since that damned gold-digger he married.' She pursed her lips.

'How I wish I could simply wave a magic wand and rid him of the baggage. If ever there was a woman deserving of a nasty accident, it's Carla Rowen.'

'I take it you don't get on with your daughter-in-law,' I comment carefully.

'Ex-daughter-in-law,' Mrs. Sinclair declared, her tone radiating satisfaction. 'Fortunately, Sebastian saw her for what and who she really is before siring any offspring.'

I really don't know what to say to that, so I draw the conversation back to the job at hand.

'So how far do you want me to go back? Isn't there some kind of record of peerages in Great Britain. Surely dukes are registered somewhere?'

'We have the writ of summons requested by the Ninth Duke Peter Sinclair when he assumed the title. But since Somerset House records only go back to 1837, we don't have an actual birth certificate.'

'What about the local church?' Alex asks. 'I take it there is one in Blackmore. All births, marriages and deaths within its parish should be held there.'

Mrs. Sinclair nods her head. 'But terribly sadly, not to mention vexingly, the original church was destroyed in another fire. This time in 1839.'

'Why is it so important?' I ask bluntly, sensing this isn't all about a birthday surprise.

Mrs. Sinclair sighs before rummaging around in her handbag, finally unearthing a large hipflask. 'Be a dear and pour me a little tot,' she orders, handing the flask to Alex. Turning back to me, she purses her lips.

'There's been a challenge for the Dukedom. According to a

man named Jeremy Sinclair, he should be the Fourteenth Duke instead of my son.'

∞∞∞

'Bloody hell, Jimmy, she wants our Teddy to arrange a nasty accident for someone called Carla.'

'Oh I can't believe that, Sir. Teddy wouldn't agree to such a terrible th…'

'Shhh, Daphers is speaking again.'

Jimmy smiled lamely at the shop assistant who returned his stare flatly. Clearly she didn't believe the Admiral had any intention of buying the tasselled harem trousers he was supposedly trying on in the tiny changing room. 'How do they fit?' she called challengingly.

'I think he might need a bigger size,' Jimmy countered desperately when the Admiral unceremoniously told her to shut up.

Fortunately, at that moment the bell jingled as the shop door opened admitting another customer. Jimmy sighed at the reprieve.

'You can't stay in there for much longer, Sir,' he hissed through the curtains.

The Admiral stuck his head through. 'It's a rum do and no mistake, Jimmy lad. I think the old baggage has finally lost it.'

'Well?' demanded the assistant shrilly, leaving the newcomer perusing a tray of nose rings.

The Admiral looked over at the assistant in irritation. Then to Jimmy's horror, he threw open the curtain and stood with his hands on his hips, like a geriatric super genie. Unfortunately he'd only managed to pull the trousers up as far as his boxers but to Jimmy's eternal gratitude, the shortfall was covered by the tails of his shirt.

'I don't suppose you've got 'em in red?'

Chapter Six

'Sebastian has entirely dismissed the charlatan's claim despite there being a familial match to their DNA. Says he could well be related to half of South Devon as it was customary for titled sons to sow their wild oats before settling down to a wife.'

Mrs. Sinclair gives a small shrug. 'To be honest, he's right. The DNA match itself proves only that they are distant relatives. But if this man insists on taking his claim forward, it could cost my son dearly.' Alex hands her a small measure of what looks like whisky, which she knocks back in one before holding her glass out for a refill.

'I wouldn't be surprised if that … that …. *bloody woman* is behind it all. She'll be doing this simply to get back at Sebastian for having the temerity to throw her out.'

'Was she unfaithful?' I can't help but ask. By now, both Alex and I are hooked. It's like an episode of *Downton Abbey*. Beats rescuing cats or investigating underground wife swapping parties any day of the week.

'More a question of how many,' is her waspish response. 'I'm simply thankful they never had any children or things would be even more complicated than they already are.' She gives the wood of the desk a resounding tap to back up her conviction.

'So,' she goes on briskly, 'we can be certain that Sebastian is a direct descendant of the Ninth Duke. But we cannot presume any further.'

'I'd have thought that's plenty far enough?' I exclaim

'One would think so, but apparently this Jeremy person is in possession of what we *think* is a letter which calls into question the Ninth Duke's primogeniture.'

'The Eighth Duke was Peter Sinclair's father?' Alex guesstimates. 'Bloody hell, I had no idea it was all so complicated.'

'Normally, it's actually quite straightforward,' Mrs. Sinclair counters, holding out her glass for another refill. 'There aren't many inherited peerages left in this country, so something like this doesn't come up often.' She pauses, clearly gathering her thoughts. 'The Register of the Lords holds records of the Seventh Duke and those who came before him. But for some reason, the Eighth Duke appears to be a mystery. We don't know his name and cannot confirm his relationship to the Ninth. He could have been illegitimate, a cousin, or…' She shrugs and takes back her glass.

'So who exactly is this Jeremy Sinclair.'

'Bourgeois middle class,' she retorts scathingly. 'A petty little man with delusions of grandeur.'

'So he could … what … claim the title should have come to him?'

'Unlikely,' is the brisk response, 'though not impossible. But in all honesty, that's not my main concern.

'Sebastian has been forced to sell much of the estate in recent years, and after the death of my husband, he made the decision to turn the house into a hotel – five stars of course. It's been a costly endeavour, and while Blackmore Grange is beginning to pay for itself, he's since had to pay off his bloodsucker wife. If he's forced to go through the courts to prove his right to the title, he could well end up completely penniless.'

I stare into space, better to think through everything she's said. 'So, let me see if I've got this straight,' I posit at length. 'You want me to somehow discover the identity of the Eighth Duke and prove irrefutably that he inherited the whole kaboodle all fair and square with no underhand tactics such as murder. Then you want me to find out who this bloke married and prove beyond reasonable doubt that said wife gave birth to the Ninth Duke. *And* that Peter Sinclair – the Ninth duke - was definitely the Eighth Duke's offspring.'

I bask in Alex's admiring look while Mrs. Sinclair takes her turn sorting through the tangled history.

'I think you've hit the nail on the head,' she beams after a few minutes. 'Just one more thing. I haven't actually mentioned my little project to Sebastian. He thinks the man is simply a fraud looking to make some easy money and that to give him any credence at all is playing into the blackguard's hands.' She gives a long sigh. 'In essence, I agree with my son's assessment. However, I've always believed it prudent to have one's ducks in a row just in case.'

She looks at me and gives a small chuckle. 'He thinks I've brought you in to dig up some serious dirt that will turn the Herald into one of those horrible sensationalist newspapers.' She shakes her head. 'Sometimes I think my son believes me a trifle unhinged. I have no idea where he gets it from. I mean, do I look eccentric to you?'

∞∞∞

'I really can't imagine Teddy arranging some kind of deliberate accident for this Carla. I'm certain you must have misheard, Sir.'

The Admiral hmphed and took a sip of his pint. In his heart of hearts, he had the same opinion. Somewhere along the line, he'd got the wrong end of the bloody stick. That didn't mean there wasn't a story there though.

The two men were sitting in the *Cherub* pub which was conveniently round the corner from the Herald.

'There's no harm in doing a spot of investigating into this Carla Rowen,' he countered. 'From what I could hear she was Dippy's daughter-in-law until the husband kicked her out.'

'Do you know anything about her son?' queried Jimmy. 'I've heard he has a title or some such, but no one seems to know much about him.'

Charles Shackleford creased his brow. 'Can't say I've ever heard him mentioned. You reckon he could be the one looking to arrange a nasty accident for his ex?'

'I'm completely certain no one is looking to do any such thing,' Jimmy argued firmly. 'If someone was thinking of doing away with this Carla, they wouldn't have been bandying it about to someone they only just met – especially as she's an ex-copper.'

The Admiral's eyes suddenly widened, and he leaned forward excitedly. 'Unless Daphers is trying to put a spanner in the works. You know, by bringing in someone like Teddy to put a stop to it...' He left the sentence hanging, and Jimmy frowned, trying to come up with something to refute his former superior's usually questionable logic. In the end, he shook his head.

'It sounds extremely farfetched, Sir. And I really can't imagine Teddy getting involved in anything so suspect. She hasn't got a private investigator's licence has she?'

The Admiral's brow creased in thought. 'I can't imagine so. If she had, she'd likely have stayed in London. But I'll have a word with Bill just in case.'

'Well,' Jimmy went on, 'as an ex-police officer, I'm convinced she'll have told Daphers to take her suspicions to the proper authorities.'

Charles Shackleford scoffed. 'I really can't see Daphers informing the old bill that she's worried her son is planning to off his ex-wife, can you? And anyway, they can't arrest a bloke for wanting to kill his missis. If they did, ninety percent of the blokes in this country would be locked up.'

∞∞∞

Sitting in Tory's old bedroom, I look down at the key in my hand and reflect on the idiosyncrasies of life. Not only do I now have a job, I also have a small flat in Dartmouth. Well, in all honesty it's basically a posh shed in Mrs. Sinclair's garden, complete with electricity, heating and hot and cold running water. It's also fully furnished in my new employers own unique mismatched style (I might have to invest in a pair of sunglasses). But best of all, the view of the river is to die for. Warfleet Creek it turns out is a small inlet in the bend of the river near to Dartmouth Castle.

What's the catch I can hear you asking - aside from the clashing colour scheme? Well, it comes with my brand spanking new job, obviously, and makes up part of my remuneration package.

According to Mrs. Sinclair, her son Sebastian (the Duke) thought she might be able to rent the *chalet* out to discerning holiday makers to supplement her allowance which she cheerfully told me she was getting through at an alarming rate.

However, also according to Mrs. Sinclair, said holiday makers turned out to be a noisy rowdy bunch of common people and while she understands that I can't do anything about my bloodline, she's sincerely hoping I won't turn out to be quite so disruptive. So, no wild parties for me then…

It also means my actual wages are pretty much pocket money.

But as Alex said, there are worse places to spend the summer. And apparently, any expenses I incur will also be paid for.

My three boxes also arrived this afternoon so, I'll be moving out of the Admiralty this weekend before starting my investigation on Monday.

I was actually quite surprised at the look of disappointment on my uncle's face when I told him my news. I imagined he'd be over the moon to be rid of me, but when he casually asked me how the interview went, I realised he'd likely been imagining us discussing my findings over the kitchen table.

Wincing at the thought of the Admiral having even the smallest involvement in the Duke of Blackmore's business, I nevertheless promised (with my fingers crossed behind my back) that I would almost certainly be requesting his expertise *very* soon. When the hell did I become so kindhearted?

Or such a bloody good liar?

I'm due at Tory and Noah's for about seven, and as the intermittent rain from the last couple of days seems to have finally moved on, I decide to walk. Given that I've not yet dusted off my repertoire of small talk, I was relieved when Alex informed me earlier that he and Freddy have also been invited. I arranged to meet them at the entrance to Darthaven Marina in Kingswear as I've only been to Tory and Noah's house once and that was in the middle of winter.

As I stroll along the track running next to the Dart, the clouds finally part and the early evening rays of the sun give a warm orange tint to the sky. The evening is surprisingly balmy, and I realise, wonder of wonders, that I'm actually enjoying the walk. I really can't remember the last time I *strolled* anywhere. In London, I was always looking for the quickest way to get from A to B.

My dad used to enjoy walking. I wonder if he still does. Since Christmas, we've only spent one weekend together when I went home to tell him I'd lost my job. I didn't cry. I think he might have felt better if I had. But I don't think I've cried since he brought me back from Japan.

The tears weren't over my absent mother. Truthfully, I saw very little of her even when she lived with us. I dare say sumo wrestling doesn't encourage maternal bonding.

The fact was, I desperately missed the well-ordered, disciplined way of life in Japanese schools. In fact when I first came to the UK, I thought my fellow pupils were completely mad. Needless to say, I only bowed to my teacher once, though I was never allowed to forget it. And of course, once my classmates discovered my mother's profession…

But on the plus side, it made me realise that the only person I can ever rely on is myself. If I have no expectations of others, then they're never going to let me down.

My thoughts turn to my upcoming investigation. I'm as yet uncertain how I'm going to find definitive proof that Sebastian Sinclair is the rightful heir to the Blackmore Dukedom, but probably the best place to start would be Blackmore itself.

It's frustrating that I'm not allowed to work with the Duke on the problem. It would be much easier all round if he was on board with the whole thing. Unless he's an arrogant knob of course, which is a strong possibility. As I pick my way through the boatyard at Darthaven, I give a low chuckle. The whole thing sounds like a modern *Grimm's* fairy tale.

Maybe I'll be able to write a bestseller once the case is over.

∞∞∞

Sebastian stared at himself in the full-length mirror. Not out of vanity, but to ensure he correctly embodied the fantasy of every woman who came to Blackmore for a dose of make-believe romance courtesy of a real live duke. He was wearing full Regency evening dress. The superb cut of his jacket and snowy white of his silk waterfall cravat would have earned a nod of approval from Beau Brummell himself. The only spanner in the works was his prematurely silver hair. But since he flatly refused to dye it, it would have to do. And anyway, he'd been told on more than one occasion that it only added to his mystique.

He gave a low chuckle. Mystique. That was actually the word used. Flattering of course but in reality, he was about as mysterious as cheese on toast. Of course, most people never saw him without the act - the persona. Sebastian Sinclair. Fourteenth Duke of Blackmore.

That was supposing he still had the title if Jeremy Sinclair had his way. Contrary to his mother's belief, he wasn't simply burying his head in the sand, but neither was he going to run around like a headless chicken. He was waiting to actually see this letter the claimant apparently had in his possession that called over two hundred years of history into question.

He bent down to give Coco one last fuss before leaving her snoring on his bed. As he walked down the hallway, he couldn't help wondering where the hell he'd be without his title. Then he gave another chuckle, this time dark. The answer of course was broke…

Chapter Seven

We arrive at Tory and Noah's just before seven. As the man of the house pulls me in for a hug, I have to fight a sudden attack of nerves. I'm definitely not used to being embraced by hugely famous celebrities, and Freddy saying with a completely straight face, 'He'll sign your boobs if you ask him nicely,' really doesn't help at all.

Fortunately, my anxiety vanishes after a glass of wine and watching Noah as he heads upstairs to put Isaac to bed. It's hard to venerate someone while they're sniffing a nappy and yelling, 'Honey, I think we've got a poonami. If I'm not out in ten, send in reinforcements.'

'How are you settling in at the Admiralty,' Tory asks, topping up my glass and offering me a bowl of nibbles. Predictably, Dotty immediately chooses that moment to say hello.

'Well, it turns out that a small flat is one of the perks of my new job, so I'm moving out over the weekend.' I hand Dotty a nacho.

'Oh, thank God,' Tory declares vehemently. 'I was dreading what would happen after his good behaviour wore off.'

'It's hardly a flat,' Freddy argues. 'More like a sort of ... hallucinogenic shepherd's hut.'

Alex grins. 'I think it's quaint,' he declares.

'Definitely trippy.'

'So how come you two have seen it?' I ask puzzled.

'My mum and dad stayed there a few weeks ago when they came down for Easter,' Alex explains. 'Everywhere else was full up so Mrs. Sinclair offered the use of the boathouse.'

'No boats though,' Freddy quips.

'Well, obviously you're taking the job,' Tory enthuses. 'What exactly does she want you to do?'

Alex and I glance at each other. 'I could tell you, but I'd have to kill you,' he states, his voice deadly serious.

'Bloody hell, get the knife, I'm all ears.' Noah enthuses as he walks back into the room.

I shake my head. 'I'm just not sure we should be sharing private information with anyone.'

'I'm not just anyone,' protests Freddy indignantly. 'And, anyway, you're not in the NCA anymore.'

'You're right, they're not,' Tory counters, climbing to her feet. 'But sharing anything with you my dearest bestie, is like sharing it with the whole of bloody Dartmouth.'

'Need any help, babe?' Noah asks as she disappears into the kitchen.

She sticks her head back round the door. 'No juicy little titbits to be shared behind my back. I'm relying on you to gag Freddy while I'm cooking.'

'Cooking? Bit of an exaggeration darling,' Freddy retorts. 'The last time you cooked anything was Thanksgiving, and we all know how that ended up.'

'I thought the sandwiches were to die for,' counters Tory,

disappearing with an indignant sniff.

'Very nearly literally,' mutters Freddy under his breath...

Contrary to expectations, the subject of my new job didn't come up again during dinner, doubtless Freddy was simply biding his time until he got Alex alone.

I was actually surprised how much I enjoyed the continual banter around the table. I was also surprised to see how relaxed Alex was. The uptight agent I knew professionally was nowhere to be seen. Clearly when he said he'd never been so happy, he wasn't being flippant.

And me? Well, let's just say I actually smiled on several occasions. I'm beginning to think I might need to see a psychiatrist.

And now, as Noah finally brings in coffee and mints, I look down at my watch for the first time since I arrived. To my surprise, it's approaching midnight. 'Look at the time. I need to think about making a move. It'll take me an hour to walk back. Particularly if I want to make it without falling over the cliff or into the river.'

Noah shakes he head. 'You don't have to walk, Teddy. I called my buddy Dave earlier. He's been on standby since you arrived.'

I raise my eyebrows. 'Dave?'

'Taxi driver,' Noah chuckles. 'He's more than happy to be on retainer.'

'I don't know why I'm not on retainer,' grumbles Freddy. 'After all, I provide all the laughter and merriment in your lives. It's not easy being me, you know.'

'Truly, we appreciate your sacrifice,' grins Tory. 'By the way, how are you two going to get back over the river?'

'God will provide,' Freddy quips. 'Or failing that, the *put-put* we've left moored up in Darthaven.

'Talking about God,' he adds, 'before we go, will you show us that family bible you were telling us about?'

For some reason, the thought of being part of a whole family history makes me uncomfortable. I know Tory's picked up on it as she looks enquiringly over at me. 'I don't mind. I'd like to see it,' I lie, nibbling on a mint.

Tory goes off while Noah carefully wipes the crumbs off the table. 'I think it might be her most prized possession,' he smiles.

Seconds later, she's back, a huge old book cradled in her arms.

'Blimey, they didn't do things by halves back in the day,' breathes Freddy, his voice surprisingly awed.

Tory carefully lays the book down on the table in front of Freddy, standing at his shoulder. 'The family tree is in the front.'

Almost reverently, Freddy opens the brittle pages until he comes to a page of spidery handwriting. Leaning closer, he reads, 'Reverend Augustus Shackleford,' before looking up excitedly. 'So the owner of the bible was a vicar? Bloody hell, can't imagine your dad being related to a man of the cloth.'

Tory gives a soft chuckle. 'Beggars belief doesn't it.' Excitedly. Freddy turns the page to reveal a long-handwritten list of names and dates. Interested, despite my earlier reluctance, I lean forward.

'He was born in 1761,' Freddy continues. 'According to this, he was the vicar of the parish of Blackmore in South Devonshire.'

'Where?' I demand, my voice coming out sharper than I intended. Surprised at my tone, the other four look at me enquiringly. 'Did you say Blackmore?' I probe.

Freddy nods, obviously baffled. I look over at Alex.

'Mrs. Sinclair's son is the Duke of Blackmore,' I breathe, reminding him of the conversation earlier.

'Her son's a duke?' chorus Tory and Freddy, almost in concert.

'Wow,' breathes Noah delightedly.

'Can I have a look?' At my urgent request, Freddy pushes the book towards me. Turning it around, I lean forward, quickly scanning the next few lines. To my disappointment, there is no mention of a duke or any other title during the time period, just a list of children born to the Reverend. He had eight daughters, poor sod. I can see where Tory gets her twin fixation from.

'This Reverend Shackleford must have been the vicar at Blackmore when the Ninth Duke was born.' I direct my comment to Alex who nods slowly.

'Where did your father unearth the bible from?' I ask Tory.

'The Admiralty attic. It's full of old stuff, mostly junk.'

'Can you remember whether there were any more old books?'

Tory frowns before nodding. 'There were a few stacks I think. I don't know how old they are though.'

'Do you think your dad would let me have a look before I move out?'

'Only if you tell us what it is you're up to for Daphne Sinclair,' she retorts, eyebrows raised. I look round at the three expectant faces, then glance over at Alex who shrugs, clearly leaving it up to me. Sighing, I reluctantly provide a brief outline of the current Duke's problem and what his mother wants me to do about it.

'So, he could be an imposter,' declares Freddy, eyes shining. 'Have you Googled him?'

I frown and shake my head. 'I've been a little busy.' Freddy looks at me as though I've got two heads.

Tory narrows her eyes in deliberation. 'I think it's better my dad doesn't know anything about this,' she comments carefully at length. 'Even you know what a loose cannon he can be if he thinks there's some kind of mystery to solve. And he's worse than Freddy at keeping secrets.'

She pauses for a second. 'I think you should move out as planned tomorrow. Dad and Mabel are taking Isaac to *Paignton Zoo* on Sunday. It's been planned for ages so dad couldn't wriggle out of it. We're dropping Isaac off at the Admiralty at eleven. That should provide a clear three-hour window.'

'I feel a bit uncomfortable going about it behind his back,' I argue with a frown.

'You're not,' Tory retorts with a grin. 'I am.'

'Don't even think about leaving me behind,' Noah adds firmly.

'Well, since Alex is part of the investigation and obviously has to be there,' Freddy pronounces, 'shall we agree on eleven thirty?'

∞∞∞

The next morning, my uncle is nowhere to be seen which is a relief since Tory reckons he's got a nose for skulduggery – especially when he's been left out of it.

Mabel's in the kitchen though and her smiling greeting makes me feel even more guilty – even though I suspect the matron would cheer us from the side-lines if she knew what we were up to.

'Are you sure you don't want to stay a little bit longer?' she asks earnestly, handing me a cup of tea. 'I know Charlie isn't the easiest person to live with, but Daphne … well, it could be like getting out of the frying pan and into the fire, dear.'

'It will be easier to get to and from the office,' I reassure her. 'And I really don't think I'll see much of Mrs. Sinclair, to be honest.'

Mabel sits down, the expression on her face clearly indicating she's wrestling over something. I look at her expectantly. In the end she gives a little cough.

'Well, I'm not sure whether you've noticed,' she begins hesitantly, 'but Daphne is a bit ... err ... strange.' Her face flushes slightly and she takes an agitated sip of her tea. Bless her, I don't think Mabel has a nasty bone in her body.

'The thing is...' she goes on, 'you know you are always welcome here, Teddy. Please don't think you have to put up with that awful, decapitated stuff she serves.'

I blink, completely at a loss for words until she adds, 'There will always be a good cup of Nescafe here for you.'

She means decaff coffee. I take an urgent swallow of my tea, while my brain tries to come up with an appropriate answer.

'I don't expect Mrs. Sinclair will be providing my hot drinks,' I comment carefully at length. 'I'll be living in a chalet in her garden, so I'll be doing my own shopping.'

'Oh, well, that's alright then.' She says, clearly relieved. She gives my hand a pat and gets to her feet. 'I'd better be getting on. Charlie's off somewhere with Pickles so I'm going to give his study a bit of a tidy. Let me know if you need anything, dear.'

'It won't take me long to get my things together,' I respond. 'Alex is coming over at ten to pick me up.'

She smiles and nods. 'He's a lovely boy, Alex. I was so pleased when he and Freddy got together. It's nice to see Freddy so happy now he's monotonous.'

By lunchtime my meagre possessions have been tidied away,

and I've managed to hide the more garish of Mrs. Sinclair's ornamentations in suitably dark corners. As I look around in satisfaction, I'm surprised at the sudden feeling of warmth that washes over me. For what is essentially a large one roomed shed – two if I count the bathroom.

The bed is separated from the living area by a large screen flamboyantly painted with various plump naked cupids. There are two small sofas scattered with brightly coloured cushions facing each other next to a woodburning stove, and a breakfast table which on close inspection appears to be stencilled with naked couples engaged in... I turn my head upside down, pretty certain that the position the figures are in is anatomically impossible. I make a note to get a tablecloth, I'm no prude but would rather not have porn with my breakfast...

Fortunately, the two chairs are simply painted – a bright red - but no naked figures to sit on. Obviously, Mrs. Sinclair was going for the whole couples' saucy weekend retreat vibe.

To complete the look, there are fairy lights everywhere. The jury's currently out on whether or not they'll provide a navigational hazard for any night sailors...

But at the end of the day, the result is actually ... well, *cosy*.

I still need to do some shopping, but as I poke my head in the fridge, I immediately spot a bottle of fizz. Pulling it out, I regard the label with delighted awe. Clearly it's a gift from Mrs. Sinclair. My new employer might have terrible taste in coffee, but she certainly knows her bubbly.

Impulsively, I pull the cork and pour myself a glass, wandering outside to sit on the small patio which looks directly over the River Dart at Warfleet Creek. The view is magnificent.

Taking small sips of my Champagne (I might not get another bottle) I sit and watch the river traffic and speculate just how much Mrs. Sinclair could be earning a week by renting this place out to holiday makers. Clearly she doesn't need the money that badly – the bottle of fizz alone must have cost her an arm and a leg.

In contrast to yesterday, the weather is warm and sunny. It really is idyllic, and I have a sudden feeling of disquiet. It wouldn't do for me to fall in love with the place. At the end of the day, the job is very likely temporary – subject to the whims of a member of the eccentric aristocracy. Getting my feet too far under the table will only end in tears. Better to simply concentrate on the job at hand.

Finishing my glass, I'm debating whether to risk another, when the sound of a car pulls me out of my reverie. Turning round, I spot a black four by four parking up next to Mrs. Sinclair's *Mini*. Seconds later, a silver haired man climbs out of the driver's seat. Watching his tall form lean back into the car, I wonder why he looks familiar.

'Sebastian darling,' Mrs. Sinclair trills hurrying round the corner towards him. 'What a lovely surprise.'

The elusive son. Feeling suddenly excited at the thought of laying eyes on a real live duke (I might have lived in London, but believe it or not, we didn't have many peers of the realm knocking around the NCA), I lean forward to get a better view. Shutting the car door, he turns to embrace his mother and for a second, I have an uninterrupted view of his face. My heart sinks like a stone. I'm almost entirely certain the Duke of Blackmore is none other than the posh knob who crashed into me at Paddington.

Chapter Eight

'Right then, Jimmy, what have you managed to find out about Dippy's daughter-in-law?'

'Not that much in all honesty, Sir. Oh she's a regular in all the society gossip pages. Mostly for her indiscretions.' Jimmy handed over a handful of online articles that had clearly come from his computer.

The two men were sitting as usual at the bar in the *Ship*, though Jimmy had made it clear he could only stay a few minutes as he was going to Zumba class with Emily. 'You should bring Mabel,' he'd suggested, hurriedly patting his former commanding officer on the back as the Admiral had nearly choked into his pint.

'Newfangled bollocks,' he'd muttered. 'What's wrong with a civilised foxtrot?'

Jimmy had hastily changed the subject.

Taking a sip of his pint, Charles Shackleford perused his friend's findings. 'Bloody hell,' he commented at length, '*Indiscretions* is putting it mildly. Her legs should be putting in for separation pay.'

'She appears to have had several male friends, Sir, despite her married status. I did find out one interesting thing though. Were you aware that Daphers's son is actually a duke?'

The Admiral raised his eyebrows. 'She's kept that one quiet. I don't reckon Mabel knows. She'd never have been able to keep that little snippet to herself.'

'Same with Emily, Sir. She had no idea.'

'What's he the duke of anyway?'

'A place called Blackmore, Sir. It's in Devon.'

The Admiral frowned, feeling a sense of déjà vu. 'Totnes way I think.' He unconsciously repeated the same words he'd used to Tory when they were looking at the family bible. He turned to Jimmy in sudden excitement. 'You know that God walloper I was telling you about – the one who's likely my great, great, great, great grandad?'

'You mean the fellow mentioned in that old bible you gave Tory?' Jimmy clarified. Charles Shackleford nodded.

'If I remember rightly, he was the vicar of Blackmore over two hundred years ago.'

'Blimey, Sir, that's a coincidence,' Jimmy breathed, all thoughts of Zumba entirely forgotten.

'Not that I think it's going to help us stop Sinclair from trying to off his wife,' the Admiral added, his excitement fading.

'I think the Duke owns a hotel there,' Jimmy piped up suddenly. 'Really posh place called Blackmore Grange. Emily keeps on at me to take her, so I've been saving up for our anniversary. Every Friday they have *Dinner with the Duke*. Never occurred to me the duke in question might be Daphers's son.'

The Admiral slapped his knee. 'That's it, Jimmy lad. It'll get us an *in*. We'll be able to quiz the bloke - discreetly of course.' Jimmy frowned. Charles Shackleford wouldn't know discreet if it hit him on the head.

'It's dreadfully expensive, Sir,' he protested desperately, cursing his idiot tongue. 'And anyway, I'm certain it's booked up for months.'

'I thought your anniversary was next Friday?' the Admiral commented. 'You were moaning about missing the *Ship*'s fish and chips.' He paused for a second, then gave a delighted chuckle. 'Jimmy my boy, you're a genius. I've been thinking about proposing to Mabel for weeks.'

'Well … I, that's wonderful, Sir,' Jimmy stuttered, a horrible sinking feeling in the pit of his stomach.

'I'd better get my skates on and find a ring,' Charles Shackleford continued thoughtfully, oblivious to his friend's look of panic.

'I … err, don't really know if…'

'I'll have a quiet word with Gerald over at the pawn shop.'

'I'm not sure that's a…'

'He owes me a favour for that horse I put him onto in the Grand Nat…' The Admiral paused, finally noticing the small man's pinched face. 'What the bloody hell's wrong with you, Jimmy? You look like you've had a brain fart.'

Jimmy squared his shoulders. 'Look here, Sir, I'm not sure exactly what you have in mind for next Friday, but…'

Charles Shackleford interrupted with a weary sigh. 'I know you're not the sharpest knife in the drawer, Jimmy, but try and keep up.

'Next Friday – *Dinner with the Duke*. We'll make it a foursome. Kill three birds with one stone. Your wedding anniversary, my proposal and a spot of interrogation. How's that for a plan to die for?

∞∞∞

Fighting the urge to duck behind the barbeque, I casually drop my eyes and step backwards. But just as I'm convinced I haven't been spotted, Mrs. Sinclair calls out my name.

'Teddy, dear, can you pop over? I'd like to introduce you to my son.'

'Shit,' I mutter wondering whether I can get away with pretending I haven't heard her. Then I stop. What the hell am I doing? This is so not me. What do I care what some stuck-up city type thinks of me – even if he has got a title? Squaring my shoulders, I turn round and march towards them, my head held high.

'Sebastian, this is my newest recruit.' Mrs. Sinclair smiles warmly at me. 'Teddy, this is my son, Sebastian.'

'How do you do,' I offer politely, directing my response to somewhere near his neck while I wait for him to comment, *'You don't look like a Teddy,'* but surprise, surprise, he doesn't.

'Teddy. That's an unusual name. Is it short for anything?' His voice is one of polite disinterest and without thinking, I look directly at his face. There is no recognition at all in his eyes, and unbelievably I feel disappointed. How bloody stupid is that? He's every bit as handsome as I remember, and irritatingly, I feel my heart thud uncomfortably as his beautiful eyes look directly into mine.

'Theodora,' I respond in my most professional (which also means brusque) tone. 'I think it was my father who shortened it to Teddy.'

'I hear you're a former police officer.'

My eyes flick to his mother, uncertain exactly what she's told him.

'I worked for the NCA in London,' I clarify, seeing no reason to lie. If he wanted to look into my background, he could do so easily.

'So, what brings you to deepest darkest south Devon?' he asks. 'I don't imagine Dartmouth is bursting at the seams with cartels – drugs or otherwise. You're unlikely to find the same level of excitement.'

'The type of excitement you're referring to is very overrated,' I answer truthfully. The fact was, I'd had enough bloody *excitement* to last me a lifetime and then some.

He looked at me then. *Really* looked at me. He didn't say the words *burnt out*, but they hung in the air.

'So, you're going to be digging up the dirt in Dartmouth instead.' His voice has gone from polite to politely scathing. My hackles rise. How dare he judge me when he knows *nothing* about me.

'Actually, I'm here to determine whether a local man buried his mother in the grounds of the Naval College as initially believed, or as my source recently hinted, over in Sandquay Woods. I'm simply waiting for the shovel to arrive. Naturally, when I discover the truth, the Herald will get the full scoop. Now if you'll excuse me.'

Of course, my intention is to simply turn my back and walk away, dignity intact. Unfortunately, my exit is ruined by the sudden appearance of a whirlwind of black and white fur round the corner of the house. I vaguely hear a deep voice shouting, '*Coco, no!*' before the dog hurls itself at my chest. I have time to give a small scream before I'm knocked backwards and fall directly on my arse right at the feet of *his grace*.

The dog proceeds to lick my face in rapturous abandon while *his knobship* bends over me as he tries to grab hold of the dog's collar and pull it off.

The weight abruptly gone, I lay there stunned for a second. 'Are you all right?'

And what does my bloody traitorous mouth mumble in answer? 'I am uninjured, thank you...'

I see in his eyes the moment he recognises me as the woman he crashed into in Paddington Station.

∞∞∞

Against my better judgement, I finished the bottle of Champagne last night and now have the mother of all hangovers. Groaning, I climb gingerly out of bed, trying to minimise the hammering in my head which is a thousand times worse when I move. My stomach roils and for a few seconds I stand still, holding onto the bed head, waiting for the nausea to pass. Shuffling to the fridge, I help myself to some fresh orange juice and hope to God there's some Alka-Seltzer in my one remaining unemptied box.

Collapsing onto the nearest sofa, I lean my head back and close my eyes, muttering, 'Bloody imbecile,' to myself. At what point did I think that drinking a whole bottle of expensive bubbly was even a remotely good idea? Especially when spending the following day crawling around a dusty attic...

This is so not like me. I'm a control freak. Getting completely smashed is something I simply don't do – ever.

I know why I did it, but I don't know *why*, if that makes even a modicum of sense.

Sebastian Sinclair. For some ridiculous reason I spent the whole evening going over and over our meeting until the bubbly turned the whole bloody thing into the equivalent of the Christmas day episode of *East Enders*.

Giving another groan, I hold my head and go over it again in the cold light of sober.

It's not like he mentioned the fact that we'd already *bumped* into one another. Simply helped me to my feet, while apologising again for his errant dog. 'She doesn't usually react so effusively to people she's never met before,' he explained stiffly, 'I can't understand what's got into her.'

The dog meanwhile paid no attention to her master as she sat staring at me, tongue lolling, tail wagging ten to the dozen. 'Her name's Coco?' I confirmed, remembering his shout. He gave an abrupt nod, clearly keen to put an end to the conversation. Coco, however, had other ideas. As I put out my hand to stroke her head, she gave a little shiver and stood up, pressing herself against me. Ignoring her arrogant owner, I crouched down.

'You're lovely,' I murmured to her softly, leaving the words, *not like your master*, unsaid. As I glanced up at him however, it was clear he knew I was thinking it. Unbelievably, his lips quirked slightly.

'This is all very unusual, my dear. Coco is usually very reserved until she gets to know one.' I jumped slightly, having forgotten Mrs. Sinclair was there. Hurriedly, I climbed to my feet.

'Of course, that's my other occupation,' I quipped. 'Dartmouth's resident dog whisperer.'

'Well, it's nice to have met you ... Teddy,' was his grace's brusque response to my feeble joke. However, his attempt to stride swiftly away was scuppered by being forced to drag Coco behind him.

I swallowed a small snigger and turned to Mrs. Sinclair. 'Thank you so much for allowing me to stay in the boathouse,' I said sincerely. 'And for the Champagne.' I attempted a winning smile. In answer, Mrs. Sinclair sighed.

'Please forgive my son's less than gracious welcome,' she stated, glancing towards the house to make sure he'd gone inside. 'I know Sebastian very often comes over as pompous and condescending. But he isn't like that once you get to know him. Despite his refusal to acknowledge the Jeremy Sinclair problem, I know that deep down, he's worried. The sooner we can expose the slippery bastard, the better.'

I blinked at her expletive, unsure how to respond. Clearly, Mrs. Sinclair's not one to mince words. For a second, I was tempted to tell her about the Shackleford bible and my proposed search of the Admiralty attic, but in the end, I swallowed the impulse. There was no telling whether it would lead to anything, and I didn't want to get her hopes up. Instead, I murmured, 'Rest assured Mrs. Sinclair, I'll do my damndest to expose him for the fraudster he is.'

Then in true *noir detective* fashion, I offered her a small reassuring nod and disappeared off into the sunset (or in this case the bottom of the garden) to pour myself another glass of the hard stuff.

Unfortunately, as I've discovered this morning, my ability to take my alcohol is nothing like *Philip Marlowe*...

Chapter Nine

Two Alka-Seltzers and a hot shower later, I'm beginning to feel a little more like a living, breathing human being. I manage to eat a slice of dry bread which is pretty much the only food I have in after abandoning all thoughts of shopping yesterday. Once we've gone through my uncle's attic, I'm going to have to brave the local supermarket.

Alex is taking his car over so I'm meeting him and Freddy at the Higher Ferry slip. I decide to set off early, thinking my delicate head might benefit from the extra fresh air.

As I make my way along the garden path from the boathouse up to the road, I keep my head down, just in case his knobship stayed overnight – all the while telling myself what a bloody idiot I'm being. This is a first for me. Very few people manage to get under my skin – my superpower has always been keeping people at arm's length and not giving a shit. But, still, my relief on discovering there's no sign of his car outside the house, is undeniable.

I actually spend the next twenty minutes as I stroll along the road towards the centre of town dreaming up scenarios where I completely blow Jeremy Sinclair's claim to the title out of the water and the Duke is explaining to the world how he'd have lost everything without me…

When I get to the fifth iteration where Sebastian Sinclair is telling me he's never met a woman like me, my imagination screeches to a halt. *Where the hell did that come from?*

Truly, I'm horrified. I stop and stare blindly over the river. I have *never* fantasised about a man (or woman for that matter). My imaginings have always been confined to solving a career-making case that would put me at the top of my profession. My head has not once *ever* been turned by a pretty face.

I lean on the wall, almost hyperventilating. I feel as though I don't know myself anymore. Since I came to Dartmouth, the careful defences I've painstakingly set in place over years and years have started to come apart.

In less than a week.

I don't know whether to cry or scream. Or throw myself in the river…

The sudden beep of a car horn cuts short my macabre thoughts, and glancing round, I see a car drive past with Freddy waving frantically through the window. Alex is driving and fifty yards up the road, he swings the car round in a nifty three-point turn.

'We were just coming to fetch you,' Freddy explains as they stop next to me.

I smile wanly in thanks and climb into the back.

'You okay?' Alex asks, looking at me through the rear-view mirror. I nod my head at him and lean back.

'Didn't sleep well,' I mumble, closing my eyes. I just can't face Freddy's brand of bouncy enthusiasm right at this moment.

The next time I open my eyes, we've stopped outside the Admiralty. Unbelievably, I fell asleep. Climbing out of the car, I realise I actually feel much better – physically at any rate.

Noah's *Porsche Taycan* is already parked outside, and when Freddy presses the buzzer next to the gate, it's Tory who answers and lets us in.

The house is strangely silent without the Admiral in it. Even when he's closeted in his study, you can't help but feel his presence. It's as if the house wants him there. Pickles on the other hand is perfectly happy in his master's absence since his one true love, Dotty is currently sharing his basket, although her eyes haven't left the plate of Danish pastries Tory's set out next to a pot of coffee.

'I thought we'd fortify ourselves with a bit of sugar before we start crawling around the attic,' she comments, eying me with a concerned look. I say nothing. I'm very fond of Tory, but we haven't got to the stage of sharing intimacies. And anyway, what would I say? *I got trollied because a drop-dead gorgeous man managed to get under my skin?* Hardly original. Although in fairness, at least I picked one with a title.

'I looked up the Duke of Blackmore online,' Freddy declares, helping himself to a pastry. 'Lots about that hotel of his and even more about his wife...'

'Ex-wife,' I interrupt, succumbing to a Pain au raisin.

'Hardly surprising - in every photo she's with a different bloke.' He shakes his head. 'But what *is* a surprise - there's hardly anything at all about Sebastian Sinclair himself. No juicy personal details at all.'

'Obviously shuns the limelight,' Noah comments. 'I don't blame him.'

'Apparently, there aren't that many inherited titles left,' Alex adds. 'I can imagine it's more of a burden really - what with the never-ending death duties and all that weight of history.'

'I could almost feel sorry for him,' Tory muses.

I give a rude snort, thinking back to the arrogant, beautiful man who looked down his nose at me yesterday. 'My heart bleeds,' I mutter, helping myself to another pastry.

Twenty minutes later, all that's left are crumbs, and we're ready to go treasure hunting. 'We're looking for something that mentions the Eighth Duke of Blackmore,' I explain. 'We have no idea of his first name, but he would have lived at the same time as your Reverend Shackleford. Apparently there was a fire in the church around 1839. The records after that speak of the Ninth Duke – one Peter Sinclair – so we can assume we are looking for his father.'

We all follow Tory into what looks like a large cupboard tucked away inside a small inner hall. The stairs inside are narrow and steep and Noah follows closely behind his wife, making sure she takes them carefully. It takes a good five minutes before all five of us finally emerge into the large attic. The only light is from a dormer window, set in the sloping roof, and a single bare bulb directly above us.

I look round curiously. There is quite a lot of old furniture, including a desk and a couple of motheaten wingback chairs. Must have been a hell of a challenge to get them up here. Beyond the bulb's reach, I can see other smaller items of furniture, all but swallowed by the shadows. Noah, bless him, insists Tory sits in one of the chairs and deposits a pile of books off the desk at her feet. I firmly stifle the sudden ache of longing that threatens to overwhelm me.

'I'll look through the other stack on the desk,' Freddy declares, peering into the shadows with a shudder. Alex chuckles, leaning forward to pick up an old walking stick.

'Never fear, dearest love of my life, nothing will harm you as long as I live,' he announces dramatically, waving the stick like a sword. 'I shall brave the dark and drag whatever lurks there back into the light… Providing it doesn't have tentacles or teeth.' The last is muttered under his breath as he steps past the desk and into the shadows.

'I'll give you a hand,' Noah laughs, setting off after him.

Shaking her head, Tory picks up the first of the books at her feet while I take the ones on the floor next to the desk.

Sitting down on the dusty floorboards, I pull the pile to me and take the one off the top.

The next few minutes is punctuated by various thumps and muttered expletives coming from the bowels of the attic along with the wild swinging of torchlight.

Most of the books in my stack are various works of fiction, from *Shakespeare* to *Charles Kingsley*. Sadly, none of them are in pristine condition so likely worth very little.

'What have you got, Tory?' I ask when my pile is exhausted.

'Nothing much so far,' she sighs, wiping her hands on her jeans. 'A couple of old accounting books, but not nearly old enough.'

'Freddy?'

There's a small silence from the other wingback chair Freddy's made himself comfortable in, then, 'You know, the Admiral was actually quite dashing in his day.'

Tory frowns. 'What are you looking at?' He holds up a large, tattered photo album.

'I thought you were intending to help,' Tory grouches, leaning forward to snatch it out of his hands. 'There are hardly likely to be any pictures of our Duke in there.'

At that moment, our two intrepid heroes stagger back into the light, their arms full of books and papers.

'There are more where these came from,' puffs Alex. They divide their hoard between the three of us and head back into the shadows.

'Bloody hell, we'll be here all day,' grumbles Freddy.

'We haven't got all day,' Tory answers, 'so no more slacking.'

I allow their voices to fade as I begin examining my new pile of books. This time, there's much more of a mixture. Old accounts – clearly my uncle doesn't hold with the idea of only keeping records dating back seven years since these go back more than thirty. The next few are to do with all things naval. If I had more time, I think I'd actually enjoy going through them.

But there's nothing at all going back to Georgian times. Sighing, I place my last book back on the pile, just as Noah returns with another stack of books, this time with a box balanced on the top. 'I found this tucked away in a corner,' he comments, placing the pile on the desk and lifting the box off the top. 'Who wants it?'

'I'll take it.' Tory leans forward in sudden excitement. 'It looks old,' she murmurs, brushing the dust off the top, just as Alex appears with another stack which he plonks on the desk with a groan of relief.

'That's it I think,' he wheezes. 'There are a few old newspapers but nothing dating back past the nineteen eighties. Is there anything in the box?'

We all watch with bated breath as Tory lifts the lid off carefully. 'Bugger,' she comments after a few seconds. 'This was mine. I remember now.' She looks up with a rueful smile. 'I didn't realise Dad was quite so sentimental...'

'He hides it well,' Freddy interrupts. She looks over at him and grins.

'That he does. These are my schoolbooks from Kingswear Primary. I had no idea he'd saved them.'

'Wouldn't it more likely have been your mum?' I question.

Tory shakes her head with a laugh. 'Definitely not, Mum never saved anything. She was scatty like that.'

'We'll take it home with us, then you can go through everything properly.' Noah leans forward to kiss her lightly, clearly picking up on her bottled-up emotions.' He takes the box and places it carefully by the door.

We go back to our respective piles. Nobody says anything but the box turning out to be a dud has definitely put a damper on the collective enthusiasm.

As I work my way down the pile, I realise the books in this stack are definitely older than any I've seen so far. I swallow a sudden feeling of hope, knowing I'm very likely to be disappointed.

Nevertheless, I examine each volume carefully to make sure I don't miss anything. By the time I get down to the last two books, my optimism has faded. Then, picking up the last but one, I look down and realise there was something squashed between the two. Putting the book I'm holding onto the floor, I lean forward. It's a small, thin booklet bound in what looks like leather. Picking it up, I blow on the dust and turn it round in my hands. The leather is worn and dirty as though it hasn't seen the light of day in ages. I carefully open it to the first page and stare down at the four lines of writing:

The year of our Lord eighteen hundred and eight.

This book is the private property of Patience Shackleford. Turn the page and you may be assured of spending an eternity roasting in the fires of hell. Indeed, you may also trust that I will do everything within my power to ensure you arrive there swiftly.

I raise my eyebrows. I have no idea who the bloodthirsty individual is, but the dramatic nature of the script suggests the writer was almost certainly young when she wrote it … *in 1808.*

Feeling almost guilty, even though the author is long dead, I turn the page. It's a diary of sorts, though there don't appear to be any more dates. My heart begins to thud in excitement as I read the first entry.

How difficult can it be to pick a deuced lock? John just watches and laughs. If the chucklehead thinks to beat me, he is sorely mistaken.

Tempy came home smelling like a privy this morning. She said she'd been to see Grace, though I cannot imagine why she should come back stinking like the old crone in the village. She said she was lost but I am certain that is a Canterbury tale. I cannot imagine what Father will do if he finds out she spent the night abroad.

Father has decided Tempy will receive lessons in etiquette from a lady named Mrs. Fotheringale. Though she protested to Father that the lady is a truly odious creature, Pru swore on Freddy's life that she heard Father telling Percy it was punishment for kicking Ebenezer Brown in the ballocks. In truth, Tempy does have the worst temper imaginable. I do not think Father knows that she spent the night out of her bed.

I am locked in my room. Father thinks to keep me confined. He does not know I am now a proper dubber. The weather is clement so I think I will spend the day at Wistman's Pool.

Tempy is to stay with Grace. Father said they are to make a lady of her. She will even have a season in London. Truly Nicholas is addled.

The house is very quiet. I think ... The rest of the writing is illegible due to what looks like a water stain, so I hurriedly turn the page over, by now completely oblivious to everyone around me.

Unfortunately, the rest of the pages are stuck firmly together apart from the final two. On the second to last is a pencil drawing of a dog. Underneath the sketch, in the same hand, is a name: *Freddy*. So this must be the Freddy mentioned earlier. He looks to be some kind of hound. Evidently Patience Shackleford was a reasonably talented artist. Swallowing my disappointment, I turn over to the final page. It's empty apart from two sentences:

There is to be a wedding after all. At this rate, Father will expect Faith to marry into Royalty.

Chapter Ten

Sebastian narrowed his eyes, better to see the computer screen in front of him. He'd be forced to close the blinds soon, once the sun came round.

Sunday was his day to catch up with the accounts. He could pay someone to do them of course, but he preferred to keep his finger on the pulse. He always knew, down to the last penny exactly what their financial position was. He recognised it came from the weeks of uncertainty after the death of his father.

Leonard Sinclair had been old school. Leaving estate managers and staff to run everything while living the same indolent life as his own father before him. By the time Sebastian had taken over the reins, the Sinclair holdings were in serious trouble. And that was without the colossal death duties owed after his father's accident. Seb still had nightmares of the months after the car crash. Especially given the rumours of suicide.

Not that he believed for one moment that his father had deliberately crashed his *BMW* into a tree. The old fool had remained blissfully unaware of their looming financial ruin right up to the very end.

By the time he left Oxford with an MSc in Law and Finance, Sebastian had clearly seen the writing on the wall. He'd tried to persuade his father to cut back, but there had been too many sycophants. And there are none so deaf as those who don't want to hear.

His mother on the other hand had taken his warnings to heart, going to extremes in the opposite direction. As far as he was aware, she hadn't spent a penny on anything actually *new* for at least twenty years. The house in Dartmouth was becoming decidedly ramshackle, though she refused to let him spend any money on it. That didn't mean she wasn't spending her allowance. Unfortunately she was spending it on her pet project – The Dartmouth Herald. No matter how much he argued with her, she simply smiled and carried on.

Building the boathouse had been his way of encouraging her to try and self-fund the newspaper, and what did she do? Gave it to her newest recruit.

Sighing, Sebastian leaned back against his chair. His mother's allowance from the estate didn't entirely cover the new reporter she'd taken on, so in many ways it was a stroke of genius to use the boathouse as part of the woman's salary. His thoughts turned to Teddy Shackleford.

What the hell was an ex NCA copper doing in Dartmouth?

He pictured her in his mind. She was well over six feet but there was nothing beanpole about her. Her curves matched her height and though her face wasn't beautiful in the accepted sense – her mouth was too generous and her jaw too rounded – she wasn't a woman one would forget easily. He thought back to their original meeting in Paddington, how he'd found himself thinking about her on the train. Her hair, a riot of chestnut waves and eyes the colour of clear water. When they'd collided, those eyes had been shooting daggers. Yesterday, they'd been haunted.

She believed he hadn't recognised her in the garden. But she couldn't have been more wrong. Her face when she realised he remembered her had been almost comical. He gave a small chuckle. It was clear she thought him an arrogant twat, but at the end of the day, it didn't really matter.

As long as she didn't screw his mother over, he was unlikely to see Teddy Shackleford again. As he climbed to his feet to draw the blinds, his eyes fell on his snoring dog. Strange how Coco had taken to her though. He'd never known the mutt to go quite so wild over someone she'd only just met.

∞∞∞

'Can you remember the names of the vicar's daughters?' I ask Tory.

She looks up at me. 'I think the eldest was called Grace. Then Temperance. I remember Faith and Hope were the first set of twins ...' She falters, her brow creased in thought.

'Was there a Patience?'

'Yes!' She nods emphatically. 'And after her, another set of twins ...'

'Charity and Chastity,' Freddy supplies.

'And then Prudence,' I add. 'She was the youngest daughter?' Tory gives another nod.

'Have you found something?' she asks excitedly.

'Listen to this.' I direct my words to the room in general as I read out Patience Shackleford's musings. When I finish, there's a small silence. I know exactly why. Somehow her words have made these people so much more than names in the pages of a book.

'I take it the Tempy referred to is Temperance?' Noah says at length with a grin. 'She sounds a riot.'

'They had a dog.' Alex smiles. 'Your namesake, Freddy.' He winks at his partner. 'And what's that about lock picking? Not the kind of pastime you'd expect a Regency lady to indulge in.'

'It says on Google that a *dubber* was a master lock picker,' Noah laughs. 'Someone actually taught Patience Shackleford to pick locks. What a hoot.'

'How old do you think she was when she wrote it?' asks Freddy. 'Her words definitely sound like the musings of a typical teenager.'

'I don't think the bible gives any of the girls' birth dates,' Tory answers. Only Anthony, the one son.'

'What about the phrase, *Father will expect Faith to marry into Royalty*?' I demand. 'Doesn't that indicate that both Grace and Temperance actually married well – maybe much higher than their station?'

'You could be right.' Noah grins. 'Maybe one of them married your Duke.'

'It would have been Grace,' I declare, suddenly certain. 'See how Patience speaks about her eldest sister - *Tempy is to stay with Grace. Father said they are to make a lady of her. She will even have a season in London. Truly Nicholas is addled.*' I close the booklet and look up. 'I think the Duke we're looking for was called Nicholas.'

∞∞∞

We manage to leave the Admiralty with our prize well before Mabel and my uncle return, actually calling into the *Steam Packet Inn* for a well-earned pint and a Sunday roast.

It's my first visit to the pub and though it's lovely, I think Tory and Noah mainly go because they're unlikely to bump into the

Admiral whose watering hole of choice is the *Ship Inn* - the only other pub in Kingswear. Naturally, the pub's owners don't particularly care why the world's most famous actor chooses to drink in their establishment. It's enough that he does. Though in the spirit of fairness, I'm told Noah makes a point of visiting the *Ship* for the quiz night. He's nice like that.

Talking of world-famous actors, while we're eating, I ask Noah when his next project is likely to be.

'Not until after the babies are born,' he smiles. 'Then I'll be filming an action movie in the South of France. Tory and the kids will be coming with me.' He says the last firmly, and I guess Tory might have put up a bit of a battle. I think Dartmouth is her safe haven. Somewhere she's away from prying eyes. I know she adores Noah, but it can't be easy always having to watch out for paparazzi looking to take the most unflattering pictures possible to splash all over the tabloids.

'We'll be renting a house in the Provence,' she tells me. 'It would be lovely if you could come and stay, Teddy.'

'You'll have to join the queue,' Freddy quips, 'I predict that half of Dartmouth will be wintering in the South of France next year.'

I smile my thanks at Tory before spreading my hands. 'I've no idea where I'll be by then. Once Alex and I have solved the riddle of the Duke for Mrs. Sinclair, there might be nothing else for me to do.'

'Oh I'm certain there are dozens of peers in the Shackleford closet just begging to be unearthed,' Noah grins.

'And failing that, we can always join forces and become Dartmouth's answer to Holmes and Watson,' Alex adds.

'Oh no, you've missed that boat,' Tory chuckles. 'My father and Jimmy have already decided they're the modern-day equivalent of the famous duo.'

I frown, wondering what she's talking about. 'You don't know?' Tory laughs. 'My father and Jimmy have solved three local murders in as many years.' I raise my eyebrows in disbelief. 'It's true,' she laughs. 'Ask anyone.'

'Well, how come I never heard that?' I comment doubtfully.

'Bit beneath the NCA I'd have thought,' Freddy pipes up.

'Murder is murder, wherever it's committed. I'll have to look them up.'

'I think there's something about their exploits in the Herald Archives,' Alex comments. 'I remember seeing a reference to a local Black Widow.' He shakes his head. 'I had no idea it was your father who solved the case.'

'Not just the guys. Don't forget Mabel and Emily,' Noah adds with another grin. 'But whatever you do, don't ask any one of them about the cases they solved.'

'Trust me, they'll give each one to you, chapter and verse and it will be just the excuse my father needs to involve himself in your missing Duke.' Tory's voice is in deadly earnest.

I think back to the Admiral's offer of help, then inwardly shudder, remembering his contribution to the ignominious ending of my policing career. It wasn't really his fault. I'd been too bloody eager to get the jump on the gangster Paul Ryan. I look over at Alex and can see he's thinking the same thing.

While, as far as we're aware, there's been no crime committed in this particular investigation, I really wouldn't put it past my uncle to invent one.

∞∞∞

The next day I arrive at the Herald office bright and early for my first official day in my new job. Our successes yesterday have both boosted my enthusiasm and piqued my curiosity and I'm determined to get to the truth about our mysterious Duke. I also really need to know what exactly this Jeremy Sinclair has in his back pocket.

By the time Alex gets into the office, I've already gone through two cups of coffee (caffeinated) and searched the web for anything I can find on our Duke Usurper. There's precious little, and I'm not convinced that Mrs. Sinclair is doing the right thing insisting we keep her son in the dark about my investigations. I ruthlessly shove back the thought that I'm just looking for an excuse to speak with him...

Nevertheless, I decide that my next move should be a visit to Blackmore, specifically the church. Despite Mrs. Sinclair's assertion that all the family records were destroyed in the fire, I need to see for myself. There may be something she or the Duke have overlooked. I'll also see if I can have a look round the hotel if it's open to non-residents.

Mrs. Sinclair has given me permission to use her old *Mini*, but when I mention it to Alex, he winces and hands me his keys. 'Take my *Range Rover*. I don't want to spend the day wondering whether you're likely to come back in one piece.' I frown, opening my mouth to argue, then look again at the seriousness of his face and take the keys out of his hand. 'It's parked in the garage at the top of Victoria Road.'

'Bloody hell,' I gripe, 'that's miles - not to mention a forty-five-degree climb. I'd be quicker to walk to Blackmore.'

'Suit yourself,' he shrugs. 'You'll need to catch a bus to Totnes, then I think they run once a day to Blackmore – or maybe you have to walk from the next village. Not sure of the name or the times though.' I look at his grinning face and grab my jacket.

'If Mrs. S. calls, can you update her about our findings?'

'Sure thing, Boss,' he drawls in an awful fake American accent. I don't lower myself to answer.

By the time I reach Alex's car, I feel as though I've spent an hour in the gym (not that I'm entirely sure what that feels like having never actually done it). I sit for ten minutes or so while I get my breath back and enter my destination in the satnav.

Googling Blackmore Grange produces a wide variety of pictures of both the inside and outside of what looks to be large classically designed mansion surrounded by formal gardens, an orchard, lake and both indoor and outdoor swimming pools. Clicking on the hotel website brings up pictures of the sumptuous bedrooms on offer – from simple doubles to enormous suites. The public rooms downstairs are furnished tastefully but more than that – comfortably, and the whole place looks wonderfully welcoming. Sebastian Sinclair is shown laughing with a group of casually dressed people, presumably guests. The theme is one of quiet elegance to be enjoyed by everybody. Colour me impressed.

Throwing my phone on the passenger seat, I turn on the engine. According to satnav. it should take me around an hour to get to the village itself. I'll park there first and hopefully visit the church before having a good old nosy around the hotel.

Chapter Eleven

It wasn't often that Charles Shackleford made the wrong decision. As far as he was concerned anyway. Others might well have different opinions.

But on this occasion, he'd dropped a bollock and no mistake. Whatever had possessed him to declare he would propose to Mabel at Blackmore? Of course it was nicely poetic seeing as his great, great, great, great grandfather happened to be the vicar there, but it only gave him four days to get the bloody ring.

While his beloved had recently made it quite clear that she wasn't averse to getting hitched, despite giving him the run-around over the last few years, she had firmly declared that her engagement ring must be a *rock*. It wasn't that Mabel had aspirations of grandeur; it was more the fact that her last husband never actually gave her a ring at all. Apparently, money had been tight when they wed, and it was still tight when he cashed in his chips.

So this time she wanted to do it right. Unfortunately, she'd also been watching reruns of *Dynasty*.

The problem was, the Admiral wasn't entirely certain what exactly constituted a *rock* in diamond terms. And the likelihood of him rustling one up between now and Friday was – well, slim. Ordinarily, he would have asked Jimmy, but well, his friend had inexplicably got a *wendy* on.

It was insubordination of the highest order and had his former Master at Arms actually answered his phone, the Admiral would have told him so. Texting him a bollocking wasn't going to plan either since he wasn't very good at texting, and the bloody auto correct kept changing deterrent to detergent.

His one last hope - Gerald at the pawnshop - had turned out to be a disappointment too. Apparently, no one in Dartmouth had recently been forced to hock their diamonds. The only rock he had in the shop was an urn with some poor bugger's ashes in it.

The whole plan was in grave danger of turning into a right load of Horlicks. The truth was, he'd have to postpone his proposal. Jimmy and Emily would be disappointed, but being a leader meant accepting when the shit had hit the fan and coming up with a self-adjusting cock-up to compensate.

∞∞∞

Forty-five minutes later, I finally approach the village of Blackmore and look for somewhere to park. It's more of a hamlet really, complete with chocolate box cottages and even a pub. The church is set back off the road and is clearly not as old as the rest of the village. Parking on a grass verge at the beginning of the village proper, I imagine how awful it must have been for the residents, seeing their house of worship go up in flames.

Climbing out of the car, I look around. It really is a beautiful spot. The rolling south Devon hills surrounding the village create a patchwork of different greens and the hedgerows along the narrow lane abound with wild primroses and crocuses. Fluffy white clouds drifting cross the otherwise blue sky, complete the delightful picture.

Locking the car door, I make my way up the track to the church. As I approach the building, I can see what look to be the ruins of the older church. Clearly it had been much bigger than its replacement. There is a small graveyard off to one side, and I venture away from the path to have a look. All of the headstones, however, are dated much later than the early eighteen hundreds – some as recent as ten years ago. Possibly the earlier tombs were destroyed by the flames.

Treading carefully back to the path, I continue on to the church itself, hesitating only briefly before pushing open the large wooden door – reasoning that since it's a Monday, I'm unlikely to be disturbing any worshippers. As expected, the church is unoccupied, and I'm able to take my time wandering along the pews towards the altar and pulpit. I can't help wondering whether they get many people worshipping here, but then perhaps this church serves more than one parish.

Though the pews are likely less than two hundred years old, they are beautifully carved and clearly well looked after and as I get to the front, I sit down to look around the sanctuary. The stained-glass window above the alter looks much older than those along the walls and I guess it was probably salvaged from the earlier church after the fire. Though peaceful, there is nothing here that's likely to help in my search and after offering a quick silent prayer to whoever happens to be listening, I climb to my feet and make my way back towards the exit.

Five minutes later, I'm back at my car where I debate whether I should go into the village itself, or head straight for the hotel. But then I realise I don't actually know where Blackmore Grange is. I know it's only a mile or so away, but there's no evidence of it in the softly curving hills surrounding the village. I look down at my phone and grimace. The internet reception is predicably non-existent.

So, the village it is then. There will doubtless be somebody I can ask. I decide to leave the car where it is and stroll towards the small village green. As I set off, I give a small inward chuckle. I've done more *strolling* in the last two weeks than I've done in, well, *ever*.

In contrast to the church, the cottages lining the main street and surrounding the village green look to have been here forever. There are a few tourists about, most of them sitting on the tables and chairs outside the front of the pub which is just set back from the green. As I make my way towards the slightly crumbling red brick building, my optimism rises slightly. It must have been standing at the time of Nicholas Sinclair.

I look up and read, *The Red Lion Inn*. There's also a sign next to the door saying, *Good food served here*. Well, whether it's good or not, it's likely to be a bit cheaper than a five-star hotel.

Pushing open the door, I step into the dim interior. The pub appears to consist of one large room with a bar running the length of it. There's a flagstone floor and a huge fireplace at one end. Despite the sunny weather a fire is crackling in its hearth. Several of the tables are taken and at the end of the bar, a lone man is standing with his back to me, laughing with the barman.

After a quick hesitation, I make my way to the bar and wait for the barman to turn and spot me. I'm just debating whether to give a small cough to get his attention, when the man he's chatting with takes a step backwards and turns to face me.

In that moment, I realise two things. Firstly, there is a dog sleeping at the man's feet and secondly, I've seen the dog before. Heart hammering, I drag my gaze upwards until I'm looking straight into the disbelieving eyes of Sebastian Sinclair.

I just have time to wonder what excuse I'm going to give for being in the Duke's backyard on a Monday lunchtime while I'm supposed to be working for his mother, when Coco lifts her head and spots me. With a joyous bark, she bounds to her feet, comes galloping towards me, before leaping into the air and throwing herself into my arms from six feet away. Unbelievably, I manage to catch her without landing on my backside, and seconds later, she's plucked from my arms by her furious owner.

'I can only apologise again for my dog's bizarre behaviour,' he comments, his tone anything but contrite. 'Perhaps your sudden appearance so far from Dartmouth took her by surprise. Does my mother know you're gallivanting around the countryside on her time? Or perhaps you have reason to believe your suspect's dead mother was buried slightly further afield than Sandquay Woods?'

The Duke's voice is clipped and accusatory, even without the sarcasm. Clearly, he's not pleased to see me. The feeling is most definitely mutual. There's no way I'll be able to ask questions while he's earwigging. And having a look round his hotel is a nonstarter. I resist the urge to tell him my presence there is none of his bloody business, because actually it is...

Biting my tongue, I give an internal sigh and see it from his point of view. It really does look as if I'm taking advantage of his mother. And alienating him will simply make my investigation that much harder. In fact, it will make it all but impossible. Whatever my employer thinks, I need Sebastian Sinclair onside. I won't find out the truth without him.

'I'm here at your mother's behest,' I offer quietly at length, and wait for his furious response. However, he opens his mouth, no doubt to throw a few more insults, then stops and creases his brow.

'My mother asked you to come to Blackmore?' I nod. 'Why?'

I look around the pub and spy a small table set into an alcove. I take a deep breath, wondering if I'm about to become unemployed again. Then I give a *what do I care* shrug and say, 'Buy me a drink, and I'll tell you.'

'So my mother has employed you to look into the family tree and come up with irrefutable proof that my ancestor wasn't born on the wrong side of the blanket?' His voice has lost its hostility but is far from friendly. It will have to do.

'Is that what Jeremy Sinclair claims?' I ask evenly. 'Your mother told me she thinks he's in possession of a letter confirming his ancestor was the rightful heir.' I take a sip of my wine and try to avoid looking at my companion. If he looked gorgeous in a suit, he looks absolutely devastating in tight fitting jeans and a crisp white cotton shirt, casually rolled up to reveal strong tanned forearms. Are dukes even allowed to wear jeans?

He takes a sip of his pint and shakes his head. 'I've no idea. I haven't actually seen the letter yet. It's apparently going through a process of authentication. If it's found to be a fake, the problem goes away. If not? Well, let's just say the bastard's keeping his cards very close to his chest.' He pauses before adding, 'Has my mother explained about the fire and the missing records?'

I nod, wondering how best to tell him about the Shackleford family bible and our subsequent discoveries. In the end, I just spit it out, and credit due to him, he doesn't interrupt until I get to the part about Patience Shackleford's diary. 'Do you have it with you?' he asks, his voice suddenly intent.

I bend down to pull the diary out of my bag. It's wrapped in a protective cloth and as I hold it out, he takes the bundle gingerly, laying it on the table before carefully unwrapping it.

'Most of the pages are stuck together. I doubt very much there's anything left of what's written on them. Especially as it's water that's done the damage.'

The Duke doesn't answer. I can almost feel his thoughts racing as he reads the juvenile words and wait impatiently as he reveals the drawing of Freddy the dog, then finally the last two sentences. At length he looks up, his expression thoughtful, before turning towards me.

'So you think my missing ancestor is the one she referred to as Nicholas.' He doesn't phrase it as a question, doing me the credit of assuming I'll have come to the same conclusion as him. I feel a ridiculous warmth and want to slap myself. I was a bloody copper for goodness' sake.

I give a small, embarrassed cough. 'It makes sense,' I respond. 'Though why a duke would consider marrying a lowly vicar's daughter is another mystery.'

'Have you eaten?' he demands unexpectedly. To my horror, I colour up. Gritting my teeth, I shake my head. 'Ploughman's okay?' he asks, getting to his feet.

I manage a faint, 'Yes, thank you,' and he strides over to the bar. I don't miss the lascivious looks directed at him by two women sitting on the next table. Title or no title, Sebastian Sinclair will always attract attention wherever he goes. Then I look down at Coco who is currently lying across my feet, gazing at me adoringly. Bending down to stroke her head, I stifle a sudden grin. There really is no accounting for taste.

Chapter Twelve

'If we follow your theory,' he continues without preamble sitting back down, 'that would make Nicholas Sinclair – my ancestor, and Grace Shackleford – your ancestor, the parents of the Ninth Duke. And we have incontrovertible evidence that Peter Sinclair really is my great, great, great grandfather.' He gives me a sideways glance before adding drily, 'It also appears we're related.'

I chuckle and nod my head. 'But we still need to prove it. And more than that. My guess is that whatever Jeremy Sinclair's in possession of somehow calls into question the legitimacy of your Ninth Duke's claim. So far I've focused my enquiries on finding the missing Duke, but I assume you've done a background check on Mr. Sinclair? Your mother described him as Bourgeois middle class, but I think she might be a little biased.'

'I can't argue with that, but in this case she's pretty spot on. He was born in Maidenhead in 1972. Parents were teachers. Studied History at university and never really left. There's no wife, and unsurprisingly his hobby is genealogy.'

'That's all?' I ask doubtfully.

He spreads his hands. 'I admit I've been burying my head in the sand somewhat,' he concedes with a grimace, 'hoping that whatever he has will be proved a forgery.' He pauses before adding, 'I've had other ... more pressing issues to deal with.' Thinking back to his dropped decree absolute in Paddington and Mrs. Sinclair's subsequent scathing comments about her ex-daughter-in-law, I assume he's referring to his failed marriage.

'You don't think your ex-wife is involved in this business somewhere?' I ask bluntly.

He narrows his beautiful eyes at me, and for a second, I think I've gone too far. Then, he shrugs. 'I wouldn't put anything past Carla,' he declares resignedly.

'I can certainly reach out to my contacts to see if there is any connection between them,' I offer matter-of-factly, shoving away the fact that I pretty much burnt my bridges when I left the NCA. I'm sure Alex will still have a couple of acquaintances he can tap for information.

To my surprise, the Duke nods his head. 'Discreetly please,' is his only caveat. 'If the press discover that my ex-wife is under investigation, they'll have a field day...' He pauses before adding ruefully, 'but that's nothing on what Carla will do if she finds out.'

'We only need to check whether there's a connection between her and Jeremy Sinclair,' I confirm. 'I assume she is ... rather money motivated?' He gives me a flat look without answering.

'I'll ask my colleague to make some discreet enquiries,' I continue, 'While we concentrate our efforts on Nicholas. Remember, you're the current holder of the title and the one with all the clout. He's an upstart nobody. I could be wrong, but my guess is that the onus will be on him to prove his claim. Not you to disprove it.'

He gives a weary nod of his head, just as our Ploughmen's arrive. We sit silently for a while as we dig in. I'm actually surprised at how hungry I am.

'So where do you suggest we look for more information about Nicholas Sinclair?' he asks at length. 'I assume you've exhausted the church.'

'Not really,' I answer. 'I had a wander around the graveyard but didn't get round to exhuming any bodies.'

He raises his eyebrows, and I grin. 'Not really into grave robbing,' I confess, 'and from what I saw, they're all too modern anyway.'

'I'm glad to hear it,' is his dry response.

'I assume this place was standing two hundred years ago,' I comment, looking up at the old beams.

He nods his head. 'I think it first became an inn around the 1750s.'

'Do they have any interesting archives – old books, accounts and such?'

'I have no idea. I'll give the owner a call and see if he can dig anything out.'

'What about Blackmore Grange itself?' I venture. 'Is there a crypt, mausoleum? I know Mrs. Sinclair said there was a fire in the library during Peter Sinclair's time.'

'There's a small chapel,' he answers, pushing away his plate. 'It's not open to hotel guests.'

'So no ancestral mausoleum?' He shakes his head.

'If there was, we wouldn't be having this conversation.'

'So have you any idea at all where your ancestors were buried?'

'I think it's safe to assume at least some of them were buried inside the old church.' He finishes his pint. 'Would you like to have a look at the chapel?'

I hide my surprise at his offer. 'That would be useful, thank you.'

I finish my glass of wine as he climbs to his feet.

'I assume you have a car?' He asks, putting his hand up to the barman. I nod, following him and Coco to the door. Naturally, he holds it open for me in true gentlemanly fashion and stepping out into the bright sunshine, I squint, wishing I'd brought my sunglasses.

'Since I walked down, perhaps you wouldn't mind giving me a lift up to the hotel.' I turn round and catch my breath. Obviously, Sebastian Sinclair hasn't forgotten his sunglasses, and he looks like he's just stepped from the pages of a magazine. I push my hair back and tug at my blouse self-consciously.

'Not at all. My car's parked up the road.'

The sudden awkwardness continues as we walk across the green. 'It's a very pretty village,' I observe at length, mostly for something to say.

'I can't imagine living anywhere else,' he replies simply. I sneak a glance towards him. His face is sombre, obviously well aware that if he loses his title, he may well have to.

We walk the rest of the way in silence, Coco dancing between us. As we approach Alex's car, I can't help but reflect how bizarre the situation is. If someone had told me a month ago, I'd be having lunch with a duke…? I smile to myself as I point the key fob at the lock.

'Something funny?' he asks, climbing into the passenger seat. I look over at him, flustered that he'd noticed. Then I shrug and tell him the truth. 'I'm not in the habit of taking lunch with peers of the realm.'

I start the car and manoeuvre away from the grass verge, then nearly crash into the hedge when he replies, 'Just be grateful I forgot the gold toilet paper, so you didn't have to dab my winkle…'

It took less than five minutes to reach the entrance to Blackmore Grange. The large wrought iron gates are closed, and as we approach, a security guard steps out of a small building to the side. He shows no surprise to see the Duke sitting in a strange woman's car and merely nods his head in greeting, pressing a small button. As the gates smoothly open he waves us on.

'Is he there to keep the riffraff out?' I ask as I manoeuvre the car carefully up the gravelled driveway.

'It's an exclusive hotel,' he deadpans. 'We don't just let anybody in.' I'm beginning to recognise that Sebastian Sinclair has a very dry sense of humour...

He directs me to a private area beyond the guests' car park. I stop the car next to what was obviously former stables, now converted to a large garage. The doors are closed, and I resist the urge to ask if he has a vintage *Bentley*. Shutting the car door I look around with interest as I follow him towards a gate set into a high wall. He opens the gate with a large ornate key, and for a second, I feel like we might be stepping into *Tom's Midnight Garden* – aside from the fact that it's two o'clock in the afternoon.

Beyond the gate is a beautiful walled garden. While I don't have even the faintest green fingers, I still stop and stare at the riot of colourful blooms interspersed with cobbled walkways, comfortable chairs and even a pond. 'The Rose Garden - my private patch,' he comments, without stopping. Coco's too, I surmise as I watch her dash around happily. I follow him towards a door on the side of the house, where he points upwards to an almost hidden balcony. 'My flat,' he murmurs with a sigh. 'As you can see, I'm reduced to two bedroomed penury.' I'm not actually sure whether he's joking, so I simply watch as he punches in a passcode and pushes the door open.

Once Coco has joined us, he leads me down a dark, narrow corridor which opens out into a small hexagonal ante-room with beautifully carved double doors opposite each other. The light floods in from a glass dome set high in the ceiling. I give an involuntary gasp, and he grins at me. 'Impressive isn't it?' I nod my head, marvelling at the intricate plasterwork around the dome.

While I gawp, he unlocks the set of doors to the left and pushes them open. 'Do people pay to get married here?' I ask, genuinely interested.

He shakes his head and repeats his earlier comment. 'It's private. As a general rule, I'm the only one who ever goes in. Apart from the cleaners.' He steps to the side and waits for me to enter.

'Did you get married here?' I ask impulsively as I step past him.

'No,' is his only terse comment, and I feel like kicking myself. *Way to go, Teddy. Back to pissing people off with the pushy interrogation techniques ...*

I wonder if I should apologise, but my attention is abruptly taken by the tiny chapel. It's plain, the only beautification coming from a small stained-glass window set high up in the wall. There are two rows of oak pews – enough for a dozen people. The pulpit is small, and the altar unadorned. The walls and ceiling are painted a calming Wedgewood blue. Simple it might be, but the whole room exudes peace. That's the only way I can describe it.

'You feel it,' he says matter-of-factly. I nod my head, suddenly unable to speak.

'I'll leave you to have a look round,' he continues abruptly, 'while I go and order us some coffee.' Then calling Coco to him, he disappears through the other set of doors. I stand and stare after him, wondering if the chapel holds unhappy memories.

Then, reminding myself I haven't got all day, I wander around the chamber. I'm not sure what I'm looking for, but I haven't entirely lost my copper's instincts, and I let my mind drift as I walk. I note absently that the floor is white marble. Clearly there are no tombs hidden underneath. There are no inscriptions on the walls or carved into the wood.

I step behind the hexagonal pulpit and climb up onto the tiny wooden platform and look across at the small altar. Perhaps Nicholas Sinclair married Grace Shackleford in this very room. I smile at the thought and look down at the pews, wondering if her father had ever preached from this pulpit.

The light from the window is shining down on one particular section of the front pew, giving it an almost otherworldly, pinkish hue. Truly it would make a lovely photograph. I'm just wondering if the Duke would object, when my eye catches a section at the very end of the row. From this distance, about three feet away, it looks like some kind of mark is carved into the wood.

Without taking my eyes off the spot, I climb down and make my way towards it. Closer inspection reveals it to be writing, but from this angle, the light is no longer shining on the bench and the script has disappeared. Crouching down, I shine my iPhone torch onto the wood. There, carved on the very edge of the seat is a small Celtic trinity knot with four interlocking circles. Inside the top circle is written a date - *1773*. In the middle circle is the name *Sinclair*. And in the left-hand circle, the name *Peter*, and in the right, *Nicholas*.

I sit back on my heels, working out the date in my head. I have no proof, but it very much looks as though Nicholas Sinclair - our assumed Eighth Duke of Blackmore - was a twin. And just to make things complicated, his brother's name was Peter.

∞∞∞

'I know you're disappointed Jimmy lad, and I dare say Emily will be distraught, but even a man of my standing has to admit defeat on occasion. The fact of the matter is, I will be unable to locate a diamond of the appropriate calibre by Friday.'

The Admiral was actually standing on Jimmy's doorstep and since the late afternoon sun was shining directly in his eyes, he didn't witness the complete and utter relief on his former Master at Arm's face.

'Are you coming for a bloody drink or not?' Charles Shackleford continued, cutting off Jimmy's entirely overdone protestations of sympathy.

'Just give me two minutes, Sir. I'll tell Emily I'm off.'

The Admiral sighed. How had he resorted to standing on a subordinate's doorstep. The world was going to the bollocking dogs. Still, Jimmy had sounded gratifyingly disappointed about Friday.

A couple of minutes later, Jimmy reappeared, and the two men strolled down to the *Ship* with Pickles ambling along the path behind them, his nose to the ground.

'I think the right diamond is crucially important to a proposal,' Jimmy declared, his tone expertly reflecting both disappointment and sympathy. 'And, naturally finding the right stone can take weeks, if not months.'

The Admiral grunted as his former Master at Arms stepped forward to hold open the pub door. 'After you, Sir,' he said using a deferential tone the Admiral hadn't heard from him in months. Stepping past, Charles Shackleford gave the small man a suspicious look causing him to pale slightly.

Less than half an hour ago, Jimmy had been completely convinced he and Emily were heading for a divorce. Though he hadn't yet plucked up the courage to actually tell her the Admiral's proposal, he'd already started a list of things he might be allowed to take with him to his future bedsit. Since the Admiral's confession, he'd felt almost lightheaded with relief.

As they seated themselves at the bar, Jimmy racked his brains to think of something else supportive to say. 'You could always book another Friday *Dinner with the Duke*,' he suggested, 'you know, a few months from now to give yourself plenty of time to find exactly the right diamond.'

Charles Shackleford ordered them both a pint, then creased his brow, thinking about the merits of Jimmy's suggestion. 'How big would you say a rock is?' he asked abruptly at length.

Jimmy stared at him uncertainly, wondering if the Admiral was finally hauling on a fouled anchor.

'I ... I'm not entirely sure what you mean, Sir,' he stuttered. 'I mean rocks come in all shapes and sizes. Did you have a particular rock in mind?'

The Admiral looked at him irritably. 'I'm talking about a diamond, you muppet, not a bloody pebble off Paignton beach.'

'Oh, a *rock*.' Jimmy nodded his head sagely, winked and gave an *how's your father* grin. Charles Shackleford stared back at him, wondering if the man had suddenly developed a twitch.

'Mabel's insisting on a *rock*,' he repeated with a sigh. 'She's been watching reruns of *Dynasty* and says she wants a *Joan Collins* moment.'

'*Joan Collins* must be at least ninety,' Jimmy frowned.

'Not in *Dynasty* she wasn't,' The Admiral countered.

'Well, Sir, in that case, *Dinner with the Duke*, will be perfect. You buy her a new dress with a split up to the top of her thigh, get down on one knee, present her with a diamond big enough to cut her fillet steak on, and *Bob's your uncle* ...' He paused before adding, 'It might be a good idea to book a room as well.'

The Admiral gave another frown. 'But what about the interrogating bit this Friday? We agreed to give this bloke a bit of a cross-examination. It's no use me booking *Dinner with the Duke* if the Duke in question is banged up. I know you mean well, lad but let's be honest, you're unlikely to put him on the rack. You couldn't pull the bloody skin off a rice pudding.' He shook his head and stared down into his pint in thoughtful silence while Jimmy looked on in mortal terror.

At length, just as Jimmy was about to throw himself in the Dart, the Admiral looked up, eyes glinting with repressed excitement. 'I've got it, Jimmy my boy. I'll take you and Emily to Blackmore Grange, and while you're hobnobbing with the rich and famous, I'll keep our suspect under surveillance, see if I can't tease out some intel.'

'But they won't just let you wander round the hotel, Sir,' Jimmy protested, his earlier relief disappearing faster than you could say *Johnny English*.

The Admiral narrowed his eyes. 'Don't you worry yourself, Jimmy lad. You go and earn a few brownie points with the dragon and leave me to melt into the shadows. You won't even know I'm there. I'll be a veritable ghost.'

Chapter Thirteen

'I've never seen this before,' Sebastian muses as he stares intently at the small carving. 'I don't know exactly when this chapel was added, but it's certainly not as old as the house.'

'Could the Seventh Duke have carved it?' I ask. 'What was his name again?'

'George,' he answered, climbing to his feet. 'We don't know much about him, but according to a letter written by the Reverend of the time, he was a taciturn man, very given to bouts of melancholy, so it's unlikely he'd be up for a spot of vandalising. It's more likely this was done by Peter or Nicholas.'

'Could I see the letter,' I ask.

'It's upstairs in my apartment,' he answers, dusting his hands, then indicating I should follow him. He carefully shuts and locks the chapel doors, then leads the way back into the corridor which eventually opens up into a small cosy alcove with a couple of wingback chairs. There's a tray with a pot of coffee and biscuits sitting on the coffee table between them.

He waves at the tray. 'Help yourself. I'll only be a couple of minutes.' With that, he whistles to Coco and disappears through yet another door. I bend down to pour myself a cup of coffee, feeling an absurd sense of disappointment. Did I really think he was going to take me to his private quarters?

'Idiot,' I mumble out loud, adding some milk and sitting down in one of the chairs. As promised, he reappears a few minutes later with a folder in his hand. 'I left her upstairs,' he murmurs as I automatically glance behind him.

'These are all that were salvaged after the library fire,' he continues, sitting down and opening the folder. He hands me a piece of old parchment paper filled with narrow angular writing.

Holding the paper closer, I study the script. The letter is dated 1765, well before our Reverend's incumbency. 'It looks as if he's pleading for someone's tenure,' I mutter, squinting at the tiny writing. I look up as Sebastian pours himself some coffee.

'It's difficult to tell, but since it ended up in our library, one can surmise the letter was intended for the estate manager.'

I look back down. 'He's worded it very carefully, but reading between the lines, I think the Duke might have unfairly thrown the tenant out on his ear.'

'That's certainly what it looks like,' he agrees putting his coffee down and carefully picking up the next document. 'This is the one that questions his temperament.' He gives a quick grin. 'Naturally, it's written by his wife.'

As I reach over to take the letter, our fingers inadvertently brush, and sensation shoots right through my body, pooling in my lower belly. Helplessly, I feel myself begin to colour up and hurriedly look down at the letter in my hand. *Bloody stupid woman.* I grind my teeth, determinedly focusing on the curving script.

'She mentions the word melancholy several times. Sounds like her husband suffered with depression.' I hand the letter back.

The next document is part of an account ledger. As I scan down it, I notice something. Leaning towards Sebastian, I hand the paper back to him, pointing my finger at a specific line. 'Skeleton suit PS & NS blue cotton.' I look up. 'The actual cost is smudged, but it's not a huge leap to assume PS and NS are Peter and Nicholas Sinclair. What was a skeleton suit, do you know?'

'Well-bred young boys were dressed in skeleton suits from about 1780,' he answers with a grin. 'Basically a jacket with fancy buttons and ankle length sailor trousers. Very fetching. We've got several portraits dotted around the hotel.'

'Could any of them be of Peter and Nicholas?' I ask. He frowns thoughtfully.

'One of them, possibly. Come on.'

I follow him through into the hotel proper, and I try very hard not to look like a fish out of water. It must cost a bloody arm and a leg to stay here. Crossing the foyer to the ornate staircase, he holds up his hand to the receptionist but doesn't stop. Trotting at his heels, I throw her a quick, smug smile, basking in her enquiring look. It's not often I'm told to follow a handsome aristocrat, so I can at least enjoy it while it lasts.

He climbs the stairs to the first floor, then stops halfway along the galleried landing. I look up at the portrait of two boys. They are almost identical and obviously wearing the proverbial skeleton suit Sebastian described earlier. The boys are unsmiling but there is definite mischief in their gazes. They are very clearly standing at the foot of the staircase we've just climbed. Unfortunately there's no date or signature. 'Do you know who painted it?' I ask. He shrugs.

'It might well have been painted by their mother. In any case, it's been here for as long as can remember.' He shakes his head ruefully. 'I'm beginning to wonder what other bit and pieces might be scattered around the house that we ... *I* haven't paid any attention to.'

'Well, we've learned a lot today,' I respond carefully. 'There might well be some other hidden gems gathering dust in secluded corners.'

'*Dust!*' He proclaims in mock horror. 'Wash your mouth out with soap, woman.'

I grin back at him, and impulsively dip into a quick curtsy. 'Forgive me yer grace, I's just a commoner wi' no manners to speak of ...' For a second I think I've crossed the line, then he laughs out loud, and I'm lost.

∞∞∞

'Do you really think I could actually be related to aristocracy,' Tory quizzed, lying on the sofa, her head in her husband's lap. Feeding her another piece of cheese on toast, Noah shook his head. 'No way, honey. Anyone who eats as much of this stuff as you do has to have working class genes.'

'I'll have you know there's a very posh version of cheese on toast. Welsh rarebit is regularly eaten by royalty.'

'And the Welsh, presumably.'

Tory frowned as he divided the last piece between her and Dotty, who was nestled in the crook of her legs. 'You know, I'm not sure,' she mused, when she'd finished chewing. 'I'll have to look it up. Anyway, don't change the subject. I think it very likely I have aristocratic blood. It would definitely explain my father's delusions of grandeur.'

'The Admiral would be unbearable if he had a title,' Noah countered with a grin, 'but I can't argue with the logic. He's a true eccentric. A dying breed, fortunately.'

'I wouldn't speak too soon,' Tory warned. 'Don't forget he's Isaac's grandfather ...'

'Please don't remind me,' Noah groaned. 'Or I might be tempted to take my son over to the States right now and get him fixed up with a shrink in case he needs one for later...'

'Don't you dare, you Yankee roughneck. Isaac is *British*. We don't talk about our feelings. Totally bad form. Especially those of us with blue blood.'

'Oh, I'm sure I can get you to talk about your feelings if I really try,' Noah murmured, lifting her hand and kissing her palm.

Tory smiled up at him and cupped his cheek with the hand he'd kissed. 'You know I love you Noah Westbrook,' she whispered, 'but I might have to insist you start calling me *Your Ladyship* in front of others.' He grinned down at her.

'If I dress up as a gardener can we role play Lady Chatterley's Lover?'

'As long as you don't forget the cap,' she quipped. 'I actually quite fancy myself as a Flapper.' She paused, then struggled into a sitting position, knocking Dotty off her lap as she swung her legs to the floor. 'Now my morning sickness has gone, we could have a fancy dress party - before I get too huge obviously. Do you think Sebastian Sinclair would come? I mean, since we're related?'

'How could he possibly refuse a chance to be in the presence of Hollywood royalty?' Noah deadpanned.

'He might ask you to sign his right buttock,' Tory added wiggling her eyebrows. 'Aristocrats are known for being a bit kinky. It's all the inbreeding.'

A sudden yell of, '*Dot Dot*,' from upstairs had Noah climbing to his feet. The subject of the shout didn't so much as twitch. Dotty had no intention of moving until her nemesis had dropped at least half the ham sandwich currently sitting so temptingly on the table.

'After we've given Isaac his lunch, I'll make a list,' Tory called after him. 'This is so exciting. If Kit and Jason have taken on a manager by then, they might even be able to pay us a flying visit. Once June's out of the way, the weather in Scotland is usually awful anyway…'

∞∞∞

As I negotiate the narrow lanes approaching Dartmouth, my earlier exhilaration abruptly vanishes. In its place is a fear so acute, I actually have to stop the car.

I've been introduced to a whole other side of Sebastian Sinclair, and I'm not sure I'll ever be the same again. I rest my head against the steering wheel and close my eyes. *Bloody idiot,* I murmur viciously to myself. 'Falling for a man who's so far out of your league, he might as well be on another planet.' I lift my head and slam my hand against the steering wheel. Then I do it again. I want to scream.

A part of me, deep down inside knows this meltdown has been coming for months. I scream at the top of my voice while hammering the steering wheel. After about a minute, my fist accidently hits the car horn and the shock of the siren piercing the air effectively shuts down my hysteria.

Panting I look around. Fortunately no one has witnessed my behaviour. Resting my forehead back against the steering wheel, I start to cry. The tears come in great breath sucking sobs, long strings of snot leaking out of my nose. I don't know how long I sit there before the tears begin to slow, replaced by hiccups and long shuddering sighs.

At long last, I lift my head, and fumble around for a tissue. Fortunately, Alex has a stack in the side of the door. Taking a wad, I blow my nose and wipe my eyes, before risking a look in the mirror.

I can't remember the last time I cried, so I have no idea what I'm going to look like. Naturally, I'm not one of those one in a million individuals who simply turns a delightful shade of pink when they sob their heart out. My eyes are swollen and puffy, and there are long black tracks of mascara smeared down my cheeks. My face is the colour of an actual tomato.

I draw in a juddering breath. There is no way I can go back to the office looking like this. Grabbing another tissue, I wipe underneath my eyes and glance at the clock. It's gone four o'clock so I can feasibly call it a day. My hands tremble as I text Alex my intent to go straight home. I tell him I'll leave the car in his garage with the keys on the back right wheel arch. I'm unlikely to bump into anyone I know between the top of Victoria Road and Warfleet.

Maybe Alex has second sight because he immediately comes back with *Don't need it. Park it tomorrow.*

Ten minutes later I'm holed up in my little boathouse. Fortunately, there was no sign of Mrs. Sinclair when I arrived home, so I left a note on the windscreen explaining why there is a strange car parked on her drive. Then I quickly scuttled down the garden path. Naturally, the first thing I do is open a bottle of wine.

My head feels like it's stuffed with cotton wool, and it's far too early to make dinner, so I take my glass outside and just sit. Gradually, my default setting of calm and composed begins to replace the hysterical stranger of the last half an hour, and I tell myself that my sobbing fit earlier was a perfectly normal reaction to the events of the last few months. It just goes to show that even a cold bitch like me has an emotional side. I think back to my colleague's quip about the mosquito and suddenly find myself chuckling, picturing her face if she'd seen me.

The fact of the matter is, I'm simply not equipped to deal with men who breathe sensuality like Sebastian Sinclair. He pierced my armour of self-preservation with barely a raised eyebrow. What I'm feeling now is lust, pure and simple. Especially given I haven't actually had sex for ... I frown and think back. I can't actually remember. Clearly, it wasn't earth shattering.

Sipping my wine, I lean back against the cushion and turn my mind to the problem at hand – *not* the one concerning my libido. Our missing Duke is the eighth of the title. But now there appears to be another complication. He had a brother. Is that where Jeremy Sinclair's claim comes from? I think back to the Celtic trinity knot. If I remember rightly, the knot represents family. Peter's name is in the left circle and Nicholas in the right. And on the accounting sheet, PS is written first. Both would signify that Peter was the older. I made the assumption that the date on the knot signified their date of birth. Though I've been trained never to assume anything, it makes sense. So we have not one missing Duke, but two. If Nicholas assumed the title, it would mean that Peter must have died. Clearly, Nicholas held his brother in high regard since he called his own first-born son after him.

So, did Peter actually assume the title before he popped his clogs, or did he meet a sticky end beforehand? And more importantly, did he sire a legitimate son? Frustrated, I knock back the rest of my wine. I really need sight of whatever it is that Jeremy Sinclair has in his pocket.

Feeling much more in control, I head back inside to start my dinner. This cool self-possessed individual is me. Not that blubbering simpleton in the car. And my reaction to Sebastian Sinclair is simply hormonal and would have happened to any woman with a pulse. Now I'm aware of it, it won't happen again.

Now, what should I have to eat. Just as I stick my head in the fridge, my phone rings. Frowning, I fish it out of my back pocket.

I don't recognise the number, but then, since I only have about three numbers saved to my phone, that's not surprising. I swipe the bottom and put it to my ear. 'Teddy Shackleford.' I'm pleased to note that my voice is back to crisp and authoritative.

'Hi Teddy, it's Seb.' My legs give way, and I collapse onto the sofa. 'My mother gave me your number; I hope you don't mind.'

'No,' is all I can manage. And it's anything but crisp and authoritative.

'I was wondering if you'd consider joining me for dinner on Wednesday evening. I've unearthed a catalogue of all Blackmore's valuable and not so valuable movables and thought it might be useful if we go over it together.'

My traitorous bloody heart slams into my chest, and for a second I can't speak.

'Teddy?'

'Err … yes, yes. That sounds … good. Yes,' Is my professional response when I finally manage to get my voice to work.

'Do you have any preferences for dinner?'

I shake my head, then manage a faint, 'No.'

'Great. My driver will pick you up at seven.' The phone goes dead.

He has a driver. Of course he does. Cool and composed has been replaced by heart-pounding exhilaration. I've never hated myself more …

Chapter Fourteen

Sebastian sank back into the sofa, absently stroking Coco's ruff. What the hell had he been thinking, asking Teddy Shackleford for dinner? Christ, he could have just suggested she come over during the day. The *working* day. He'd made it look like a bloody date which was absolutely the last thing he needed.

He gave an irritated sigh and climbed to his feet. Heading into the small kitchen, he made himself a large gin and tonic, and took it out onto his private balcony, gazing over the hills and valleys of Blackmore, allowing the peaceful stillness of the early evening to gradually ease his tension. He could hear voices in the background. Guests laughing and chatting in the garden, but they felt a million miles away. This was his sanctuary. The only part of the house still his.

Coco ambled out and sat at his feet, unconcernedly scratching behind her ear. He wondered what it was about Teddy Shackleford that the dog liked. For that matter, what was it about her that *he* liked. She was prickly, rude, dismissive – all the things he normally despised. But for some reason he hadn't been able to get her out of his mind. He leaned against the balcony railing, sipping his drink. She was all those things, but underneath he sensed a vulnerability. Out of nowhere, his mind conjured up a vision of her lying naked on the crisp cotton sheets of his bed, and he felt himself go instantly hard. *Shit*! That really was a complication he didn't need.

He'd have dinner with her on Wednesday but he'd make sure to keep the whole evening on a professional footing. They would discuss the investigation and nothing more. And as soon as they'd looked into the inventory, he'd have Jamie drive her home. The whole thing could well be over and done with by the end of the week since he was expecting to hear from Jeremy Sinclair's solicitor on Thursday and would finally discover what the bloody swindler had over him.

∞∞∞

'So, he's buying you dinner?'

'I don't think he has to buy it. He owns the hotel.'

'Mmm, bit of a cheapskate then. I'd dump him.'

'It is *not* a date.' I glare at Freddy nonchalantly leaning back in Alex's chair. 'Why are you here anyway?' I ask rudely.

'You really are going to have to work on your conversational skills sweetie if you want to blend in with A listers.'

I grit my teeth. Where the bloody hell is Alex? I'll throttle him if he's much longer.

The office door abruptly opens as the object of my murderous thoughts walks in with our lunch. He takes one look at my thunderous face and shakes his head. 'I don't know why you rise to the bait,' he comments mildly, putting the goodies on the table before turning to his partner. 'And you, stop with the wind up.'

'Me!' Freddy squeaks indignantly. Alex just looks at him flatly until he gives a small unrepentant grin.

'She's just so easy to provoke. Like a little porcupine…' He pauses before adding, 'well, not so little, more like a …' he falters, clearly having run out of prickly metaphors.

I sigh, picking up my chicken shawarma. I do like Freddy. And he's right, I *am* far too easy to poke. So instead of retaliating, I tell him what I discovered yesterday.

'I've checked the General Register Office at Somerset House,' Alex chimes in, 'and confirmed they have no records prior to 1837 and since all the parish records in Blackmore were destroyed in the church fire ...' He tails off. Basically there is no record of the death of a Peter Sinclair on or around the turn of the century.

'Mrs. Sinclair mentioned a writ of summons,' Alex continues, 'so I looked into it. Apparently, before the creation of the Roll of Peerage in 2004 all peers were required to petition the Lord Chancellor for a writ of summons requesting a seat in the House of Lords. Basically, once the old Duke died, the new one had to prove he was the son and heir.

'As Mrs. S was saying, it really is more complicated than that, but the fact is that no writ of summons was requested by the Eighth Duke – according to the Register of the Lords Spiritual and Temporal, which I'm guessing is quite unusual to say the least.'

'Sebastian didn't say anything about a writ of summons,' I frown. Freddy sniggers at my use of his Christian name, and I grit my teeth.

'He must be aware though,' Alex continues thoughtfully. 'If the missing duke was in the register, you wouldn't be looking for him.'

'And there's no record of a brother either,' I muse thoughtfully.

'The plot thickens,' Freddy declares dramatically, taking a bite of his shawarma. He follows it by a long keening moan.

Alex jumps to his feet, yelling, '*What's wrong*?'

'I've got bloody tzatziki on my Hugo Boss sweatshirt.'

I spend the rest of the day Googling Blackmore, the Sinclair family and the House of Lords (bloody hell they're a pompous bunch). As I look at the aerial view of the village, I study the vicarage. It certainly looks much older than the current church and could well have been inhabited at the turn of the nineteenth century. It might be worth approaching Blackmore's current vicar to ask if he's in possession of any historical records.

I look down at my watch. Just after four. Alex has been absent all afternoon chasing a lead on Mrs. Perrin's missing underwear. Before he went out, he made some discreet enquiries as to whether there might be a connection between Jeremy Sinclair and the Duke's ex-wife. Hopefully, we'll have more information by the end of the week.

Impulsively, I google Carla Rowen, and ten minutes later, sit back and shake my head. Bloody hell, she's certainly a lady of the evening. Oh, she's beautiful, right down to her Jimmy Choos, but it looks to be a beauty that's well and truly only skin deep. No wonder Mrs. S. was pleased when she and Sebastian got divorced - though instinct tells me, he may not have heard the last of her.

After what I've just read, it wouldn't surprise me at all if she isn't involved in this business somewhere. She looks the type who prefers her revenge cold.

My thoughts go back to my dinner at Blackmore tomorrow evening. My elation when Sebastian called yesterday was undeniable, but deep in my gut is a knot of dread. I might argue that the attraction is purely physical since I can't actually remember the last time my bed saw any action that didn't involve sleeping pills - and he *is* the most handsome man to have crossed my path in ... well, *ever*. But deep down inside, I know it's more than that. The truth is I'm falling for him.

I've spent my entire life keeping my distance from people.

Carefully guarding my heart. Getting close to someone equalled getting hurt. But I've been in Dartmouth a couple of weeks and already my armour is cracking. I have *friends*. And it terrifies me.

I know I'll end up getting hurt by Sebastian Sinclair. How could it possibly be any different? But the most frightening thing of all – at this moment, I don't really care. The thought of not seeing him again is infinitely worse.

Rubbing my hand across my face, I shut down the computer. I'm beginning to get a headache from too much screen time. The fine weather is holding, and some fresh air will do me good. I grab my bag and decide to wander down towards the riverfront and grab an ice cream before heading home.

And there's the other scary thing. I never thought of my flat in London as home. I've been living for less than a week in what is essentially a shed, and I'm more comfortable than I've been in years. It won't last. It can't. Life doesn't work like that. Not for me anyway.

An hour later, I finally reach Warfleet Creek. This morning I discovered a set of steps that cut up to Mrs. S's House from Warfleet Road. They might challenge anybody over the age of twenty-five but providing you don't have a heart attack before reaching the top, they do cut out a good few minutes' walk up the steep winding road to the parking area. I'm not really sure which is the lesser of two evils to be honest. Amazing views obviously don't come without cost, and at least my thighs get a bit of a workout. The steps come out near to the boathouse too, which is useful if I'm planning a bit of sneaking around!

Naturally, I'm puffing and panting by the time I finally push open the gate into the garden. My intention is to go straight into the boathouse, but as my feet turn away from the path to the main house, I suddenly have a thought.

I have gone directly against my employer's wishes by informing her son what I'm up to. I stop, frowning. Not only that, but he's actually involved himself in my investigation. What if he speaks to his mother? While she might be delighted he's finally taking a stand, she'd also be quite within her rights to dismiss me on the spot. But, hang on, he said he'd asked her for my number - so he might already have told her everything. But then, if *I* say nothing, that will make it worse …

Damn it, I'm going to have to come clean.

Reluctantly I redirect my steps towards the house, and a couple of minutes later, I'm knocking hesitantly at the door. I can't help but wonder if I should have used the tradesman's entrance…

After a couple of minutes, I knock again. I know Mrs. Sinclair is in because her ancient *Mini* is parked in the drive. As another minute passes, I'm beginning to worry something might have happened to her. Then I hear the sound of feet and breathe a sigh of relief. Short lived as it happens. The door is abruptly thrown open, and I take a startled step back. Standing in the open doorway is an elderly man with a shock of white hair – wearing his vest and underpants.

Fortunately, I'm not left for long wondering whether he's escaped from the local care home as Mrs. S. arrives seconds later donned in a long, pink, frothy negligee and odd slippers. To say I'm mortified would be a gross understatement. Obviously, I've interrupted my employer having a spot of afternoon delight.

'I'm so sorry to disturb you,' I stutter, 'It's not important, I'll come back later.'

'Nonsense darling. Do come in. Roger will make us both a gin and tonic.'

I have absolutely no idea what to say to this, but *Roger* gives a winning grin and nods his head before giving a little bow and sweeping his hand backwards in a gallant welcome. Giving a small, self-conscious cough and wishing I was anywhere else but here, I step past him into the hall.

'We'll have our drinks in the drawing room, Rog,' Mrs. Sinclair trills. *Rog*?

She sweeps through a large set of double doors to the left and after offering a mumbled, 'Thank you,' to the smiling Roger, I follow her.

'Oh, and do put some clothes on darling,' she calls over her shoulder, much to my relief.

The drawing room is a delightful, high-ceilinged room filled with an eclectic mix of furniture, all of which had seen better days. She sits down on the large sofa and pats the seat next to her. 'Have you got news for me, dear?'

I tell her the progress I've made so far, and fortunately she doesn't flinch when I mention the help I had in the attic. 'How fascinating,' is all she murmurs. 'Who'd have thought we might be distantly related?' Then she waves me to continue, and I take a deep breath.

'I went to Blackmore yesterday.' She stares at me expectantly. 'I … err … spoke to the Duke.' She raises her eyebrows but says nothing, and I blunder on. 'He showed me the chapel … and … err … and…'

'Did you get married?' she asks mildly when I stumble to a halt.

'No, no, of course not. I … we…' Oh bugger it. I take another deep breath and blurt, 'I told him everything.'

For a second, she doesn't respond, just stares thoughtfully at me. 'I do hope he didn't throw you out on your ear,' is all she says in the end.

'He was actually very helpful, and I found something in the

chapel.' I tell her about the carving and my belief that there was another son. Just as I finish, Roger comes in with the drinks. He's now wearing a pair of Bermuda shorts and, bizarrely a shirt and tie. He puts the tray onto a large coffee table and hands us both a large gin and tonic. Taking a sip, I almost spit it back. There must be at least three measures of gin in it.

'Teddy's only been on the job for two days Rog, and she's already discovered I'm related to Charles Shackleford.'

'Good grief, not closely I hope.'

She gives a tinkling laugh. 'Not as closely as Teddy – he's her uncle.'

'Oh, I do beg your pardon.' He bends his head towards me in an old-fashioned gesture of apology. 'Unfortunately, one can't choose one's relatives.'

I'm tempted to raise my glass and say, '*Amen to that,*' but in the end I take another sip instead. I'll be trollied at this rate.

'Mabel's a lovely lady,' Mrs Sinclair adds. 'A little eccentric, but then one would have to be to put up with Charlie Shackleford.' She takes a sip of her gin and gives a thumbs-up sign to her elderly paramour. 'So, tell me,' she quips, her voice taking on a conspiratorial tone. 'What's the son-in-law like? The actor chappy?'

'He's actually lovely,' I smile. 'Just ... well, *normal*. You wouldn't think he's famous at all.'

My employer, who's anything but normal, claps her hands together and gives a girlish sigh. 'Such a handsome young man.'

I want to say, 'Not as handsome as your son,' but of course I don't. Reluctantly, I turn the subject back to Sebastian's invitation. I've no idea how she'll take it. 'The Duke has suggested I go over to the hotel tomorrow evening,' I reveal carefully. 'He's unearthed an inventory of items that might provide us with more clues.'

'Then of course you must go, my dear,' she responds with a wink. 'I must say, seeing Sebastian not stuck up his own arse for once is actually rather refreshing.'

Chapter Fifteen

Naturally, I spend the next day entirely unable to concentrate on anything other than the evening to come. My internal voice keeps reminding me that it's *not* a date. And I know that, I really do. There's no way someone like Sebastian Sinclair would even look twice at someone like me under any other circumstances.

But by six p.m., I'm ready and waiting, pacing the boathouse and nibbling at my fingernails. I daren't have a drink – turning up at Blackmore squiffy doesn't even bear thinking about. I catch sight of myself in the mirror. I can't actually believe I'm wearing a dress. I think the last time I wore anything that showed my legs was at school. It's a floaty number too – another of my charity shop finds.

Unfortunately, I don't own any heels, but at least I won't be taller than him. I've put my hair up in a kind of messy up do which in reality took me nearly an hour to achieve with the dubious help of YouTube, and I've even gone for some lippy. All this for someone who'll likely not even bloody notice.

I mean, it's *not* a date.

The car turns up at exactly seven p.m. The driver's obviously well trained - he doesn't even blink when he stares up at me but simply murmurs, 'Good evening, Ms Shackleford,' and opens the car door. We sit in silence most of the way. Small talk has never been one of my strengths, and I'm far too nervous to make an effort. I want to ask him what the Duke is like to work for, but that would be the height of bad manners.

By the time we arrive, my internal monologue has talked me into a semblance of calm. Most of my life I've been accustomed to giving very little away. Hiding my feelings is another of my superpowers. The touchy-feely stuff that's been rammed down my throat since I got to Dartmouth isn't me at all. Cool, composed, unruffled under pressure. That's the Teddy Shackleford I'm comfortable with. Oh and forthright. Don't forget forthright.

Naturally, I've decided not to dwell on yesterday's childish episode.

As I climb out of the car, I'm able to thank the driver calmly and even offer him a pleasant smile. Unfortunately, my composure takes a bit of a knock as the gate to the Rose Garden opens and Sebastian Sinclair steps through. He looks good enough to eat, and the welcoming smile on his face turns my insides to something resembling custard.

Fortunately, before I do something stupid like curtsy, Coco shoots through the gate and bounds joyously towards me. I've really got no idea why she's taken such a liking to me, but I crouch down to fuss her anyway. It gives me something to do other than stand there like a lemon. And she really is rather sweet.

'Thanks, Jamie,' he says to the driver. 'I'll call you when Ms. Shackleford's ready to leave. Shall we go in?' It's a second before I realise he's directing the last sentence to me, and I awkwardly clamber to my feet, surreptitiously wiping Coco's drool off my fingers and onto my dress I've been here less than five minutes, and my cool exterior's disappearing faster than you can say cucumber.

'I trust the drive was comfortable,' he enquires politely as

I follow him inside, Coco sniffing rapturously at my nether regions.

'Very,' I manage as we step through another door and come face to face with a small lift tucked out of sight in the reception area. Although I'm unable to see much of the reception from this angle, the underlying murmur of conversation clearly implies the hotel is very busy.

'I hope you don't object to having dinner in my private quarters,' he comments as the lift door opens. To my absolute horror my face suffuses with colour. Anybody would think he'd just suggested we eat in his bedroom.

Fortunately, he's preoccupied stepping into the lift and I'm able to keep my face averted as I mumble, 'Of course not.' As the lift starts to climb, he asks if I've discovered any other skeletons in his family's closet. Relaxing slightly, I smile and shake my head.

'I had a chat with your mother yesterday,' I mention casually.

'Ah, then you met Roger.' I look over at him in surprise. His expression is serious, but his eyes are practically dancing.

'My mother's solicitor,' he adds, his voice completely straight-faced. 'Comes to the house every Tuesday afternoon to review her *investments*.' I can't help it, I burst out laughing.

'You don't mind?' I ask incredulously as the lift stops.

He grins back at me. 'I'm certain you've already realised that my mother is a law unto herself, and I've learned the hard way that any disapproval I show, generally tends to make her worse. And of course, it's not really any of my business.' He waves his hand as the door slides open. 'After you.' Naturally, Coco doesn't have the same manners.

I resist the urge to gasp as I step out into the Duke of Blackmore's private quarters. The apartment has clearly been refurbished by a master craftsman - from the beautiful parquet flooring to the pale grey walls, ornate plasterwork and huge picture windows overlooking the estate. 'It's beautiful,' I murmur appreciatively.

He smiles at my observation but makes no comment. Instead, he walks towards the windows, and I realise they're actually French doors leading out onto the large balcony he pointed out on my last visit. 'I thought we'd have drinks out here first if you're agreeable.'

I step out onto the terrace and make my way to the edge. The view is stunning. 'Wow,' I breathe, for once not even trying to hide my reaction. I feel him step up beside me.

'The estate used to encompass everything you can see from here,' he states without any trace of conceit. 'But over the years most of it has been sold.' I look up and he adds, 'Taxes,' with a *what can you do* shrug. 'Gin and tonic okay?'

'As long as you don't make it quite as lethal as Roger's,' I quip.

'Now there's a challenge,' he grins and waves towards the large 'L' shaped sofa. 'Make yourself comfortable.'

I linger for a few minutes longer, watching the beginnings of a spectacular sunset. Everything is silent apart from the occasional birdsong and bleating of sheep. Almost the complete opposite of the constant noise that is central London. Walking across to the sofa, I see Coco has already made herself comfortable.

Impulsively, I sit down next to her and curl my fingers into the soft fur at her neck. She wags her tail sleepily and rests her head on my lap with a contented sigh. Quashing a sudden wish that I could do the same to her master, I bite my lip and turn my attention to a folder lying on the coffee table.

Twisting my head to the side, I manage to read the word, *Inventory*. Assuming it's there for me to read, I pick it up, just as Sebastian returns with the drinks.

'That has a complete list of everything not nailed down that belongs to the family,' he explains, putting the drinks down on the table. 'Whether every item is still where it should be...' He trails off before adding, 'I've been remiss in the last couple of years. My attention has been elsewhere I'm afraid.'

Since he's all too obviously talking about his ex-wife, I don't comment. The inventory is fascinating. It contains a photograph of each item and exactly where in the hotel it was placed. 'Perhaps you might have been better putting these things into a safe?' I suggest quietly.

He leans back against the sofa and frowns slightly, taking a sip of his drink. I find myself staring at his mouth. 'You're probably right,' he says casually at length. His careless dismissal of what are likely valuable artifacts, drags my eyes back to his in sudden annoyance.

'How come I've never heard of you?' I question, changing the subject abruptly.

He raises his eyebrows at my belligerent tone, and I wince, my annoyance giving way to embarrassment.

'Is there any reason you should have?' he responds coolly.

I bite my lip. 'No, I ... it's just that, well, you're a *Duke*.'

For a second I think I've overstepped the mark. 'I use my title very rarely,' he finally answers. 'And choose not to participate in the political merry-go-round.'

I think back to the ridiculously few images of him on Google. Clearly he prefers to keep a low profile.

Hurriedly, I pick up my drink, kicking myself mentally. When will I learn to lose the attitude? I really have to stop speaking to everyone like they're a bloody criminal. I take a large swallow of my drink, waiting for him to politely ask me to leave.

Instead, he nods towards the inventory and asks if I think there might be anything useful.

'There are a couple of drawings that look to be from the right period, and I noticed you have a cabinet filled with miniatures on an upstairs landing.' I hope my voice is suitably contrite. He nods thoughtfully.

'I thought we'd do the Sherlock bit before dinner. Just tell me if either of the drawings we need to look at are in the restaurant. If they are, I'll be examining them by torchlight around three o'clock tomorrow morning.'

At my enquiring look, he adds, 'We're completely full up tonight. If I so much as stick my head through the door, we'll be there for the rest of the evening.'

'And *Dinner with the Duke* is not until Friday,' I joke.

'You've been reading the brochure.'

I look down at the inventory and shake my head. 'One's in a small sitting room and the other says it's in the library. Don't you have some kind of disguise?' He grins and climbs to his feet.

'Watch and learn,' he jokes, striding back inside, only to return a couple of minutes later complete with Elvis Presley black hair and glasses. I nearly choke on my gin and tonic.

'Bloody hell, your own mother wouldn't recognise you in that wig. It's dreadful.'

'Isn't it,' he laughs. 'And yet I wander through the hotel like a ghost when I'm wearing it. Nobody gives me a second glance.'

'I'm surprised they don't kick you out.'

'My staff know it's me, naturally.'

'Then I'm surprised they manage to keep a straight face. You look like *Roy Orbison*.'

'I think I look quite suave,' he counters. 'Come on, let's get this over with, and no sniggering while we're examining the priceless artwork.'

Leaving Coco snoozing on the terrace, we head back down in the lift. 'Are they priceless?' I ask curiously.

He shakes his head. 'No. I've not been *that* preoccupied. Believe me, my ex-wife had every picture in the building examined by experts as soon as she had the ring on her finger.'

'So, no Rembrandts then?'

'You think I'd be doing *Dinner with the Duke* if I had a couple of Rembrandts stashed away?'

I have no answer to that.

Fortunately, we manage to reach the sitting room without anyone seeing through his disguise. I think most people were actually looking at me in sympathy.

The drawing is situated above a large sideboard. The sketch is of a handsome, stern-faced man leaning on a stick. Behind him is a large colonial building complete with Grecian columns. 'Is there a date?' I ask.

He lifts the frame down and stares at the drawing. 'It's funny, but I don't ever remember actually looking at this before.'

'It doesn't look as though he's in England,' I guess. 'If this is the Nicholas we're looking for, he might have spent some time abroad.

'What about the stick?' Sebastian adds. 'Could he have been injured?'

I nod. 'Looks like it. He's very handsome, but he really doesn't look happy.'

The Duke lifts the sketch closer. 'It says *Gibraltar 1806*. So, you're right, he wasn't in England.' He props the drawing on the sideboard and takes a photo before turning it over to look at the back. Unfortunately, there's nothing more to give us a clue. 'I don't think this was commissioned. The sketch looks a little too rough and the frame too simple.'

'Perhaps he brought it with him when he came home to Blackmore,' I speculate as Sebastian hangs the drawing back up on the wall. 'Do you know exactly when the Seventh Duke died?'

'It's difficult to say.'

'No Writ of Summons,' I murmur. He nods in surprise before walking towards another door. 'The library's through here.'

I make a mental note to ask Mrs. S. if she has any idea when the Seventh Duke died as I follow him through into the small library. Unfortunately, there are no drawings on the wall at all, just a small photograph of Blackmore Grange complete with smiling guests. After a couple of minutes fruitless searching, he suggests we head up to the first-floor landing.

The cabinet of miniatures is at the very end of the hall. After looking furtively around, Sebastian produces a key. 'I don't think you'd make a very good gentleman spy,' I murmur, crouching down. He gives a low chuckle and unlocks the glass cabinet for me to reach inside.

Most of the miniatures appear to be late Victorian. Ladies with nipped in waists and huge bustles. There's no identity on any of them. We're just about to give up when I spot a small tatty looking picture at the very back of the cabinet. The frame looks to be satin, but it's grubby and worn, faded almost to a nondescript grey with nothing left of its original colour.

The picture is tiny but is almost certainly the same man in the sketch. It shows just his head and shoulders. It has obviously been painted with loving care, and this time the man looks smiling and carefree. For some reason my heart lifts. Turning it over, I read in small, curving, obviously feminine writing,

> *To my dearest Nicholas. You have my whole
> heart, my body and my soul.*
> *I am eternally, your wife, Grace.*

'So he *did* marry the vicar's daughter,' I exclaim triumphantly.

Chapter Sixteen

Fifteen minutes later, we're back in the Duke's private quarters. After carefully placing the miniature onto the table out of Coco's excited reach, I study the Inventory photograph of the missing drawing in frustration. 'It's really too small to see anything clearly, but it looks to be a church. Perhaps it's the one that burned down.' I wave the folder at the Duke as he brings us both a glass of wine.

'I've asked for dinner to be brought up in twenty minutes,' he comments, sitting down. 'I hope you're hungry.'

I nod enthusiastically, realising I haven't actually eaten since breakfast.

Thankfully he's ditched the hideous wig and glasses, and I can't help but notice his silver hair is attractively mussed. As he makes an attempt to straighten it with his fingers, I feel a tightening in the pit of my stomach and quickly turn my attention to my glass of wine. Somehow I have to crush this bloody, idiotic ... *infatuation*. I swallow and take refuge in history.

'I think we can say with a fair degree of confidence that Nicholas Sinclair was the Eighth Duke of Blackmore,' I declare briskly, 'and that he married Grace Shackleford, the local vicar's daughter. The question is – can we prove that the Ninth Duke was definitely Nicholas's son and what the hell happened to the twin brother?' I have a sudden, unwelcome thought. 'Could the drawing in the sitting room be Peter?'

He gives a shrug. 'Possibly, though the drawing looks very like the man in the miniature.'

'But if the portrait on the landing really is Nicholas and Peter, they were almost identical.' I shake my head and give a frustrated sigh. 'For every strand we manage to unpick, we just seem to uncover another tangle.'

Unexpectedly he lays his hand over mine. Startled, my gaze flies to his, my face flaming at the brief contact. 'I think we've done enough for one evening,' he murmurs. 'Nicholas won't mind waiting until tomorrow.'

Swallowing, I give a quick nod, wondering what the hell we're going to talk about. I needn't have worried. He might be a bit of a loner by choice, but Sebastian Sinclair is still a peer of the realm and was undoubtedly perfecting his conversational skills with his nanny.

The meal is delicious. Simple but superb and, in my honest rookie opinion, completely worth its Michelin star. The steak melts in my mouth and the bread-and-butter pudding bears absolutely no resemblance to the one my dad used to make when he wanted to use up a stale loaf.

And it isn't just the Duke who talks. I tell him stuff about my childhood that I've never shared with another soul. And he's interested. I mean, not simply going through the motions, but genuinely engrossed. But then I daresay he hasn't met many women whose mother was a sumo wrestler. And neither does he say that's obviously where I get my big bones from ...

As he takes the dessert bowls into the kitchen, I find myself thinking back to Mrs. Sinclair's comment about her son being up his own arse. The Sebastian I've met this evening isn't like that at all, but of course, it could just be the alcohol. I look down at my watch, surprised to note it's approaching ten o'clock. He's obviously going to suggest I leave soon. Should I mention it first? I've no idea of the correct etiquette.

He smiles at me as he walks back towards the table which has been set up to take full advantage of the magnificent sunset. It's not yet fully dark, but the very last streaks of orange and gold have almost disappeared below the horizon.

I open my mouth to suggest it's time for me to leave, but as he approaches the table, instead of sitting down he asks if I'd like to go with him to take Coco for a last walk. It wouldn't be too much of a stretch to say I practically scramble to my feet in my eagerness. I haven't brought a jacket with me, so he lends me one of his sweaters and I have a moment of mortification that it doesn't actually hang off me that much.

A few minutes later we're back in his private garden, but this time Coco leads the way to the far wall and a gate I hadn't noticed before. As we step through, the path forks.

'Down that way is the orchard,' Sebastian clarifies. 'It was almost certainly here during the Eighth Duke's tenure.'

I look towards the shadowed trees and imagine the vicar's daughter, my ancestor, sitting under their canopy, perhaps reading a book. 'Obviously it's too dark to go that way, perhaps another time.'

Perhaps another time. I allow his words to enfold me in a warm glow. A sober me would have undoubtedly realised that he was simply being polite, but squiffy me has already written the tabloid headlines.

He takes the left-hand path, illuminated by the soft light cast by the hotel. It really is a magnificent building, and as we walk, I can't help but channel my usually well-hidden inner Jane Austen, imagining the balls and routs that must have taken place within its walls.

'It must have been wonderful growing up here,' I comment. He looks down at me and I can just about see the nod of his head.

'It was,' he murmurs simply. Neither of us mention the spectre of Jeremy Sinclair looming over his head. The prospect of losing Blackmore must be too painful to even contemplate. Coco dashes past us and he laughs softly. 'This is her favourite time of the day. Lots of rabbits.'

'Has she ever caught one?'

'Not so much as a cotton tail. She wouldn't know what to do with it if she did.' We walk along in silence until he turns towards the house, and I realise we've nearly come full circle. My stomach clenches as we approach the Rose Garden. It's getting late and there's no real reason for me to go back up to his penthouse. But as we finally reach the door back inside, he slows, and I look up at him enquiringly. 'Nightcap?'

The darkness almost completely hides his face, and I can't tell if he's simply being polite. Then he steps closer and the lamp above the door shines onto his face. His eyes are intent. Focused.

My heart slams against my ribs as he lifts his hand and brushes a stray curl off my face. Then he bends his head, oh so slowly, until his lips lightly touch mine. 'Say yes,' he murmurs against my mouth. His voice is astonishingly almost rough with whispered need and a sudden heat unfurls deep down in my core.

In answer I turn my head, the tiniest bit, until his mouth is once again directly over mine. It's enough. With a low groan he pulls me to him, and our lips finally fuse together, gentle at first, then, as I slide my arms up around his neck, he presses me against his hard length.

Almost academically I think just how perfectly his large body fits against mine.

A small whine breaks us apart and I stare at him, my chest

heaving. With a ragged sigh, he steps back and takes my hand. We don't speak on the way up to the penthouse and the voice inside my head is screaming at me to leave. To get out while the going's good. Before I'm completely lost. As the lift door opens, Coco trots out and goes straight to her basket. Clever girl. Sebastian steps out, pulling me gently with him. As the lift door closes, he looks down at me, the question clear in his eyes.

The choice is mine.

Except there isn't really any choice at all. I give an almost imperceptible nod and the desire in his eyes almost sends me to my knees. Seconds later we're in his bedroom.

I have time to notice there is nothing left of his ex-wife, then his hands are on me, and I'm lost in a sea of hot satin skin, tangled breaths and oh so skilful fingers until somehow we're both naked on the bed. Rising over me, he strokes, touches and kisses his way down my body until I'm almost mindless. And then, at last, the glorious feel of his nakedness pressing hard against me then deep inside as he takes me to heights I've only ever dreamed of.

Much later, as we lie amidst the tangled sheets, my head on his chest, I try so very hard not to think about what comes next. He doesn't speak and I know I have to leave. This was never anything other than a brief interlude. Dukes don't date ex-coppers with emotional baggage -especially when they've only just extracted themselves from a disastrous marriage.

But still, I don't regret one moment. As one-night stands go, this was one to remember when I'm old and grey. I just need to be adult about the whole thing. Squeezing my eyes shut, I revel for one last moment in the warmth of his body, before slowly extracting myself from his embrace.

He looks up at me, eyes inscrutable, but he doesn't try to stop me. 'It's late,' I murmur. 'Could you ask Jamie if he's ready to take me home now?'

∞∞∞

As I walk into the office, two pairs of eyes immediately zero in. 'Why are you here again?' I growl to Freddy, throwing my bag onto the desk. He grimaces and sags back against his chair.

'Ouch, that bad was it?' he sighs. I purse my lips and swallow, trying to force back the sudden onset of tears.

Sitting at my computer, It's a good minute before I finally manage to speak past the lump in my throat, 'It wasn't a date,' is my flat response.

'Did you find out anything important?' Alex asks quietly.

I take a deep breath. 'Actually, yes.' I tell them about the drawing and the miniature.

'When I got home, I searched on Wikipedia for buildings in Gibaltar in 1806. The one in our drawing came up immediately. It's now the *Gibraltar Heritage Trust*, but back then, it was known as *Main Guard*. Unfortunately we can't confirm whether the man leaning on the cane is Nicholas or his brother.'

'Well, for the sake of argument, let's assume the man in the drawing is Nicholas. It means he may not have been in England when his father died.'

'That could have been why he didn't apply for a writ of summons.'

I nod. 'It makes sense. I've sent a message to Mrs. S. asking if she has any idea when the Seventh Duke died.'

'If Nicholas Sinclair had been injured in some way as the drawing suggests, it might have been quite some time before he got home,' Freddy adds.

A sudden ping on my phone indicates I've received a message. Forcing back a sudden flare of hope, I look down at my phone and have to stifle the disappointment when I see it's Mrs. Sinclair. 'Mrs. S. doesn't know exactly when the seventh Duke died, but she thinks it was towards the end of 1805.'

'So if Nicholas was in Gibraltar when the old Duke popped his clogs, it could have been months before he got back to Blackmore. Likely the funeral had been done and dusted, so the writ of summons could have just been overlooked.'

'Okay, let's assume that's the case. There's still the problem of the twin brother. If Peter was born first, he must have died before he had the chance to inherit. We just need to find out when.'

My phone pings again. Another message from my employer. 'Sebastian has finally heard from his solicitor,' I murmur, reading the text. 'Apparently Jeremy Sinclair is in possession of a letter written by one Peter Sinclair, Heir Apparent to the Seventh Duke of Blackmore, to a woman named Fannie who he addresses as his wife. It's dated the 17th of February, 1805 and he gives thanks for the safe delivery of their child. A boy by the name of Nicholas Arthur.' I look back up. 'He's apparently also in possession of birth certificates from 1846 proving the line of succession as it *should* have been.'

I crease my brow in thought, picking my way through the convoluted facts. 'So now, just to complicate matters even further, we have two Peters and two Nicholass. If Jeremy Sinclair's documents are correct, it would mean we've been barking up the wrong tree.

'Perhaps our Nicholas Sinclair wasn't the Eighth Duke at all – his older twin, Peter was. So Grace Shackleford could have married the younger brother.' I shake my head. 'It would still have been considered a very advantageous marriage for a vicar's daughter.'

'No, that doesn't work,' Alex intervenes. 'We still have the problem of the second Peter – the Ninth Duke. He applied for a writ of summons remember, so was legitimately accepted as the holder of the title.' He rummages around for a pen and a sheet of paper and begins sketching out the Sinclair family tree. Climbing to my feet, I look over his shoulder.

'The only Duke we have no record for at all, is the Eighth,' he explains. 'We know the Seventh Duke was George Sinclair. All the evidence points to him having twin sons - Peter, the firstborn and Nicholas.' He sketches the names in. 'We are also certain of the Ninth Duke, Peter the younger.

'In our timeline, Peter – the older twin – dies before his father, and without issue, leaving his brother, Nicholas as the Heir Apparent. Nicholas inherits the title and becomes the Eighth Duke. His firstborn son, Peter the younger, becomes the Ninth Duke.'

Frowning in thought, I pick up the thread. 'But in Jeremy Sinclair's timeline, Peter the older still dies before his father, but not before fathering a legitimate child – Nicholas the younger.'

'So that's where we get to the sticky wicket,' Freddy intervenes. I realise he's been trying to peer under my armpit.

I move to give him a better view and nod. 'Presumably, Jeremy Sinclair believes that Nicholas the younger was cruelly deprived of his rightful title by his uncle – Nicholas the older. Bloody hell, it's like trying to put together a puzzle without any picture.'

'So the birth certificates in Jeremy Sinclair's possession must begin with Nicholas the younger's son – after 1837 when the records were first held at the General Register Office.'

'The first certificate he's got dates from 1846,' Alex reiterates. 'So Nicholas the younger's son was presumably born then.'

'If Nicholas the younger was born in 1805 as the letter suggests, it would mean that he didn't have a son until he was forty. That's quite old.'

'It's also quite feasible. He may well have had girls up to that point.'

'All these olders and youngers are making my bloody head ache.' Freddy throws himself back into his chair. 'I could do with a drink.'

I return to my own chair, mulling over the evidence. 'Presumably the documents have been authenticated to the time period at least. So the only way we're going to be able to blow Jeremy Sinclair's claim out of the water is by proving that Peter the older died before he could have fathered any children.' I give a frustrated shake of my head. 'But since there are no records, we have absolutely no idea of how or when he popped his clogs.'

Chapter Seventeen

Despite this sudden pretty bloody catastrophic development, I don't hear from Sebastian. Could be he's concerned I'll turn out to be a bit of a bunny boiler. But I can't imagine the man I met yesterday giving up his title without a fight and he's unlikely to let any embarrassment over a quick shag with the hired help get in the way.

My guess is that the first thing he'll do is bring in some experts of his own to examine Jeremy Sinclair's so-called evidence. So while he does that, I'll get on with my investigation - focusing on Peter the older.

For Sebastian's legitimate claim to the title to be incontestable, we need to prove that Peter Sinclair the older died before he reached adulthood.

My gut tells me that despite their declared validity, Jeremy Sinclair's documents are forgeries. And in my previous line of work, I learned very quickly never to ignore what my stomach was telling me.

So, aside from the fact that Sebastian Sinclair might well have turned out to be a bit of tosspot after all, I'm more determined than ever to get to the bottom of the mystery.

Much, much better to keep my bloody stupid heart out of it.

First of all, I make a phone call to Blackmore vicarage and explain that I'm looking into the Sinclair family tree on behalf of the dowager Duchess – all perfectly true. When I ask if any records survived the destruction of the old church, she promises to ask her husband and call me back.

Then I call the Red Lion with the same spiel. This time the voice on the end of the phone is not quite so helpful. He tells me there might be a box of old papers and such up in the attic, but he doesn't know when he'll get the time to look.

Hanging up, I look over at Alex. 'You fancy coming with me to Blackmore after work?' I think turning up in person might encourage the landlord.

'Freddy will want to come too,' he warns with a grin.

'Oh goody, a threesome,' I retort. Then impulsively I pick up my phone and text Tory to ask if she and Noah would like to join us for an early dinner. Her answer comes gratifyingly quick, but she warns I'd better book a highchair.

'Doesn't hurt to bring the big guns out,' I say to Alex. 'Nothing like having a world-famous actor in the party to inspire a little goodwill.'

∞∞∞

By lunchtime Sebastian had arranged for independent experts to examine the documents in Jeremy Sinclair's possession. The situation was worse than he'd envisaged. Where the hell had the swindling bastard unearthed the letter from? Sebastian ran his hand through his hair in weary frustration. He couldn't afford the sleepless night he'd just had – especially since the reason for it had nothing at all to do with his current predicament.

He never acted impulsively. *Never.* Eight years of second-guessing every word that came out of Carla's mouth had taught him first hand the devastating consequences of acting rashly.

And yet, despite his earlier avowal, he hadn't even hesitated when it came to having Teddy Shackleford in his bed. He might tell himself it had simply been too long since he'd relaxed in a woman's company, that he'd been desperate for the physical contact. Though both were true, there was far more to it than that.

But what if she went to the press? He could almost see the lurid headlines. Instead of *Dinner with the Duke*, they might read *Doing it with the Duke*. Suddenly, despite everything, he found himself chuckling. Knowing the tabloids, they'd likely favour *Rumpy pumpy with the Duke*, or even *Hanky panky with the Duke*.

He laughed and shook his head. When had he begun to take himself so seriously? A one-night stand hardly constituted a marriage proposal, and he didn't really believe Teddy was the kind of woman to kiss and tell.

Against his will, an image of her Junoesque curves came into his mind, and he found himself replaying their lovemaking in his head.

Once hadn't been nearly enough.

His laughter died. He knew her body intimately, but what did he know about *her*? He knew she was smart, independent, and took no prisoners. But underneath the tough exterior was the vulnerability he'd sensed from the beginning. Having a bloody *sumo wrestler* for a mother must have cost her dearly over the years. He didn't even dare think about the newspaper headlines if that came out …

Sebastian shook his head and forced his mind back to practical matters. Teddy Shackleford also had excellent investigative instincts. It had taken her less than a week to uncover their missing Duke. He didn't know why she'd left the NCA and he didn't care.

Jeremy Sinclair had finally laid his cards on the table and his gut told him that Teddy Shackleford was his best chance of bringing the charlatan down without the whole world knowing about it. That was all that mattered.

He'd see the bastard in hell before he gave him the keys to Blackmore.

∞∞∞

'This place is awesome. I can't believe we've never been here before. How old did you say this pub is?' Noah Westbrook's delight is unfeigned as he carefully eases his son into the highchair, completely oblivious to the incredulous stares of the pub's other patrons. Dotty immediately stations herself directly underneath to catch any future crumbs.

'It first became an inn in the 1750s' I inform him, parroting Sebastian's earlier comment.

'Can you believe we could be distant relatives to an actual Duke?' Tory breathes, bending down to give me a quick hug before sitting down next to the highchair. 'It didn't really hit me until a couple of days ago. Whatever you do, don't tell my father, he'll be completely impossible to live with.' She reaches down into a bag whose last owner might well have been Mary Poppins and pulls out a huge selection of toys - to keep Isaac entertained presumably – or possibly Freddy.

'What are you drinking guys? Do they have any real ale?'

'Jail ale on tap,' Alex declares in a tone that could only be described as reverential, 'and Freddy's driving. My life is complete.' Noah laughs as he makes his way to the bar.

'It's alright him sniggering,' Freddy gripes. 'He's got months of being chauffeur driven.'

Tory looks down at herself – I swear her bump's bigger since I last saw her. 'Depends how much longer I can get behind the wheel. Could be mere weeks ...'

'Has the morning sickness disappeared yet?' I question her.

'Kicked into touch,' she crows. 'I think it happened when I discovered my blue blood – it was either that or get a new bucket. One couldn't possibly continue vomiting into a plastic vessel. it's ...'

'...so proletarian,' Freddy interrupts, taking a reluctant sip of his sparkling water.

'They used to call it casting up one's account back in Regency times,' I grin.

'That sounds much better,' she laughs. 'Anyway enough of my bucket adventures in public, how are you getting on in your investigation?'

I pause, wondering exactly how much I should say. Since I'm the lead on this investigation, Alex is again leaving the decision to me – as evidenced by the fact that his head is buried deep in his pint glass. I bite my lip. Mrs. S. didn't seem to have any concerns about me sharing, but I was admittedly vague about who accompanied me on my attic adventure to Sebastian. Then again no one here is a blabbermouth – with the exception of Freddy, and I'm certain Alex will have read him the riot act if he so much as breathes a word.

And of course there's the actual reason I'm here at all – clearly I didn't think the whole family jaunt bit through... But then, having diverse perspectives is often very useful. I look round at my expectant audience as Noah comes back with the drinks. Oh bugger it...

By the time I get to the discovery of the older twin brother and Jeremy Sinclair's subsequent claim, my listeners are clearly enthralled.

'Blimey, the plot thickens,' Tory breathes.

'So, do you think this upstart guy really could be the rightful Duke?' Noah asks, getting to the nitty gritty.

'Definitely not,' Tory scoffs. 'We couldn't possibly be related to such a weasel.'

'His evidence is compelling,' I answer with a shrug. 'But something tells me it's fake. I don't have the resources or the expertise to go looking into forged documents – that's down to Sebastian. My best bet is to find evidence that Peter Sinclair could never have married or produced an heir.'

'And how will you do that?' Noah probes.

'By proving he popped his clogs before he was old enough for any of it to have happened.'

'You think he did?'

I nod. 'My instinct tells me that Peter Sinclair died young, while his father, the Seventh Duke, was still alive, leaving Nicholas the Heir Apparent. I just need to find the evidence. It…' My account is abruptly halted as a toy car comes sailing over my head.

Tory turns to her son with a smile. 'We'd better order. Isaac's obviously ready for his dinner, and the next missile could be the fire engine.'

The food turns out to be excellent. My lasagne is very obviously homemade and I'm just mopping up the last of the sauce with my garlic bread when the sound of a familiar voice has my stomach contracting with dread. I look up and freeze, my last piece of bread poised halfway between the bowl and my mouth.

Shit. What is the bloody likelihood of Sebastian Sinclair being in the pub at six thirty on a Thursday evening? Then I kick myself. He's obviously here for the same thing I am. For a second I'm actually tempted to simply crawl under the table. Then he turns round and sees me. Or rather, Coco does.

With a delighted bark, she charges towards our table before suddenly pulling up short as she catches sight of Dotty hoovering up under Isaac's highchair. The two dogs stare at each other and almost hysterically I wonder if we're about to witness a canine version of the Gunfight in the O.K. Corral. But after a few seconds, both tails start wagging and the two of them begin time-honoured doggie greeting traditions.

Unfortunately, Sebastian's tail is not so much as twitching, and his face can only be described as wooden as he walks over. Hurriedly I get to my feet, catching sight of Tory's raised eyebrows from the corner of my eye.

'Sebastian,' I declare in my best, brusquest police manner. He doesn't answer immediately but looks round the table. 'Family outing?' he observes impassively. The easy banter of the night before might never have existed.

I give a self-conscious cough, feeling as though I'd just been caught stealing from the biscuit jar. It's no good, I'm going to have to do the introductions.

'This is my colleague Alex and his partner Freddy,' I reel off, pointing awkwardly around the table 'and my cousin Tory and her husband Noah.' I look down at my companions before adding stiffly, 'Sebastian Sinclair ... the Duke of Blackmore.'

Chapter Eighteen

I've never been one to shy away from awkward situations, though my answer has generally been to simply bulldoze my way through. And when I'm embarrassed, I get especially belligerent. 'What are you doing here?' I ask bluntly.

He raises his eyebrows at my rudeness, then looks down at my companions. Noah of course, being the uber nice guy that he is, jumps up and holds out his hand. 'Great to meet you, Sebastian,' he enthuses with a welcoming smile. I see the moment the Duke relaxes. With a rueful smile, he takes Noah's proffered hand.

'Likewise,' he responds. 'Has Teddy told you what she's up to?' I wince inwardly. This is getting better and better. But before I dig myself a hole I can't possibly get out of, Noah jumps in smoothly.

'Not really, just that she's helping you look into your family tree.'

Sebastian nods and turns his devastating smile on Tory. 'It seems we might well be related.'

Despite already having bagged a drop-dead gorgeous, world-famous actor, my cousin goes pink and actually titters. I shove down the irritation. 'Noah and I are holding a fancy dress party,' she says breathlessly. 'We would so love it if you could come.' I frown. *What bloody fancy dress party?*

I immediately look over at Freddy who's regarding Tory as though she's just committed murder. I take it he doesn't know about it either.

'If I'm free, I'd love to,' Sebastian answers smoothly with another warm smile that makes me want to thump him. Then he looks down at Coco, enthusiastically joining in Dotty's game of eating Isaac's leftovers. The little dog is magnanimously allowing her new friend to have the dropped peas. I feel ridiculously miffed that she hasn't even given me a second glance. Giving a rueful shake of his head, he adds, 'Please forgive my dog's manners. I starve her at home.'

'We've found bread and water works best,' Noah quips back. The two men grin at each other, and I feel another onset of the warm fuzzies. I ruthlessly shove them down.

'It's great to have met you all,' Sebastian comments finally, politely making sure to encompass both Alex and Freddy.

'Who's your stylist? I'd die to have hair your colour.' Naturally Freddy can't resist a parting shot.

'Entirely natural I'm afraid,' the Duke replies before adding drily, 'The joys of an ex-wife.'
He turns to me. 'If you've finished eating, Teddy, could I borrow you for a couple of minutes?' His eyes give nothing away and I'm unsure whether to be elated or terrified. With a last nod around the table, he turns and walks back to the bar. After swiftly hoovering up the last pea, Coco finally favours me with her presence. Trotting over, she noses my hand for a quick fuss and wags her tail encouragingly.

My companions regard me silently with collective raised eyebrows. I give a small, embarrassed cough and mutter, 'I'll only be a moment.'

I can feel their eyes on me as I walk towards the bar, followed by Freddy's heated, 'You never told me about a bloody fancy dress party...'

Sebastian picks up his glass as I step up next to him. 'Lime and soda?' I question for want of something to say. He glances down at me, his expression inscrutable. I expect him to berate me for sharing his personal business, but he grimaces and comments flatly, 'One won't be enough.'

'Have you spoken to the landlord?' I ask, guessing that's the reason he's here.

He nods. 'I think he's crawling around in the attic as we speak.'

'I called him earlier, but he wasn't quite so helpful to me.'

'So you thought you'd bring along a world-famous actor to give him a bit of incentive,' he returns coolly.

I shrug. 'Something like that.' Then I take a deep breath. 'Do you still want me to continue the investigation?'

'Why - because we slept together?' I blink. Clearly Sebastian Sinclair is just as adept at bluntness. 'My apologies, that was unnecessary,' he adds after a few seconds. 'Yes, I still want you to continue.' He glances back towards our table. 'They seem ... nice.'

I look up at him and suddenly realise something. Sebastian Sinclair is as bereft of friends as I am. I want to laugh at the irony of it. Instead, I nod my head. 'They're lovely, but I have to confess that I'm not really used to being around *nice*.'

'You don't think I'm nice?' he teases. My eyes fly to his. The intentness of his whisky gaze does strange things to my insides. I actually want to slap him. Instead I take a deep breath and direct the conversation back to the business at hand. A sudden irritable yell in the background indicates Isaac has finally had enough.

'Will you let me know what the landlord unearths?' I ask, preparing to take my leave.

To my surprise, he suggests bringing it to the office in Dartmouth tomorrow. I swallow and manage a casual nod. As I turn away, I have a sudden thought. 'I also called the vicarage this morning to find out if anything survived the fire in the old church. I spoke to the rector's wife, and she promised to call me back. If I don't hear from her, I'll call again in the morning. If they have anything, could you pick it up on your way through?' Nothing like sending a peer of the realm on errands.

'You have my number,' he responds, his tone back to brisk and business-like. 'Just let me know.'

I nod my head, bend down to give Coco a last fuss, then walk away.

∞∞∞

Charles Shackleford decided it was absolutely crucial he blend in on Friday, so while Mabel was at bingo, he dragged out his old Mess Dress, complete with white waistcoat, bow tie and tails.

Unfortunately, when he tried them on, he discovered he couldn't get the trousers past his knees. He didn't dare tell Mabel or she'd put him on another diet.

After a bit of thought, he swapped them for the bottom half of his new black track suit. The end result might well have seen him court-martialled when he was in uniform, but he was fairly certain most people nowadays wouldn't be able to spot the bloody difference.

Naturally, Friday would be a long day since he wouldn't be meeting Jimmy at the *Ship* for their Friday lunchtime fish and chips, and he'd have to make do without a pint. Bloody hell, the lengths he'd go to prevent a heinous crime. Especially as it could be argued that the strumpet on the receiving end of the heinous crime, might be well overdue her comeuppance.

Still, it wasn't up to him to judge. He simply wanted to make sure that Dippy's son didn't do something he might regret, or worse, get strung up the yardarm for - duke or no duke.

∞∞∞

I tell myself that my decision to wash my hair and put on a dress has nothing to do with Sebastian's intended visit. I just hope and pray that Freddy is too busy to grace us with his presence, though I don't hold out much hope since I made the mistake of mentioning the Duke's intention on the way home.

As I come out of the shower, I realise I've missed a call from Blackmore vicarage. Clucking in frustration, I prepare to call back when a sudden ping tells me they've left a voice message. My excitement surges as I listen. The vicar has apparently unearthed a folder of some architect's drawings. I text a message asking if it would be convenient for the Duke of Blackmore to pick them up this morning sometime. It takes me mere seconds to send, and a simple thumbs up comes back immediately.

My follow up message to the Duke however takes nearly an hour. By the time I press send, my hair is completely unmanageable, and I'm late for work.

Alex is already in the office by the time I pole up, hot and sweaty. He doesn't waste any time asking where I've been but announces he's heard from his contact.

'On the face of it, there doesn't appear to be any connection between Carla and our man Jeremy, but digging a little deeper, it seems they both grew up in Maidenhead. Possibly a coincidence.'

'Don't believe in them,' I retort, collapsing into my chair. 'But if Carla is the brains behind this scheme, how the hell did she find out about the missing Duke?' I have a sudden thought. 'Can you find out if she's a member of *Ancestry.com*?'

He frowns. 'I think there has to be a connection for someone to show up.' Then he creases his brow thoughtfully. 'Leave it with me.'

I look down at my own computer and add to my notes of what we've discovered so far. I'm more convinced than ever that Sebastian's ex-wife is involved somewhere. But that would mean she not only discovered there were no records of the Eighth Duke but must have subsequently done her own investigation and unearthed the same evidence as us - which leaves me with *how*, *why* and *when*.

I'm still deep in thought when the doorbell suddenly pierces the quiet. I know it's not Freddy – he would simply have barged in. Immediately, my heart begins to thud. *Idiot*, I berate myself, climbing to my feet. The doorbell rings again. Impatiently. I know exactly who's out there. Throwing open the door, proves me right. The Duke is carrying a box which is beginning to come apart. Clearly that's why he couldn't open the door. He steps forward and plonks it on the nearest desk. 'Thought I was going to lose the lot,' he mutters.

'Have you had a sneak peek?' I ask excitedly.

'Once. After nearly hitting a bus just outside Harberton, I decided I wanted to live more than I wanted answers.'

'Where's Coco?' I quiz him, peering through the still open door.

'I left her with my mother. There's no way she'd have been able to keep her paws off lots of nice crinkly old paper.' He reaches into the box and pulls out a folder. 'This came from the vicar,' he explained. 'The rest is from the Lion.'

'Would you like a coffee?' Alex questions, ever polite. I give an internal wince. I hadn't even thought to ask.

'God yes, you're a lifesaver,' Sebastian answers, opening up the folder. There appear to be four architect's drawings in total. He lays the first one flat on the table. I lean over and look at it upside down.

'Can you tell what it's of?' I ask. 'The vicar didn't say.'

'I think it might be of the proposed new church,' he answers, laying the second one next to the first.

'The one that's there now?' I question. He nods without looking up.

'Is there a date?'

He peers down for a moment, then tuts, straightens and reaches inside his jacket. I quash a sudden grin as he pulls out a pair of glasses. What do you know, his knobship needs reading glasses like the rest of us mortals... Unfortunately, I then have to suppress a gasp as he puts them on. The arrogant bastard looks even sexier. Gritting my teeth, I look back down at the two drawings.

'The date on them is 1839, so almost immediately after the original church burned down.'

He quickly lays down the third. 'I think they're the proposed designs for the replacement,' he murmurs, shuffling between the three before picking up the fourth sheet. 'This one has a signature at the bottom.'

I watch with bated breath as he holds the last sheet closer. 'I think there might well have been a seal over the top of the signature once upon a time,' he murmurs. 'All that's left now is a small blob of wax. Unfortunately, the residue it's left makes the actual signature difficult to decipher.'

Unable to help myself, I step over to him and peer down at the document in his hand. I can smell his cologne. It makes me want to bury my nose in his neck and sniff him.

I reach over and point at a flourish at the beginning. 'That looks like an *N* to me.' He looks over at me and sighs.

'Interesting, but ultimately it proves nothing,' he declares with a grimace, laying the sheet back on top of the others. 'I would guess the signature is that of the Eighth Duke signing off on the chosen design. Likely he'd have had to foot the bill.'

Alex hands us both a coffee. Nodding his thanks, Sebastian leans back against the table. 'The only thing that will stop Jeremy Sinclair in his tracks is for us to prove that Peter Sinclair died without issue.' Obviously, he followed the same thought process we did and came to the same conclusion. Clever man.

He gives a despondent nod towards the dilapidated box from the Red Lion. 'I can't imagine that's going to contain definitive proof Nicholas Sinclair didn't steal the title from his nephew. I doubt the Duke even set foot in the pub.'

I give a shrug. 'But we may as well look at what's in there. You'd be surprised at the bizarre places I've gotten evidence from.'

I pull the box towards me and peer inside. On the top is a small tin box. I reach in and take hold of it.

'Do you think this held tobacco once upon a time?' I question.

'More likely snuff,' Sebastian answers. 'Is there anything inside it?'

I prize open the lid and dip my head to sniff. 'It still has a sweetish smell.' I lift out the small object. 'It looks like a pipe. But a bit small for a man.'

'Women smoked pipes as well,' Sebastian clarifies. I pass it to him. 'Definitely a woman's,' he muses.

I stick my head back into the box and lift out a folded piece of paper. Opening it carefully, I quickly scan the contents. 'It's a licence to keep a common Ale house or a Victualling-house at the Red Lion in Blackmore, Devonshire.' I peer at the tiny script. 'I can't read the name, but it's dated 1765.'

Interested despite himself, the Duke puts down his coffee and pushes himself away from the table. Reaching inside the box, he pulls out a small wad of documents tied together with a ribbon. I watch avidly as he carefully unties the length. 'Letters,' he clarifies. He hands the first one to me and opens up the second.

'This one's from someone called Percy,' I comment after a second. 'It's addressed to a man named Harry, but that's all I can tell. Something's been spilled over the rest of the letter.'

'And this one,' Sebastian murmurs. 'I think Harry may have been the landlord of the Red Lion.' He picks up the next two letters and hands one to me.

'It looks as though the subject of both letters was this Percy's mother, Mary,' the Duke continues. 'Both of them appear to be expressing her son's concern over his mother's immortal soul. Seems she elected to live in sin with Harry.' He looks up. 'I think the writer might have been your Reverend Shackleford's curate.'

'Wow, his mother's indiscretion must have rankled,' I wince, picking up my second letter and scanning its contents. 'This one follows much the same theme. Lots of concerns about eternal damnation and everlasting fires of hell. This Percy must have been a bundle of laughs.' I put the letter down and watch as he opens the last one. He's silent for so long, I know he's found something.

'What does it say?' I ask, impatiently.

'The curate married them,' the Duke murmurs, 'on his mother's deathbed.' He looks up. 'The two witnesses were one Nicholas Sinclair - His Grace, the Duke of Blackmore and Peter Sinclair – His Lordship, The Viscount Holsworthy and Heir Apparent to his father the Duke.'

We both stare at each other, trying to work out the ramifications. Sebastian is the first to sag.

'It makes no mention of the older brother. Obviously, it puts to bed the possibility of the Ninth Duke being illegitimate.' He gives a mirthless chuckle. 'The fact that Nicholas called his firstborn son after his twin brother does sort of disprove the theory that he was a conniving greedy bastard who stole his nephew's inheritance.'

'The nephew who was also named after his uncle you mean,' I quip.

'If we go along with Jeremy Sinclair's version of events, it's possible Nicholas never actually knew his brother had actually had a son,' Alex chimes in. 'If he was abroad at the time, he may never even have known his brother was married.'

'That's true, but at the end of the day, it doesn't really matter one way or the other. As much as we dislike the idea that our Nicholas might have been a blackguard, ultimately all we're interested in are the facts.

'And put simply, the only fact that matters to us is when Peter Sinclair the older actually kicked the bucket.'

Chapter Nineteen

We go through the rest of the box but there is nothing else relevant to our investigation with the oldest of the remaining documents only going back as far as the late eighteen nineties.

Reluctantly, we put everything back into the box. 'Would you like us to keep the contents in our archives?' Alex asks.

'As long as you don't use the information for a future scoop,' Sebastian retorts drily.

With a grin, Alex takes hold of the box, muttering, 'Damn, another nefarious plot skuttled.' Seconds later he disappears into a walk-in cupboard.

'Speaking of nefarious plots,' I comment carefully, 'I have a very bad feeling that your ex-wife might be involved somewhere in this one.'

'What makes you say that?'

'Nothing concrete as of yet,' I respond, 'aside from the fact she was born in Maidenhead – the same as Jeremy Sinclair.'

'That's a huge leap,' he replies evenly. 'Lots of people are born in Maidenhead. It doesn't mean they know each other.' He looks down at his watch. 'I have to be back in Blackmore before five thirty…'

'*Dinner with the Duke?*' I mock in my best upmarket accent.

'The show must go on,' is his dry response. 'Have you got time for a quick drink before I go?'

My traitorous heart gives a leap. Clearly I should tell him to do one, but what actually comes out of my mouth, 'Yeah, sure.'

I'm doomed.

∞∞∞

Admiral Shackleford was tempted to go ahead with his Friday lunch time fish and chips even without Jimmy, but somehow he didn't fancy sitting in the *Ship* with just Pickles for company.

Instead, he decided to pop into Dartmouth to see if he could get one of these new-fangled recording devices he'd read about in Amateur Detective Weekly. Apparently they now came so small they were practically invisible. Easy to stick in a suspect's pocket without 'em being any the wiser. If he could get close enough to the Duke, he might be able to pop one into the fellow's pocket.

Pickles on the other hand was clearly not happy about missing Fish and Chip Friday, as evidenced by his complete refusal to board the upper ferry. No amount of pushing or shoving could get him to move. At last, in exasperation, the Admiral promised to buy the spaniel a bowl of chips at the Floating Bridge once they'd finished shopping. Seconds later, to the ferryman's complete astonishment, Pickles trotted up the ramp quite happily.

'You're a bloody embarrassment,' Charles Shackleford muttered crossly as the ferry began to move. Pickles simply looked up at him, and for a second, the Admiral could swear the bloody dog was grinning.

In the end, it took a bit longer than he'd bargained to find what he was looking for – specialist electronic shops being in singularly short supply in Dartmouth. Eventually, he popped in to see Gerald at the pawnshop where he found a second-hand portable cassette recorder that even had a cassette tape inside it. 'It's been used, but you shouldn't have any problem recording over it,' Gerald explained, magnanimously throwing in a couple of free batteries.

Unfortunately, being more than forty years old, it wasn't quite as *inconspicuous* as the Admiral had hoped, and the chances of him slipping it undetected into the Duke's pocket was about as likely as him winning a bloody *Tom Cruise* lookalike competition. He'd just have to stick it under his jacket and turn it on while he was interrogating the bloke. He and Jimmy had used something similar in *Operation Murderous Marriages*, so he was quietly confident.

Mission complete, Charles Shackleford was following Pickles back towards the Floaters, when all of a sudden he spotted Teddy about fifty yards in front. He was just about to shout at her when he realised she wasn't alone.

Narrowing his eyes, he yanked up the hood of his anorak and pretended to look down at his shoelaces. Who was the bloke she was talking too? He looked up furtively. Whoever it was, was as tall as his niece, and had a full head of silver hair. Charles Shackleford thought back to the few pictures he'd seen of Sebastian Sinclair.

Teddy Shackleford was walking and talking to none other than the Duke of Blackmore himself.

He hurriedly put Pickles on a lead. If the springer caught sight of Teddy, he'd be off. Then the Admiral carefully kept his distance as he followed the couple along the river front. As they reached the higher ferry slip, he hid behind a large bush, keeping them under surveillance as they crossed over the road to the pub. On reaching the few picnic tables set up outside, Teddy sat down while the Duke continued on inside. This was too good an opportunity to miss.

Suppressing his excitement, the Admiral continued from bush to bush, keeping Teddy in sight until he reached the ferry slip. There was no sign of Sebastian Sinclair as he hurriedly weaved through the cars boarding the higher ferry taking care to give the Floaters a wide birth, so his niece stayed upwind of Pickles. His destination was the small yard at the back of the pub. From there, he could get inside and hopefully have a word with his suspect who was very likely at the bar.

A couple of minutes later he emerged into the front bar – a bit winded but still reasonably chipper. Unfortunately, his suspect was just taking his drinks back outside. For a second, the Admiral thought he'd missed the boat, then he spotted a table next to the window, right behind where Teddy Shackleford was sitting. He could just see her head. Capital. And to top it off – the window was open.

Tying Pickles to the table, he covertly placed the cassette recorder on the windowsill behind Teddy's head, and pressed record. Then he quickly ordered a pint and two plates of chips at the bar.

Once back at the table, he sat on the chair next to the window, so he'd have a better chance of earwigging their conversation. The Duke was sitting facing the window, so the Admiral took care to keep his head down. It wouldn't do for the bloke to recognise him during his interrogation later.

Taking careful sips of his pint - he was due to pick Jimmy and Emily up at five thirty so he couldn't afford to have another one – Charles Shackleford settled down to listen.

∞∞∞

I have to say, it feels a bit surreal sitting outside the Floating

Bridge with the Fourteenth Duke of Blackmore, especially as he's currently eating a bag of salt and vinegar crisps. I'm a cheese and onion girl myself.

'What makes you think Carla's involved in this ... whatever it is?' Sebastian is saying. I pop a crisp in my mouth before answering, giving myself time to phrase an answer that's neither rude nor inflammatory.

'We have to assume the birth certificates in Jeremy Sinclair's possession are genuine,' I declare at length. They would have been relatively easy to get hold of, and he might simply have done so while researching his family tree online. But a letter purporting to be from a man whose existence has been forgotten for more than two hundred years? Where the hell did he get that from? And how did he even find out about it? He has to have had inside help.'

I watch as he stares into space for a moment, brow furrowed, clearly processing my words.

I take a deep breath and add, 'How long was Carla aware that the writing was on the wall – with your marriage I mean? I don't want to pry, but I assume it was you who finally ended it?'

For a second, I think he's not going to answer, then he sighs and nods. 'For the last year of our marriage we were barely speaking. She spent most of her time in London.'

'So she never came down to Blackmore?'

'Likened it to being buried alive.' He gives a rueful shrug. 'We were totally unsuited from the get-go. She hates walking, loves partying. I'm the exact opposite.' He pauses, obviously thinking back. 'She sometimes came down for the weekend. Loved being *her grace* to the commoners.' The last was said drily, and I can't help but grin.

'I don't think Carla Rowen was born with a silver spoon in her mouth.'

'Ah, you've been doing some digging,' he responds, taking a sip of his pint.

I give an *of course* shrug.

'She did start coming down a little more frequently towards the end. I assumed she was making sure she didn't leave any of her personal belongings behind.' He pauses and pulls out another crisp. 'Naturally, she might also have been helping herself to the odd family heirloom at the same time.'

'Like that drawing that was missing?'

He frowns. 'I can't imagine it's worth much. If I remember correctly it was just a sketch of the old church.'

I nod, thinking back to the small picture in the inventory. 'Is she clever?' I ask abruptly.

'Well, she manoeuvred herself into the role of a Duchess without much trouble,' he answers wryly.

Since I can't think of a response that isn't insulting, I decide to plough on with my train of thought. 'I think she could well have been looking to lift a few bits and pieces she could stockpile for a rainy day, but I think she found something else. I think she found out about Peter and Nicholas.'

'I can't imagine how,' he retorts. 'I don't think Carla ever even stepped foot in the chapel.'

'Could there have been anything on the missing church drawing?'

He shrugs. 'I have no idea.'

'Well, just because we haven't found any evidence in Blackmore, aside from the carving and the ledger, doesn't mean there wasn't anything.' I pause, getting my thoughts in order. 'She could have followed the same breadcrumbs as us. Discovered there was no writ of summons from the Eighth Duke and found herself a patsy to land you right up bollocking shit creak as my uncle would say.' I spread my hands in a *voila* motion, before adding, 'I assume she hates you?'

'With a passion,' he responds. 'This uncle of yours sounds interesting. Is he another Shackleford?'

I can't help it. I laugh. 'A retired Admiral. He's my cousin Tory's father and one of England's great eccentrics.'

He raises his eyebrows. 'A bit like my mother then?'

'Oh, much, much worse. I could fill a book with the number of his self-adjusting cock ups – another of his quaint colloquialisms.'

'I can't wait to meet him,' is Sebastian's droll response. I feel my heart lurch, torn between sheer terror at the very idea of him meeting the Admiral, and exhilaration that he actually might want to meet one of my relatives. In the end I give an inelegant snort and drag the conversation back to our more immediate problem.

'Alex is looking into the possibility of any connection between her and Jeremy Sinclair,' I tell him.

'Aside from the fact that they were both born in Maidenhead?' he counters sardonically.

'Trust me, I've started investigations with much more tenuous links than that,' I retort. 'If we can prove a connection between them, it might be enough to cast doubt of the validity of that letter he has – which is almost certainly a forgery.'

'You think Carla's really behind it all?

'Oh I don't doubt it. Not even for one second. Your ex-wife is doing her damndest to take away your title and hopefully leave you destitute while she's at it.

∞∞∞

'You'll never guess what I discovered today, Jimmy lad.' The Admiral's excitement as he and Emily climbed into the car had the small man quaking in his dress shoes.

'Good evening, Charlie,' Emily intoned, in her best *lady taking dinner with a Duke* voice.

Giving her an irritated glance through the wing mirror, the Admiral's less than gentlemanly response was fortunately lost as he turned the key in the ignition.

'What did you discover, Sir,' Jimmy asked, interested, despite his misgivings.

'Old Carla's only trying to diddle our Duke out of his title and all his dosh. No wonder the bloke wants to do her in. And Teddy's helping him.'

'What, do her in?'

'Get a bloody grip, Jimmy, of course not. She's helping him catch the strumpet in the act. I overheard 'em talking about a missing picture and someone writing a summons – I think they're setting a trap to catch the baggage red handed.'

'Where did you hear all this, Sir?'

'I overheard 'em talking in the Floaters earlier today.'

'Forgive me for questioning your word, Sir, but are you sure you've got your facts right?'

The Admiral stiffened at his former Master at Arms' insubordination. Such was his outrage that he totally forgot to slow down as they boarded the lower ferry and almost overshot the platform completely, only just managing to brake before the car flew out into the Dart on the other side. Those in the vicinity said later it had been just like watching *Fast and Furious 8* all over again.

'I'll have you know I taped the whole bloody lot,' Charles Shackleford declared with an indignant sniff once he'd turned the engine off.

'Perhaps we can listen to it,' Jimmy mumbled, finally plucking up the courage to open his eyes. He was actually beginning to question the odds of them surviving the journey. He turned round to Emily who was staring white-faced into space. 'Would you like to listen to a tape dear?' he shouted.

'Is it *Neil Diamond*?' she managed faintly.

Jimmy turned back to the Admiral. 'I don't suppose you've got any Neil Diamond have you, Sir?'

'What's *Neil* bollocking *Diamond* got to do with the Duke of Blackmore's dodgy ex-wife? It's a tape recording of the bloody shenanigans I was listening to today. I had it on the windowsill behind Teddy's head.'

Jimmy sighed. 'Go on then, Sir, let's hear it.'

'Just let me get off this ferry first. You wouldn't believe how many bad drivers there are on the roads today.'

Chapter Twenty

As Sebastian put the finishing touches to his Friday night fancy dress, his mind kept replaying his morning in Dartmouth. Or more specifically, the time he spent with Teddy Shackleford. He told himself he was glad they'd put the awkwardness of their foolish intimacy behind them and were now firmly on a purely professional footing. If desire shot through him as soon as he caught sight of her – well, it was simply a male reaction to an attractive woman. He shied away from the thought that it had never happened when he'd looked at Carla - even at the very beginning...

He picked up his gloves. Both the hotel and the restaurant were absolutely rammed tonight, with over half the guests being unattached ladies of varying ages. He'd be unlikely to see his bed until the small hours. He bent down to give Coco a fuss. 'Tom will be up to take you for a walk,' he murmured, kissing her soft head briefly. 'So don't wait up.' Then, chuckling softly, he made his way down the hall to the lift.

His first port of call would be the reception desk where he'd pick up the list of guests along with their interests. It was useful to know if Mr. Smith was into flower arranging, or Mrs. Jones was a judo champion. It also helped him know which topics to avoid.

His next stopover would be the bar and a stiff gin and tonic. He made a habit of spending at least fifteen minutes chatting to Bob, the head barman, while keeping his back determinedly to the room. He could gauge when the room was full by the level of titters at his back. But more accurately when Bob declared it was time for him to piss off.

It was going to be a long night.

∞∞∞

'Right then, the recorder's in the glove box. You'll need to rewind it. I'm hoping there'll still be plenty of space left for me to do a spot of recording later while you and Emily are doing the business.'

Without answering, Jimmy picked up the small player and pressed the rewind button. He could only pray to whoever might be listening that the Admiral didn't end up getting arrested. Otherwise he had no idea how they were going to get home.

The tape stopped, and he prepared to press play. 'Make sure you turn the volume right up before you start,' the Admiral ordered.

Jimmy did as he was asked, then pressed play. For the first few seconds, there was a faint crackling sound. Then all of a sudden, they heard a long-drawn out moan followed by a series of gasping noises. 'Yesthereyesyesyesaahgiveittomebigboy…'

'Is she speaking French?' asked Emily from the back.

'It doesn't sound much like Teddy,' Jimmy commented doubtfully.

'It's not bloody Teddy. It must have been what was on the tape before. Fast forward it a bit.'

Jimmy obligingly pressed the fast forward button for a few seconds, then started the tape again. This time there was a series of rhythmic banging noises accompanied by low rough grunting.

'He really should get something for that cough,' Emily chimed in.

Jimmy hurriedly pressed the fast forward button again. 'Aaaah, ooooh, yeeeessss.' The banging noise got faster, now accompanied by a loud recurrent squeak.

'He could really do with some WD-40. Have you got any with you, Charlie...'

∞∞∞

As I sit on the patio eating my *Marks and Spencer's* chilli for one, my head replays the last few hours for the nth time. Somehow the Duke and I seem to have settled into a constructive working relationship which is exactly how it should be. And I hate it.

Sitting across from him today at the Floating Bridge was delicious agony. Listening to his deep voice, watching the myriad of expressions cross his face. Hearing him laugh... Dear God, if this is love, I really don't want it.

I push away my unfinished chilli. After years of hardly even noticing members of the opposite sex, how the bloody hell could I have allowed myself to fall for someone so... *unsuitable*. My brain finally acknowledges what my heart has known since I first laid eyes on him. I've fallen in love with Sebastian Sinclair. I grimace and shake my head. Truthfully, I didn't think I had it in me.

I have to get away from Dartmouth. How on earth can I stay here? Then I look towards the river, at the early evening sunlight dancing on the water and realise I don't want to leave. Ever. For the first time in my life, despite my farcical unrequited love, I'm actually happy.

There's no reason I should come into contact with Sebastian at all once all this is over. We move in entirely different circles, and Blackmore is far enough away from Dartmouth that I'm unlikely to bump into him as long as I keep to my little boathouse and stay well away from the main house.

And if I have to get another job and another home – well, so be it. For the first time in my life, I actually have people who *like* me. My friends here don't care if I'm prickly – they simply dish it back. *My friends.* I practice the word out loud and chuckle. And besides, if I'm to be Alex's best man … I shift my thoughts to the possibility of delivering a speech that doesn't end up with, *You have the right to remain silent…*

∞∞∞

'I'll be having a quiet word with Gerald at the pawn shop,' the Admiral muttered, once the security guard had waved them through the gates into Blackmore Grange. 'It's a bloody good job I didn't need to use the tape as evidence. If I took that to the Old Bill, there'd be a right cake and arse party.'

'I think it's probably best if you throw the tape away, Sir,' Jimmy suggested. 'You don't want it to fall into Mabel's hands. She might think you're having an affair.'

Charles Shackleford hmphed. 'If that had been me, she'd be giving me the third degree in the bloody mortuary.

'Right then, here we are. I'll drop you two lovebirds off at the front door, then go and park the car. Make sure you keep in full radio contact, Jimmy.'

'Please don't do anything imprudent, Sir.' As usual, the small man's desperate entreaty fell on deaf ears.

'Don't you concern yourself, Jimmy lad,' was the Admiral's cheerful response. 'I know you're as observant as a blindfolded mole, but you can depend on me. I'll melt into the shadows just like that bloke from the *Milk Tray* advert...'

∞∞∞

As he got out of the car, the Admiral couldn't help reflecting how much easier it would have been if standard Mess Dress trousers had been made out of polyester. No chafing, no wondering if his nether regions were in danger of turning into a boil in the bag frankfurter, and best of all, no risk of accidental castration while easing springs during a Mess Dinner. Win, win as far as he could see. Perhaps he'd suggest it the next time he bumped into the First Sea Lord.

Right then, where to start. Did he walk in the front door, bold as brass, or sneak in round the side. Both had merits when doing a recce. Abruptly, he found himself wishing Jimmy was with him. All his snooping over the last few years had been done in the company of his former Master at Arms, and it seemed strange to be sneaking about on his own. Still, he was only going to have a bit of a scout around. If what he'd heard about Carla this morning was true, it definitely upped the stakes a bit, and while he wouldn't dream of admitting it to Jimmy, the Admiral wasn't actually sure what he was looking for. Truthfully, he was feeling a bit out of his depth. Nevertheless, he didn't want his grace tossed out on his ear until after he'd had a chance to propose to Mabel.

In the end, he decided that looking as though he had every right to be there, was the best way to remain invisible, so he started towards the front. Just as he turned the corner, he nearly bumped into a woman coming the other way. Startled, the woman dropped a package she was carrying. Before he could help, she swiftly bent down to pick it back up, waving away his mumbled apologies. As she straightened, he saw her face clearly for the first time and only just managed to suppress a gasp. It was Carla Rowen, the Duke's ex-wife. The one who was looking to ruin him.

What the bloody hell was she doing here? He turned to watch as she hurried on her way. Whatever she was up to, he'd bet his right arm she hadn't had a bollocking invitation. As she turned the corner, he suddenly came to his senses. He wasn't going to find out standing there like a complete plank.

Hastily, he trotted after her. As he reached the corner, he stopped and poked his head round, just in time to see her unlocking a set of French doors. He'd wager her ex-husband didn't know she still had a key. Seconds later, she disappeared inside.

Hoping she hadn't relocked it, the Admiral hurried to the door and peered inside what looked to be a small sitting room. There was no sign of her, but a door to one side stood half open. Cautiously, he tried the handle of the French door. It was unlocked.

Stepping through, he gingerly approached the open door and peeped through the crack in the frame, just in time to see his quarry hanging what looked like a picture on the wall. Baffled, he watched as she stepped back, clearly making sure the picture was straight. Then she turned, picked up the bag the picture was in and hurried back towards the sitting room.

Panicking, he got onto his hands and knees behind a small sofa and listened as she went back through the French doors, locking them behind her.

The Admiral waited another few seconds to make sure she was gone, then with a grunt, he took hold of the back of the sofa and heaved himself back to his feet. He'd definitely have to rethink the whole getting down on one knee bit of his proposal to Mabel. Having to be winched back up really wouldn't add anything on the romance front.

Wincing, he hobbled into the next room to have a look at the picture Carla Rowen had left. As far as he could tell without his glasses, it looked to be a sketch of a church. He reached up and lifted it from the wall to have a closer inspection. To his layman's eyes, it didn't look to be anything special. There was some writing at the bottom. Squinting, he read, *Blackmore Church*. After that were the initials *GS* and a date – *1837*. He turned the picture over but there was nothing on the back.

More mystified than ever, he hung the picture back up and looked round the room. With the number of books, he guessed it was a library. He hoped there was a way out since the bloody woman had relocked the French doors behind her. He didn't fancy being stuck here until Jimmy came looking for him.

Fortunately, the exit wasn't locked and after opening the door a crack, he stuck his head through and breathed a sigh of relief when he realised he was looking out into a broad corridor which was obviously part of the hotel.

Hurrying down the hallway, he wondered how he was going to let his grace know that his ex-wife had been skulking around the place using her own key. It would take a bit of explaining since he'd also have to come clean about why he'd been following the strumpet in the first place.

Emerging into the main reception area of the hotel, Charles Shackleford slowed down to a formal walk. At the end of the day, he hadn't got to be an admiral without knowing how to look as though he owned the place. Nobody questioned him as he followed the signs to the restaurant. Since it was *Dinner with the Duke* night, it was a good bet that was where his grace was holed up.

The restaurant was a masterpiece in understated elegance. He could see why it was so popular. Mabel would love it here. Hovering at the door, he could see Jimmy and Emily in a nice, secluded corner. Sebastian Sinclair was chatting to a group of diners in the middle of the room, and it was clear they were hanging off his every word. The Admiral had to hand it to him, the bloke had magnetism. Not like Kit's husband, Jason Buchannan. He still thought the Scot had all the charm of a bloody verruca . Still, there was no accounting for taste.

'Can I help you, Sir?' The Maître D' looked down his nose as he caught sight of the tracksuit bottoms. 'I'm afraid we do have a very strict dress code, Sir, which does not include *leisure wear*. I'll have to ask you to leave.'

The Admiral sighed. Just his bloody luck to run into a pompous gopher. He doubted the bloke could count past ten without taking his shoes off, but he'd literally fall on his sword before letting anyone in who wasn't adhering to the appropriate dress code.

His only recourse was to make a scene and hope the Duke would take direct action to remove him.

'I'd like to speak with his grace on an urgent matter,' he announced loudly.

'Keep your voice down,' the attendant hissed with a flustered glance back towards the Duke who was already looking up with a slight frown. The Admiral caught sight of Jimmy's panicked face and gave him an encouraging thumbs-up sign.

'KINDLY INFORM HIS GRACE THAT ADMIRAL CHARLES SHACKLEFORD IS HERE TO SEE HIM,' he thundered abruptly. It had the desired effect, and with satisfaction he saw the Duke hurriedly excuse himself and rise to his feet.

With a broad wink at the Maître D' who looked as though he was about to faint, the Admiral watched Sebastian Sinclair stride towards him, his face stony.

'The Uncle, I presume,' was his only comment.

'At your service, your grace.' The Admiral gave a small unrepentant bow.

The Duke raised his eyebrows but didn't answer. Instead, he strode through the door, clearly trusting the Admiral would follow.

'This is not a good time, I'm afraid,' Sebastian growled when the restaurant was finally out of sight. 'How can I help you, Admiral Shackleford? Your niece is not here.'

'I'm not looking for Teddy,' Charles Shackleford answered. 'I just thought you might be interested to know that your ex-wife was here a few minutes ago getting up to no good in your library.'

'Carla was here?' Sebastian's composure slipped completely for a second.

'In your library,' the Admiral repeated helpfully. 'She hung a picture on the wall.'

'Show me.' This time the Duke's voice was clipped and authoritative as he turned and strode back towards the small library. Charles Shackleford trotted after him, making sure to give Jimmy another enthusiastic thumbs-up as they passed the restaurant.

'It's a church,' the Admiral commented as the Duke stared silently at the picture in question. 'She had it in a bag until she took it out and hung it up there.'

'The missing drawing,' Sebastian murmured, realising for the first time that Teddy could well be right in believing his ex-wife was up to her elegant neck in the whole bloody business. Stepping towards the picture, he took it down to examine.

'You didn't know she had it?' Sebastian shook his head. Aside from the fact that it was dated in the crucial time period, and looked to have been done by Grace Sinclair, he couldn't see anything interesting about it at all. Nevertheless, it looked to be the missing picture from the Inventory, and the fact that Carla had it... He turned towards the Admiral.

'How did she get in – did you see?'

'She came through the French doors in the sitting room next door. Had her own key.' Charles Shackleford followed the Duke through the connecting door. Once there Sebastian stared at the French doors thoughtfully.

'What were you doing in this room?' he asked the Admiral at length. Finally.

'My friend and his wife are here for dinner,' Charles Shackleford responded guilelessly. 'So I offered to drive 'em both. Thought I'd have a bit of a shufti while I was hanging around.'

'How did you know it was my wife?'

For a second, the Admiral's mind went completely blank, then suddenly he caught sight of another drawing, this time on the sitting room wall. It looked familiar. Ignoring the Duke's impatient sigh, he stepped closer.

'You know what? I've seen that bloke somewhere before.' The Admiral took out his reading glasses and leaned towards the drawing. 'That looks like *Main Guard* and the *Parade Square* in Gib. Hang on a bollocking minute - 1806...'

He gave triumphant slap of his thigh. 'Shiver me timbers and call me Woody, that's the Captain of HMS *Temeraire*. Finest captain in the bloody fleet he was. Badly wounded in the battle of Trafalgar and had to resign his commission.' Charles Shackleford shook his head in admiration. 'I can't believe it, Nicholas Sinclair. How come you've got a drawing of him here...?' He stopped and looked over at the Duke with a frown. *Sinclair* -that's your family name. Was he an ancestor of yours?'

Chapter Twenty-One

'There's a large painting of Captain Sinclair in the Naval College at Dartmouth. I reckon this drawing might have been the initial artist's sketch. Probably worth a bob or two I'd say.'

To the Admiral's relief, the subject of how he'd recognised the Duke's wife seemed to have been forgotten. In fact the Duke's face currently had the look reminiscent of a fart in a trance.

Then abruptly Sebastian started to laugh. The Admiral eyed him in concern. It wouldn't be the first time a member of the English aristocracy had lost his bloody marbles.

'So Nicholas Sinclair's actually famous?' the Duke chuckled a minute or so later.

'I wouldn't say that exactly. He's very well known in Naval circles,' the Admiral clarified. 'He captained *Temeraire* at Trafalgar. She was second in the line and when *Victory* came under heavy fire, it was *Temeraire* who came to her rescue – ended up not only saving *Victory's* bacon but capturing two French ships while she was at it. In a terrible state at the end of the battle though. Barely managed to limp into Gibraltar. Suffered well over a hundred casualties and Sinclair himself almost cashed in his chips.'

'When exactly was the Battle of Trafalgar?'

'Twenty first of October, 1805.'

'Do you know what happened to Sinclair after he was injured?' Sebastian asked, feeling his excitement begin to build.

The Admiral shook his head. 'I'm not entirely sure. I know it was touch and go whether he'd survive. All the severe casualties were treated in Gibraltar, and as far as I'm aware, Sinclair was among them.' He gave a thoughtful pause. 'Your drawing suggests he was still convalescing there in 1806 and I think it was around that time he resigned his commission, presumably due to his injuries.' He shrugged. 'If you're interested, I'd have thought the full details will be in the *Naval Archives* at Kew.'

'Will they have information on what happened to Nicholas Sinclair *after* he recovered?'

The Admiral creased his brow in thought. 'Well, they've hung onto pretty much every bloody thing, so any correspondence between Sinclair and the *Admiralty* should be in there.' He gave a small chuckle. 'That's the *actual Admiralty*, not the one I live in.'

'Admiral Shackleford, you're a genius. I could kiss you.'

'Steady on,' Charles Shackleford commented, his chuckle fading. He hurriedly leaned back just in case.

'I have to get back to the restaurant. Are you free tomorrow?'

Charles Shackleford thought for a second. 'Well, I was going to take my other half to Paignton, but that can wait.'

'I take it you know your way around the *Naval Archives* at Kew?'

The Admiral nodded. 'Spent a bloody month there as a two and half. Could find my way round blindfolded.'

'Then I'd appreciate your help. I'll pick you up around seven if that's convenient.'

'I take it you'll be bringing the sandwiches?'

∞∞∞

My phone ringing at midnight is not something I've been used to in recent weeks. When I was in the NCA, it rang at all hours, and for a few seconds, I'm back in London. I scrabble for my mobile, still half asleep and bark, 'Shackleford,' when I finally get it to my ear.

'It's Seb. I'm sorry to wake you.' At the sound of the deep voice, I'm abruptly wide awake.

'Is something wrong?'

'Exactly the opposite,' he laughs. 'I think we may have had the breakthrough we needed.' He proceeds to tell me about his evening.'

'My *uncle*, the Admiral?' I can't help but interrupt. I can almost feel him nodding.

'He happened to spot the drawing of the man we thought was Nicholas Sinclair. Turns out we were right. But that's not all. It seems before he became the Eighth Duke, our man was quite a big noise in Naval circles. Your uncle's coming with me to the *National Archives* tomorrow, and I was hoping you'd be able to come too.'

The Admiral spending the whole day with Sebastian Sinclair without anyone to chaperone him? Wild horses wouldn't keep me away...

∞∞∞

Having spent the rest of the night in sleepless anxiety, I'm naturally not looking my best when Sebastian turns up the next morning – in a chauffeur driven *Sedan* no less. As the car slows to a stop, the Duke opens the door for an excited Coco to jump out. 'You're taking her with us?' I question as she capers around my feet.

He shakes his head. 'She's staying with Mum. Make yourself comfortable while I take her into the house.' Somehow, his use of the word Mum makes him seem a little more human. As he drags the reluctant dog away from her new favourite toy – me - I slide onto the luxurious leather seat and smile through the glass at Jamie, the driver.

Seconds later Sebastian re-appears and slides in opposite me. 'Very nice,' I murmur bouncing a little on the seat.

He gives an almost embarrassed smile. 'I don't use it often. But the thought of driving in London traffic.' He shrugs, adding, 'We'll need to brief your uncle.'

'About that...' I pause and cough slightly. 'I should warn you that the Admiral is a bit of a loose cannon. I wouldn't trust him as far as I can throw him.'

'He's untrustworthy?' Sebastian frowns, and I hurry to explain.

'Not exactly. It's just that he follows a different set of rules to the rest of us. His ability to go off half-cocked is legendary - spontaneous, half-baked schemes are his speciality. He's reckless, thoughtless and prone to putting his foot in it. Need I go on?'

'I think I've got the picture,' he returns drily.

'As long as you keep him on a short rein, I'm certain he'll be fine. But whatever you do, don't let him go off on his own.'

'I'll pick up a lead on the way.'

We sit the rest of the way to the Admiralty in silence, and I wonder if I've done my uncle a disservice. Perhaps I should have allowed the Duke to form his own opinions. Then I think back to the stories Tory has told me - even overlooking my own experience of the Admiral's *help* - and shudder. I can't allow Sebastian to bring the ticking time bomb along without some kind of warning. I watch with trepidation as the driver gets out to press the buzzer next to the gate.

A couple of minutes later, my uncle appears. 'Oh, hello, Teddy,' he puffs, climbing into the car. 'Wasn't expecting to see you here. Come for a bit of jaunt have you?' I smile sweetly at him through gritted teeth.

'You're very cheerful for so early in the morning, Uncle Charlie? How's Mabel?'

He creases his brow in thought as though I've asked him the winning question on *Who Wants to be a Millionaire*. 'I haven't asked her,' he answers at length.

The Duke gives a small cough. 'Thank you for coming today, Admiral. It's very good of you to spare the time.'

'My pleasure,' the Admiral returns before suddenly leaning forward and tapping on the window separating us from the driver. 'Turn right up here my good man.' He looks back at the Duke who's regarding him in bemused silence. 'We just need to pick up Jimmy. It won't take a minute.'

To his credit, Sebastian doesn't actually lose his temper at the knowledge that the Admiral has invited a complete stranger along, and when I hurriedly explain who Jimmy is, he merely gives a small, *what the bloody hell have I done*, sigh. I wince in sympathy.

By the time we've collected Jimmy and the small man has made himself comfortable, it's nearing eight o'clock and we still have to go back over on the ferry. 'At this rate, we'll reach Kew by about midnight,' Sebastian mutters under his breath.

'So, what exactly is it we're looking for and why?' the Admiral demands when we're finally en route to the A38. I really hope the Duke didn't spot the broad wink he gave his partner in crime seconds earlier.

For a moment, I think Sebastian isn't going to answer, then with another sigh, he brings both men up to speed. I'm actually surprised he doesn't hold anything back.

'So you're saying we're related,' the Admiral gloats delightedly. My heart sinks as I think back to Tory's insistence her father never got wind of the connection.

'By marriage, it seems,' Sebastian clarifies. Of course the distinction doesn't even register with my uncle who's likely already wondering if there might be a title in the offing.

After another gleeful chuckle, the Admiral comments, 'What a cake and arse party. It's a bloody good job you've asked for our help lad. Old Teddy's good at her job, but between you and me, she's a bit of a social hand grenade.'

My sour comment of, 'I'm right here,' goes straight over his head, so I grit my teeth and close my eyes. Less than five minutes later, I'm asleep.

We finally reach the *National Archive* building just after lunch. Fortunately we only had to stop once on the journey when my uncle announced he was so desperate for a pee his back teeth were floating. Sebastian also supplied a picnic reminiscent of *Brideshead Revisited*, so we're all actually quite cheerful by the time we arrive.

I visited the *National Archives* on several occasions in my previous life, but never had occasion to view any of the naval records. As we walk into the document reading room, a sudden excitement grips me. The discussion in the car brought home to me that these records are about my family too.

The room is very busy – obviously being a Saturday. However, I suspect that not many of the groups busy looking through the archives can boast either a Duke or an Admiral in their party, and I know my uncle at least will be entirely shameless about name dropping.

I'm absolutely right, and ten minutes later we're sitting in a small private room with a jovial chap called Rupert assigned to assist us.

'Right then,' the Admiral states. 'We're looking for everything you have on HMS *Temeraire* and her Captain - Nicholas Sinclair between the dates of ...' He pauses looking at the Duke enquiringly.

'Let's start with 1804 to 1806,' Sebastian suggests. The Admiral looks back at our researcher.

'You heard his grace. We want despatches, reports of proceedings, letters in and out. That should do for a start.'

'Err, you do realise that's likely to fill half of this room,' Rupert stammers

'Well, you'd better get started then.' I wince at the Admiral's high-handed manner and suddenly realise he must have been a force to reckon with in his day.

'Thank you, Rupert,' the Duke adds drily, soothing any ruffled feathers.

An hour later, the boxes are stacked high, and we've discovered that Nicholas Sinclair took over as Captain of *Temeraire* in 1803 and was ordered to report to the Channel fleet. In 1805, he apparently joined Nelson's blockade of the Franco-Spanish fleet in Cadiz and was part of the chase across the Atlantic to the West Indies and back which ultimately ended in the Battle of Trafalgar on 21st October 1805.

There's an incredibly detailed description of the ship's actions during the battle, and we learn how Nicholas almost lost his leg and took several life-threatening injuries to his torso from flying shards of wood. Sebastian reads this part, and we're all silent for a few moments. Nicholas Sinclair has suddenly become a real, living breathing person. Not simply a name.

Finally, we turn to the last couple of boxes. *Letters In and Out*. According to the Admiral, these were mostly correspondences between the *Admiralty* in London and Captains and Lieutenants throughout the fleet, though at least some of them were personal. Obviously, the only letters we're interested in are those to and from Nicholas Sinclair.

As we all wade through the mounds of paper, many of them recording mundane things such as the cost of gunpowder and salt beef, I think we all begin to get a little desperate. It's nearly four p.m., and the Archive closes at five. The last thing we want is to have to come back tomorrow.

With only half an hour to go, Jimmy suddenly holds his letter up in the air with an uncharacteristic whoop. 'Look at this, your grace,' he grins.

We all watch as Sebastian takes hold of the document, scanning it quickly. When he looks up his face is wreathed in smiles.

'It's a letter informing Nicholas of the death of his father – the Seventh Duke of Blackmore and acknowledging his accession to the title.' Then he gives a small grimace. 'There's no mention of his twin brother.'

'Still, it indicates that Nicholas was the acknowledged inheritor,' I comment. 'That's got to be worth something.' He lays the document carefully to one side and we feverishly go back to our search.

Almost immediately, the Admiral turns up several letters of commendation which though interesting, contain nothing to help us.

Then at four forty-five I finally unearth what we're looking for.

Nicholas Sinclair's letter resigning his commission. In it, Nicholas sites both his injuries and his upcoming duty as the new Duke of Blackmore as the reason for his resignation.

Attached is a note from the Admiralty Dated 11th January 1806, referencing the forwarding of a missive from one Jacob Howells of Howells and Sons, solicitors in Exeter. Dipping excitedly back into the box, I finally discover the actual letter.

In a nutshell, it's an entreaty for Nicholas Sinclair to return home forthwith. Mr Howells expounds at length of the duties unfortunately thrust upon the new Duke *due to the unfortunate accidental death of his twin brother Peter in a riding accident when only fifteen.*

'That's it, we've nailed the strumpet,' the Admiral growls.

I couldn't have put it better myself.

Chapter Twenty-Two

We weren't allowed to take any of the documents away from the Archive, but they were photocopied and certified as genuine.

By the time the driver drops off my uncle and Jimmy, it's past nine p.m., and I've spent most of the journey asleep. As we approached Dartmouth, Sebastian finally turned into the Duke of Blackmore, absolutely forbidding both men to so much as breathe a word of our actions. His orders were clipped and to the point. Jimmy, of course, was quick with his assurance. The Admiral however, looked as though he was having a colonoscopy when he finally mumbled his guarantee to keep the whole matter to himself.

As we cross over on the ferry, I suddenly realise that except for fifteen minutes this morning, we're completely alone together for the first time since I left his bed. Sebastian is looking out of the window, watching the last rays of sunlight sink below the mouth of the river.

'What do you intend to do now?' I ask quietly. He turns to look at me.

'First thing on Monday morning, I'll return to London and personally hand over the letters to my solicitor. I'm hoping that will put the whole bloody business to bed permanently.' He gives a small frown which I can just about see in the gloom.

'What?' I ask without thinking.

'It's just … that drawing. Why did Carla take it, then bring it back? I didn't study it carefully, but on the face of it, there was nothing to further her patsy's claim.'

'Could the one she returned be a fake?' I ask. 'Perhaps there was something on the original drawing Carla didn't want you to see.'

The Duke nods slowly. 'That's the only thing that makes sense. While I'm in London, I'll ask my solicitor to have it checked.' He gives a tired shrug. 'Not that it will make much difference one way or another, but if my ex-wife has the real drawing, I'd like it back.'

We pull off the ferry, and five minutes later, the car is cruising up Warfleet Road towards his mother's house.

'I would offer you a nightcap,' I murmur impulsively, 'but I don't think your driver would appreciate it.'

He stares at me, and my heart gives a dull thud at the intentness of his scrutiny. Helplessly, I feel myself colour up. I'm not sure I'll ever get used to being around this man. Suddenly, I want the case over and done with. I desperately need to get on with my life, to somehow put Sebastian Sinclair behind me.

The car turns into the drive and comes to a stop. Hurriedly, I scramble out, only to turn round and discover he's followed me. I stand and watch as he bends towards the driver's window, suggesting Jamie grab a bite to eat in the town. He finishes by asking to be picked up at eleven. Then he straightens and looks at me, his whisky gaze inscrutable.

I'm vaguely aware of the car manoeuvring back out of the driveway, as I lead the way to the boathouse. Directly in front of us, the lights from Kingswear on the other side of the river have turned the Dart into a kaleidoscope of colours dancing in the ripples. It feels almost surreal, as though we've stepped through a portal into another world. 'Would you prefer to sit outside?' I murmur as I turn the key in the lock. Abruptly, I feel the heat of him behind me and stop.

'Why can't I get you out of my head?' he whispers, his breath a soft caress on the back of my neck. I feel an answering throb, deep down in my core. Dropping my bag, I turn to face him, my breasts almost brushing his chest. I don't speak, just lift my hands and slide my fingers around the nape of his neck, letting the tips caress the soft hair above his collar. I only have to lift my head slightly to see into his eyes, and my heart slams against my ribs at the desire in them. Wordlessly, I give a slight tug. That's all it takes to pull his head down, for him to cover my lips with his.

As he plunders my mouth, his hands grip me to him, pressing me against his hardness. Feverishly, I slip one hand inside his shirt, sliding it against his hot skin. The hardness of his chest, the smattering of hair awakens a need that won't be denied.

Impatiently, I feel behind me for the door handle. As the door opens, we stumble inside and somehow make it to the bed. Seconds later, he's pressing me into the mattress, our bodies fused together, skin to skin, every nerve ending alive with sensation. With a small moan, I rake my hands down his back and part my legs, wanting, *craving* the feel of him deep inside me. To forget everything but this desperate, aching need that only Sebastian can fulfil.

I stare into his eyes, heavy lidded and dark with desire as he accedes to my wishes. I watch as he lets out a small groan, eyes closing briefly at the exquisite sensation. For a second, he stills, and it's my turn to close my eyes as I savour the blissful feeling of fullness. And then he begins to move, and I cry out as he takes us both to a crescendo of pleasure that's so intense it's almost pain.

Great, heaving breaths rock us both as I stroke the cooling strands of his hair, relishing the feel of his naked weight on top of me. And this time, when he rolls onto his back, he takes me with him, pulling me into his side. He doesn't flinch when I lay my arm across his chest, but instead strokes it absently with his free hand.

Neither of us speak. There really isn't anything to say. But instead of the unease of last time, there's a sense of peace. I know he feels it too. I still have no idea whether Sebastian and I have a future together. At the end of the day we come from different worlds, but I'm finally okay with it. I'm prepared to accept whatever he has to give for as long as he can give it.

∞∞∞

'I've been thinking, Jimmy.' The two men are in the *Ship* having a crafty pre-Sunday lunch Yorkshire pudding whilst discussing their findings of the day before. 'What was Carla doing with that drawing – you know the one of the church? The Duke reckoned she must have taken it earlier. But why would she bring the bloody thing back?'

Jimmy gave a thoughtful frown. 'Do you think the one she returned was bogus, Sir?'

'That's exactly what I'm thinking, lad. Now since she's got no bloody idea that our Nicholas Sinclair was a hero in the Royal Navy, that drawing must have been important. There has to have been something in it or on it that she didn't want her ex-husband to see. Something that completely quashes Jeremy Sinclair's claim.' The Admiral taps his nose, before dipping a bit of Yorkshire pudding in some gravy for Pickles.

'I think you're probably right, Sir, but it doesn't really matter, does it? I mean since we discovered the letters yesterday.'

'That depends on whether his grace wants the real drawing back.'

'Well, I can't imagine his ex-wife coming clean about having it, so I reckon the picture's likely gone forever.'

Unless we go and collect it ...' Jimmy looks at the Admiral's perfectly serious face.

'You want us to go up to London and knock on Carla's front door and demand the Duke of Blackmore's real drawing back?'

'Well, I wasn't thinking of *asking* her exactly.'

'We don't know where she lives,' Jimmy countered desperately.

'We do actually. There was a picture of her coming out of her pad in Islington a couple of days ago. I could see a sign up on the wall. It said *5, Borough Mews*. It didn't look a very big place, so it won't take long.'

'I'm really not sure this is a good idea,' Sir,' Jimmy declared with as much authority as he could muster.

The Admiral looked at the small man tetchily. 'Sometimes Jimmy, you're as wet as a bloody otter's pocket.' He speared his last piece of Yorkshire pudding before adding, 'I thought we could have a shufti at some diamonds while we're at it. Have a look to see if we can find Mabel a rock that doesn't cost me the same as a small bollocking country.'

'I doubt you'll find a bargain in London, Sir,' Jimmy scoffed.

'That's as may be Jimmy lad, but as my best man, it's your job to bloody well find me one.'

∞∞∞

I lie for a couple of minutes completely disorientated. The sun is shining through the edge of the window blind casting two shafts of light onto the bed. One of them shining directly onto my face is what woke me. For a second, I wonder what's different, then I notice the soft snoring coming from the left of me. Sebastian.

Unbelievably he asked if he could stay the night – with me. When did I fall down the bloody rabbit hole?

Turning over onto my side, I stare at his sleeping features. He looks much younger, and I can't help but notice the silver stubble of his beard is losing its sharp definition, making him look less like he just stepped out of the pages of *Hello*. I think back to last night. To his hesitant request to stay. The seriousness of his gaze told me he couldn't promise me anything, but I said yes anyway. Seconds later he told Jamie to go home, and it was too late to wonder whether I'd made a mistake.

We made love three more times before we both fell into an exhausted sleep. In between, he asked me what it was like being brought up in Japan, and I asked him was it was like to grow up with a silver spoon in his mouth. It's strange really, despite the dissimilarities of our childhood years, we had one thing in common. Loneliness.

I suddenly realise his beautiful brandy-coloured eyes are open and he's regarding me sleepily. I recognise the exact second he actually *sees* me. His eyes darken and he reaches out to gently thumb my nipple. I stifle a gasp as the sudden sensation slams between my legs, then he reaches for me, and I stop thinking altogether.

It's practically lunch time before we finally get up. I can't actually remember the last time I stayed in bed after nine. I make us both some toast and coffee, then, '*Coco!*' I gasp, suddenly remembering the collie is still with Sebastian's mother. 'How could we have forgotten about her?'

'I think we were otherwise occupied,' he responds drily. 'Don't worry, my mother wasn't expecting me to collect her last night. She's usually in bed by eight thirty with re-runs of *Inspector*

Morse, Coco apparently adores *Lewis*.

'Should I be jealous?'

He chuckles. 'I can't actually remember her fawning over anybody in quite the same way as you.' He pauses, then adds. 'She hated Carla, and the feeling was definitely mutual.'

'Impeccable taste, obviously,' I deadpan.

'Do you fancy taking her for a walk up to the Castle?' he asks. I shove down the ridiculous delight that swamps me at his suggestion.

'What will Mrs. S. say if you turn up to collect Coco without a car?'

'She won't even ask. And anyway, it's none of her business – in exactly the same way it's none of mine that she's bonking her solicitor.'

I can't help it, I grin. 'Bloody hell, that was embarrassing,' I recall.

He laughs. 'I never visit on a Tuesday afternoon.' Then, popping the last piece of toast in his mouth, he climbs to his feet. 'If you don't mind I'll use your shower, then go and pay a call on my mother.'

'Will you tell her what we found at Kew?' I ask, handing him a towel.

'I'll let her know we think we've put Jeremy Sinclair's nose out of joint,' he answers, 'but I'll keep the rest of the sordid details from her until after I've spoken with my solicitor. I wouldn't put it past my mother to give Carla a very public punch on the nose which would undoubtedly go down a storm with the tabloids ...'

By two p.m. we're walking a delighted Coco along the road towards Dartmouth Castle. Everything feels very odd, as though I'm participating in a dream. I've actually never done this before

– ever.

It's another beautiful June day and there are lots of cars parked along Castle Road. Sebastian turns off onto a footpath signposted *Gallants Bower*. Once we're away from the road and walking along a wooded path, he unclips Coco's lead. I can't help but smile as she dashes backwards and forwards through the carpet of bluebells still covering the forested hillside. To our left are glimpses of the River Dart though the trees as the path begins to rise steeply. I have to say I'm puffing a bit as Sebastian gives me a brief history lesson about the earthworks of an English Civil War fort that ring the top of the hill.

'This isn't the Castle then?' I wheeze, sitting down to get my breath back.

He grins at me, shakes his head and points back towards the river. 'The Castle's that way. Not far now.'

'You've taken me the bloody long way haven't you,' I accuse as we start our descent through the trees.

'I didn't think you'd want to walk along the road with all the cars,' he answers.

And he's right. The views of the estuary and beyond are amazing and the bluebell covered woods are a delight.

At length we drop back onto the road and walk the last few yards to Dartmouth Castle. Perched on a rocky outcrop at the mouth of the river, the castle is almost surrounded by the sparkling waters of the estuary.

Casually putting his arm around me, Sebastian points out the World War II gun shelter below us, and above it, St. Lawrence's Tower – a Napoleonic lookout. 'I wonder if Nicholas Sinclair was ever here,' I muse, savouring in the feel of his body so close to mine.

Across the river is Kingswear Castle. The two would have

guarded the entrance to the estuary once upon a time, though according to my guide, Kingswear Castle is now a holiday cottage. I imagine what it would be like to stay there with him and Coco. Just the three of us.

After investigating the castle's gun tower, winding passages and climbing to the top of the battlements, we indulge in a delightful cream tea in the Castle tea rooms.

'Are you a jam and cream person or a cream and jam?' I quip as they bring over the scones.

'Cream and jam all the way,' he grins. I'm a true Devonian.'

'Cornish way for me,' I respond. 'How the hell do you put jam over the top of all that cream? It offends my sense of neatness.'

'Finicky, with rebellious Cornish leanings,' he retorts. 'I'll make a note.'

As we eat, he finally asks me about my time in the NCA. My replies are guarded, but I think he gets the gist.

'So basically you weren't the flavour of the month,' he comments as I trail off.

'Not even the decade,' I answer drily, bending down to give Coco a fuss.

'So, why did you lose your job?' My head snaps up. His gaze is enquiring but there's no challenge in his eyes. He's curious, no more.

'I was too eager to nail the bad guy,' I sigh at length. 'Forgot my priorities for a little while. Since I was about as popular as a dose of syphilis, it was just the excuse they needed to be rid of me.'

'Their loss is my mother's gain,' he banters. I raise my eyebrows doubtfully, before popping the last piece of scone in my mouth. He does the same and my heart stutters a little as he glances down at his watch. 'Do you want to have a look round the church?' I nod - anything to stretch it out a little longer.

Climbing to my feet, I walk over to lean on the castle wall and drink in the view. I really don't want the day to end. I stare over the river, past Kingswear to the far right of the headland, and as Sebastian joins me, I point out what I think is Noah and Tory's house. 'It's Edwardian and absolutely beautiful,' I murmur. 'I think you'd love it.'

He doesn't answer and I glance over at him enquiringly, only to see his face closed and withdrawn. My heart sinks and I know our interlude is nearly over.

He doesn't speak as we walk over to the small church of St. Petrox, nestling into the edge of the cliff and I swallow my disappointment when he leaves me to explore on my own while he waits outside the churchyard with Coco. Although interesting, the pleasure has gone out of the day, and I'm not surprised when on my return he tells me quietly that he's called Jamie and the driver will be picking him up in an hour.

Time to return to the real world.

Chapter Twenty-Three

'I'm going to bite the bullet and send a formal invitation to Sebastian Sinclair,' Tory declared. 'Do you think that's terribly sycophantic?'

'Bloody hell, that's a big word,' Noah teased. 'Don't you be forgettin' I'm jus' a good ol' country boy, darlin'.'

Tory tossed him a droll look before continuing, 'I mean he *is* practically family,' she mused, chewing the end of her pen thoughtfully.

'That's a disgusting habit, hon,' Noah retorted, bending down to kiss her head. 'You can't be toadying to members of British aristocracy with chewed up pens lying all over the place.'

'I'll say Dotty got hold of it.'

Noah laughed out loud. 'Dotty wouldn't demean herself by chewing on anything that doesn't have any calories.'

Hearing her name mentioned, the little dog lifted her head and gave a hopeful wag of her tail. When nothing tasty appeared, she gave a doggy sigh and rested her head back on her paws.

'Have you spoken to Kit about the fancy dress party?'

Tory snorted. 'I'm certain you've already made it quite clear to Jason that to ensure your continued harmonious existence with your hormonal other half, he is, under pain of death, not to refuse the invitation.'

She looked over at Noah's grinning face and added, 'Mind you, Kit did tell me she'd consign Jason to the spare room if he said they couldn't come.'

Noah winced. 'The poor guy's been out manoeuvred. I doubt he'll take it well.'

'It'll do them good to have a nice relaxing weekend down in here.'

'Because of course Dartmouth is so quiet and tranquil during the summer months,' Noah scoffed.

'You love the buzz of Dartmouth in the summer. Besides, you know you're just dying to show Jason your Batman costume.'

'How dare you mock the Caped Crusader.'

'Darling, that Batman suit is thick rubber. You'll be sweating your nuts off within ten minutes.'

'We actors are made of sterner stuff. And besides it's the only way I'll ever get to be the Dark Knight.' Noah gave a dramatic sigh.

'You're still sore they chose *Robert Pattinson* over you. Poor baby.'

'I would have made a great Batman,'

'The director said you were too pretty as I recall. Anyway, talking of pretty faces, did you sense anything between Teddy and our drop-dead gorgeous Duke?'

Noah frowned and shrugged. 'Just that Teddy didn't look comfortable.'

'Teddy never looks comfortable. Didn't you notice the way he looked at her?'

'Can't say I did, honey.'

'You know for an actor, you're not very observant.'

'I'm also a man, so by default I'm not very observant. You think there's something between them?'

'I'm not sure, but it'll be fun to invite them both and watch to see if there are any fireworks …'

∞∞∞

'I'll let you know what happens tomorrow.' I nod, trying for a smile as we stand awkwardly at the door to the boathouse.

'What will you do about Carla?' I can't resist asking. 'The evidence we found yesterday won't prove she put Jeremy Sinclair up to the whole thing.'

The Duke shrugs. 'Unless Sinclair points the finger, nothing at all. My hope is she'll chalk it up to experience and move on.'

'Don't take on a powerful Duke and hope to win,' I joke.

He raises his eyebrows, regarding me quizzically. 'As I recall, our success has had nothing to do with my influence, and everything to do with your determination.'

I give a light laugh. 'Dogged is the word you're looking for I think. It was one of the better ones used to describe me at the NCA.'

He stands and stares at me for a second as though he's committing my face to memory. A sudden cold terror grips me.

'Thank you, Teddy, for everything,' he murmurs, stepping forward to press a light kiss on my cheek.

I step backwards, giving a small cough to hold back the tears. 'You're welcome,' I manage gruffly. 'Now your little problem's sorted, I can turn my attention to the missing body in Sandquay Woods.'

He gives a soft laugh. 'Mr. Parkinson must be quaking in his boots, and if he isn't, he should be.'

I bend down to give Coco a last fuss. I can't bear the thought that I might never see her again. 'Be good sweetie,' I mumble into her soft fur. Her answer naturally is to jump up and plant a resounding lick on my nose and I straighten, laughing. 'Take care, Sebastian …' I pause before blurting in a rush, 'Don't forget to let me know what happens.'

He nods without speaking, then turns to walk up to the driveway. He doesn't look back, but at least I have the satisfaction of watching him having to drag Coco away …

∞∞∞

'What excuse did you give to Mabel?' Jimmy asked when they finally climbed onto the London train at Totnes.

'Told her I was off to get her a surprise,' the Admiral chuckled. 'What did you say to Emily?'

'Almost the same, word for word,' Jimmy responded with a wince. 'I hope they don't speak to each other today. We're both for the high jump if they do.'

'Couldn't you have thought of something a bit more original?' the Admiral grumbled.

'Like what, Sir? What excuse could I possibly give for going up to London again with you? We only went two days ago.'

'Nothing that wouldn't have 'em smelling a bloody big rodent,' Charles Shackleford agreed with a sigh. 'So where did you say you were going?'

'Exeter,' Jimmy answered.

'Same here.'

The two men stared at each other for a second, clearly running possible excuses through their heads. 'We've got plenty of time to come up with something,' the Admiral commented at length. 'And anyway, we're not talking total bollocks. Especially if we manage to find a ring for Mabel.' He paused before adding, 'We just need to keep schtum about the whole breaking and entering bit.'

'Provided we don't end up in prison,' Jimmy retorted sourly.

'Don't you worry yourself, Jimmy, lad. We're good at this. And it's not like we're going to pinch anything. Just get back that picture that wasn't hers in the bloody first place.'

'You try telling that to the police, Sir,' Jimmy muttered. 'Especially as it's not ours either.'

'Sometimes the end has to justify the means,' the Admiral responded grandiosely. 'Just think how happy his grace is going to be when we hand it back to him. He might even give me and Mabel a free dinner.'

Jimmy refrained from mentioning that less than a week ago, his former commanding officer was convinced the Duke was planning to arrange a nasty accident for his ex-wife. Instead, he sighed and leaned back against the back of his seat. With a bit of luck it would take them so long to find a diamond for Mabel, they wouldn't have time to indulge in a spot of robbery.

∞∞∞

Sebastian looked blindly out at the coastline as his train gathered speed towards Exeter. With a bit of luck he'd be in London before ten and at his solicitors by eleven. The photocopied documents they'd been allowed to take from the

National Archives were safely inside in his briefcase. He was hoping they'd be enough to ensure the challenge was quickly and quietly withdrawn.

Inevitably his thoughts turned to Teddy Shackleford. After Carla, he'd believed himself incapable of really loving someone, but almost from the very moment Teddy crashed into his life he'd been unable to get her out of his head.

Or his heart.

But if Carla found out about her? Sebastian closed his eyes. His ex-wife had shown her true colours very early on, but her recent attempts to see him brought to his knees, culminating in an attempt to actually have him stripped of his title… That spoke of a woman more than a little deranged. He couldn't prove Carla was behind the whole complicated business and as he'd told Teddy, it was his fervent hope that once she realised the scam was over, she'd dust herself down and finally move on.

But hatred didn't follow logical rules and thinking about the extraordinary lengths Carla had been prepared to go to see him brought down - that spoke of a deep abiding hatred that was unlikely to simply go away.

And first and foremost he had to protect the woman he'd so unexpectedly fallen in love with…

∞∞∞

'I give you very good deal, Sir!'

The diamond merchant hadn't got as far as salivating or rubbing his hands with glee, but he was leaning so close, the Admiral could count the number of hairs growing out a particularly large wart decorating the little man's top lip. He also suspected the merchant had been weaned on pickles.

However, despite his often-buffoonish behaviour (Emily's description), Charles Shackleford was actually very much more than a chinless wonder (also Emily's description). He straightened up, narrowed his eyes, pushed up his sleeves and said, 'How good ...?'

All in all, to Jimmy's despair, the whole transaction took less than half an hour, leaving them plenty of time to indulge in more than just a spot of breaking and entering.

'I must say I was a bit disappointed in your negotiating skills,' the Admiral commented when they finally got off the tube in Islington.

'In fairness, Sir, you didn't give me the chance to get a word in edgeways.'

'True, Jimmy my boy. But then it's difficult to hang back when one is automatically assumed to be the one in charge. It's not easy being the dog's bollocks you know.'

'Have you got a plan for when we get to Borough Mews, Sir?' Jimmy asked, thinking it prudent to change the subject. 'I mean we've only got until five before we have to be back in Paddington.'

'Well obviously first things first, we'll have to knock at the front door to ascertain if the subject is at home.'

'And if she is?'

'We run like buggery.' The Admiral stopped on the corner of a well to do narrow street. 'This looks like it, Jimmy. We'll have a bit of a shufti, see if we can find Number Five.' He set off determinedly down the street. After dithering for a couple of seconds, Jimmy followed.

'And if she's not in, Sir?' Charles Shackleford didn't answer, being too busy staring at a familiar tall, silver haired figure just about to knock on Number Five's door.

'What the bloody hell's he doing here?' the Admiral muttered. Jimmy followed the direction of the large man's gaze.

'That chap looks exactly like the Duke of Blackmore.'

'That's because it is,' the Admiral answered, darting behind a tree and dragging Jimmy with him. 'Could be he's after the picture, same as us.'

'Oh, that's alright then, Sir. Perhaps we should leave him to it.' Jimmy couldn't hide the relief in his voice, earning him an irritated look.

'Sometimes Jimmy, I swear you're as bloody spineless as a length of wet spaghetti. We can't just bugger off. He might need our help. Hang on – is that Carla answering the door?'

The two men watched as seconds later the Duke disappeared inside, the door slamming like a death knell behind him.

'I don't like this at all,' the Admiral mumbled after ten minutes had passed without the Duke reappearing. 'Come on, Jimmy.'

Without waiting to see if the small man followed, Charles Shackleford hurried up the street. He didn't know why, but all of a sudden he felt a sense of urgency the like of which he hadn't experienced since the disaster with Doris in Thailand all those years ago.

Pushing open the gate to Number Five, he bypassed the front door and crouched down under the small Georgian window to the left. Seconds later, Jimmy crawled up beside him. 'Are they in there, Sir?'

The Admiral rose up and peeped over the edge of the windowsill. After a moment he shook his head. 'Negative,' he muttered. 'Come on Jimmy, there's a passageway round the back. The two men crawled away from the window, only standing upright when they got to the narrow alley to the right of the front door.

'Do you think she's killed him?' Jimmy asked fearfully as they hurried through to the small back garden.

'Well, if she has, she's going to have her work cut out burying him out here.' The backyard was completely patioed over.

The Admiral tried the back door. It was locked. Then he peered through the kitchen window. The small room was empty. He was just about to turn back to Jimmy when he noticed one of the knives in a wooden block was missing. 'What a bloody cake and arse party,' he muttered, fear gripping him. 'Can you see anything through that window Jimmy?'

The small man shook his head. 'It looks like a dining room, but it's empty.'

'Right then, lad, we've got no choice ...'

'... Are we going to break in?'

'Don't be ridiculous, Jimmy. You're going to have to get through that window.' He pointed upwards to a small window halfway up the wall in between the ground and first floor, the top part of which was slightly open.

'I'm not sure I can squeeze through there, Sir.'

'Well I bloody well can't. Come on lad, there's a reason your nickname was *the Snake*.'

'They didn't call me that because I could squeeze through windows,' Jimmy blurted.

It wasn't often the Admiral was completely lost for words.

A sudden bang took them both by surprise.

'Bloody hell, I think she's shot him,' Charles Shackleford breathed. 'There's no time to lose.'

Hastily he took off his coat and wrapped it around his hand and arm. 'Stand back, Jimmy,' he ordered before striking his covered fist at the glass and punching straight through the Kitchen door.

Jimmy watched in admiration as the large man gingerly reached through the hole to unlock the door. He sometimes forgot the Admiral had been no mamby pamby officer.

The two men hurried through the kitchen and into the hall. The noises were coming from upstairs. Grabbing a large tray off a coffee table, the Admiral turned to Jimmy and put his finger across his lips. Then they tiptoed to the bottom of the stairs and looked up.

Sebastian Sinclair was holding onto his right arm with his left hand. Blood was seeping through his fingers.

'For God's sake Carla, you can't possibly think you'll get away with this.'

'Why not,' she spat, brandishing the gun in her hand. 'I'll say you hit me. Injuries are easy to fake. I acted in self-defence.'

'We can settle this amicably,' the Duke stated hoarsely, 'like two civilised human beings.'

'I don't think so.' Carla's face was twisted in hate as she raised the pistol.

With a yell, the Admiral abruptly charged up the stairs, holding his tray in front of him like a battering ram.

Carla's shot went wild as she swung towards the oncoming threat. Pointing the pistol she fired again. The bullet ricocheted off the tray and a second later she gave a cry and fell forward, dropping the gun. As if in slow motion, she toppled forwards towards the edge of the stairs. Sebastian jumped towards her, trying to grab her with his good arm, but he only managed to grasp the end of her cardigan. It wasn't enough to stop her momentum.

The Admiral dropped the tray and braced himself for the impact as she fell towards him. He grunted as she fell against him, but after wobbling for a couple of seconds, he managed to steady himself and sank to his knees, Carla's prone body in his arms.

'Call an ambulance, Jimmy,' he ordered huskily. 'Mabel's going to have my bollocking guts for garters if I get blood on this new shirt.'

Chapter Twenty-Four

The last thing I want to do this morning is drag myself out of bed and go to the office. But, in fairness what else am I going to do? I'm not actually sure if I've closed my eyes at all in the last sixteen hours, having spent it fruitlessly going over and over my last day with Sebastian.

My last day with Sebastian. It's actually a pretty good title for a book. Or maybe, *My last day with the Duke* would read better. Truthfully the whole bloody thing sounds as though it came out of the pages of a romance novel. I give a mirthless chuckle and force down a piece of toast, then grabbing a light sweater, I make my way down the steps to Warfleet Road.

It feels like a typical Monday. Overcast, with the threat of rain and I wonder if the recent spell of good weather is coming to an end. It seems fitting really. It's hard to believe I'm actually in this situation. Teddy Shackleford mourning an unrequited love – well, maybe not the unrequited bit – but definitely the falling in love bit.

It's only been a few weeks, but I've changed. My ex-colleagues would be gobsmacked. But as I've discovered to my cost, developing a soft side comes with a health warning.

I spend the entire walk wallowing in self-pity and by the time I reach the town, I'm ready to throw myself in the Dart. Fortunately, I opt for the local bakery and three large pain au chocolats instead.

When I finally push open the door to the office, Freddy is predictably sitting in the spare chair and without commenting, I hand him one of the warm pastries. He eyes me in concern.

'Are you okay?' Alex asks as I give him the second one. Clearly my bloodshot eyes and tangled hair speak volumes. Most men wouldn't notice, but when both of them are gay …

'Peachy,' I respond, dropping into my chair and taking a huge bite out of my pastry.

Since I updated Alex on the way back from Kew, both of them are completely up to speed with the investigation. But the rest of it? Well, to be fair, they just sit and wait, until at long last, I put my head in my hands and begin to cry. For the second time in my life.

Two hours later, I'm feeling a little better. I don't actually look better. In fact according to Freddy I could audition for a bit part in *The Walking Dead,* and while ordinarily he'd offer to take me to the pub, on this occasion he's more than happy to bring the alcohol to me.

Blowing my nose into the last but one paper hanky, my heart starts to pound as my phone suddenly rings. Realistically I know Sebastian won't have any news as yet, but the desperate desire to hear his voice – well let's just say I'm pathetic and leave it there.

But the voice on the other end is Mrs. Sinclair. At first I have trouble understanding what she's saying. Her words are garbled, and her voice is almost hysterical. Then I make out the words, *Sebastian* and *shot* and feel as though I'm about to throw up.

I'm not exactly sure how my uncle ended up hero of the hour. According to Mrs. Sinclair, Carla tried to kill Sebastian and the Admiral somehow thwarted her attempt. The incident apparently happened in Carla's London townhouse. All I could make out from my employer's jumbled explanation was that both Sebastian and Carla are in hospital. The Duke has a gunshot wound in his arm which is fortunately not serious, but his ex-wife is fighting for her life after being shot in the stomach. I can only imagine that Sebastian was there to request his drawing back or possibly trying to make peace. Why the Admiral was in Carla's house is anybody's guess.

Naturally, my instinct is to get to Sebastian as soon as possible. I even get as far as picking up the phone to order a taxi, but Alex gently puts his hand over mine and shakes his head. 'You'll just complicate matters by being there,' He murmurs. 'Mrs. S. said he's okay. It's not serious. But if his ex-wife dies … You can't get involved, Teddy.'

I swallow a sharp retort and snatch my hand away angrily. I know he's right. I have no claim on Sebastian and would likely be turned away from the hospital anyway. Shoving my hair away from my puffy face, I grit my teeth and determinedly get on with some work. There must be something happening in Dartmouth worth reporting - other than my uncle's bloody heroics.

But the most awful thing is - while I hope Carla survives, a very small part of me is saying she bloody well deserves everything she gets. Clearly, the old Teddy Shackleford hasn't entirely vanished from the face of the earth …

∞∞∞

'So, come on then, Teddy what are you going as?'

'You'll just have to wait and see.'

'Ha, you haven't got a clue have you?' Freddy is back to being annoying.

'I've got better things to do than think about a fancy dress party,'

I respond tartly. 'And anyway what are you going as?'

'Alex and I are going as Captain Kirk and Mr. Spock,' he retorts. 'But don't ask who's who.'

I raise my eyebrows. 'Well you know what they say about a man with big ears ...' Freddy preens himself. Clearly he's going as Mr. Spock. I repress a snigger and add, 'Now bugger off, I've got work to do. This month's paper's due out at the weekend.'

'Has the Admiral given you an exclusive yet?'

'You know very well he's not allowed to talk about it.' That much is true at least.

It's been over a month since the shooting and as far as I'm aware, Sebastian has made a full recovery and Carla is finally out of the woods. Despite being bombarded with questions from the national tabloids down, my uncle has firmly refused to speak about what happened. Especially since the whole episode appears to have brought up an earlier news story to do with a Thai prostitute. An internet search followed by a chat with Freddy surprisingly brought up very little, so I'm intending to corner my uncle about it at the earliest opportunity ... Freddy actually laughed when I told him I was going to talk to the Admiral about what happened - I think he might have since started a sweepstake.

I haven't seen anything of Sebastian. I had held out some hope that he would be coming to Tory and Noah's fancy dress party, but according to my cousin, he declined the invitation.

At least I know the claim on the Blackmore Dukedom has been withdrawn. Mrs. S. brought two bottles of fizz into the office and by the end of the day, all three of us were decidedly squiffy. Of Jeremy Sinclair, there's been no sign. And since the Duke has refused to press charges, the press have finally lost interest.

Despite my snappy response to Freddy's questioning, I have

actually given some thought to my costume. Naturally, my height makes Wonder Woman an obvious choice (I shied away from the idea of the jolly green giant – I do have some pride) but a boob tube and shorts really isn't me – and that's without taking my cellulite into consideration. So I think I'll stick with the whole Amazon warrior vibe. Gives a bit of a nod to WW without having to take my kit off. Win, win.

And I'm glad that Sebastian isn't going. No matter how much I long to see him, being close to him without being *close* to him really won't do anything to heal my aching heart. And standing on the side-lines, worshipping him from afar really isn't very Amazon warriorish.

I repeat this to myself several times during the next few days until eventually I almost believe it.

∞∞∞

The day of the party is dry and warm – perfect July weather. Tory has offered me a bed for the night, so I decide to go over early with my costume hidden away in a bag. Crossing over the river dressed like *Zena Warrior Princess* is not likely to add anything to either my self-esteem, or my reputation. Especially as I end up looking more like *Princess Fiona* from *Shrek* by the time I reach their house.

After answering the door, Tory immediately grabs my arm and drags me outside onto the patio where Kit and Jason Buchannan are enjoying the early evening sun along with Noah, Isaac and Dotty. The little dog gives an enthusiastic bark and dashes up towards me. My thoughts turn briefly to Coco, then I determinedly swallow the pain and pick her up, smiling brightly at the newcomers.

Kit immediately jumps up and folds us both in a warm hug. 'It's so lovely to see you again, Teddy, especially without the handcuffs.' Her delight seems totally genuine, and my false smile softens into something a little more authentic.

'I've hung up my handcuffs,' I respond ruefully, putting Dotty back down, just as Jason comes over to give me a hug of his own. As I succumb to the handsome Scot's embrace I can't help thinking, *bloody hell, I've never been hugged by so many people in my life.*

'I'm not sure I ever said thank you for saving us from my housekeeper's psychotic niece,' he murmurs, 'so, just in case, please accept my heartfelt belated gratitude.'

Ridiculously I feel myself start to redden but am saved from having to answer by a small hand pulling at my jeans. Looking down I see Isaac holding out a small *Paddington Bear*. 'Teddy,' he says, holding it out to me.

Unsure whether the three-year-old is actually cracking a joke, I laugh anyway and bend down to pick him up. Then pointing to myself, I say 'Aunty Teddy,' which he repeats solemnly while trying to stick *Paddington* up my nose.

I sit down with Isaac on my knee. This is the first time I've had any interaction with my sort of nephew, and for some reason I really don't want to blow it.

'How are you enjoying Dartmouth, Teddy?' Kit asks, sympathy evident in her voice.

Fighting my instinctive urge to close up, I begin taking *Paddington's* coat off on Isaac's instruction. At length I murmur, 'It's nice. The pace of life is much slower than London.'

'Just a bit,' Kit laughs. 'But if you think it's slow here, you should come up to Loch Long.'

'How's the hotel going,' I ask, genuinely curious.

'The exact opposite of slow,' Jason comments drily. 'I wouldn't mind having a chat with your Duke sometime about Blackmore Grange. He's had the kind of success the rest of us can only dream about.'

I swallow the urge to say, 'he's not *my* Duke,' and instead find myself saying, 'I'm certain he'd be happy to speak with you.' Of course I don't know anything of the sort. I wince internally and busy myself putting *Paddington's* coat back on again.

'I'm glad to hear the whole succession problem's gone away,' Noah comments, handing me a welcome glass of wine. 'I hear his grace is giving you the credit for debunking the guy's claims. Way to go Teddy.'

'I did read something about a challenge to his title being discredited,' Jason responds. 'There was quite a large piece about his ancestor being Captain of HMS *Temeraire*. Nicholas Sinclair's a bit of a legend in naval circles due to his heroics at Trafalgar. I didn't know you were involved.'

'Teddy might have hung up her handcuffs, but she's not been loafing around doing nothing,' Tory chimes in. 'Is it okay to tell Kit and Jason about our attic adventure, Teddy? I've been dying to tell them we might well have blue blood.'

Kit gives a snigger of disbelief.

'No taking the piss, Kitty Kat or I may be forced to end our friendship now I'm possibly related to royalty.'

'Royalty?' I frown. 'Where did you get that from.'

'Her head,' Noah grins.

'So, spill,' Kit orders. Tory looks over at me enquiringly.

I give a small shrug, seeing no harm in it. I know that she won't divulge what she knows about Carla. 'We also found a little bit more about Blackmore in your Reverend's time,' I add. 'Nothing about any *Royal marriage* before you get your hopes up. There was a box of bits and pieces from the Red Lion pub. I'll have Alex check with Sebastian, but I'm sure he won't mind you having a rummage. There are a few letters that look to have been written by the old Reverend's curate.'

'Ooh, fascinating,' Tory enthuses. 'I'll ask Sebastian when he gets here.'

When he gets here?

'I thought he wasn't coming,' I comment carefully.

'Oh, didn't I mention it? Tory frowns, then shrugs. 'I must have forgotten.' I faintly hear the doorbell ring and my cousin jumps to her feet. 'That must be him now.' She turns to Kit and Jason and drawls in her best plummy accent, 'Do try not to be too uncouth, darlings.' I vaguely register Kit's response which is about as uncouth as they come, but for the moment can't get past *That must be him now.*

I carefully put Isaac back down on the floor and wait, my heart banging against my ribs. A minute later I watch as Noah, Kit and Jason get to their feet. I know the minute Sebastian steps through the door and I finally force myself to rise and turn to face the man who's haunted my dreams since the day I bumped into him in Paddington station.

I stand awkwardly as Noah makes the introductions, until finally Sebastian turns to me. 'How are you feeling your grace?' I manage, grateful that my voice sounds almost normal.

I note with satisfaction his wince at my use of his title. Petty, me?

'I'm well, thank you.' His deep voice does something to my insides and all of a sudden I want to burst into tears again. Why the bloody hell has he decided to come? I'm conscious that everyone is regarding us curiously.

'Have you brought Coco?' I ask, looking behind him as if I expect the dog to appear.

'She's with my mother,' he answers. Then, 'I wanted to see you.'

I have time to register that his voice is slightly hoarse, when abruptly Tory yells, 'Kit, Jason, I could really do with your help in the kitchen. Noah, can you bring Isaac?' Seconds later the patio is empty apart from Dotty who's finishing off Isaac's potted beef sandwich.

'I got the drawing back.'

'Do you know why she took it?'

He gives a small chuckle. 'If we'd seen it, Jeremy Sinclair wouldn't have had a leg to stand on. There's a family tree on the back. I think Grace did it when the old church burned down. It clearly states that she married the Eighth Duke of Blackmore on the 20th of April 1806.

They had three children. The first was Peter, then came Jennifer and lastly Nicholas. It was the Nicholas connection that Carla tried to alter. The birth certificates provided were perfectly legitimate. But they were the heirs of the *third* son of the Eighth Duke.'

'That's wonderful,' I murmur, not knowing what else to say.

We stare silently at each other, until unexpectedly he sighs. 'I had a whole speech planned,' he murmurs, shaking his head, 'but now, all I can think is how much I've missed you.'

'I've missed you too.' My answer comes out in a whisper.

His dark, starkly handsome gaze almost takes my breath away and my heart begins pumping madly. Then suddenly, *ridiculously* the tears start to flow. And this time I don't try to stop them. With a low groan, he closes the gap between us and drags me into his arms. 'I love you, Teddy Shackleford,' he breathes into my neck. 'For God's sake tell me I'm not on my own.'

'You're not,' I manage before turning my face up to his and meeting his lips. He presses me to him as though he wants to fit me into his skin, his kiss almost harsh, demanding my complete and utter surrender.

But surrendering is not something I've ever been able to do. And for the briefest of seconds I want to pull away. To run from this *yearning* that threatens the whole identity I've painstakingly built over so many years.

Then abruptly, the fragile house of cards collapses, dissolving the last of my fear. I give myself to him fully, finally accepting that I'm loved. And even more astonishing - that I love in return.

Chapter Twenty-Five

'Have you got the ring, Jimmy?'

'You haven't proposed yet, Sir. You don't need to give me the ring until the wedding.'

'Oh, yes. Bloody hell, I've never been so nervous in my life. When I asked Celia to marry me, I think I had a bit more bottle.'

Jimmy refrained from mentioning that since the Admiral had been committing bigamy at the time, he'd really needed a bit of extra bottle.

'Right then, Jimmy lad, the Duke has given us that nice table in the corner. Before we sit down, can you make sure you move that statue a bit closer. You know, the one with the fig leaf covering his bits.' Jimmy nodded, helping the Admiral on with his tails.

'Then make sure the rest of 'em aren't too close. I don't want to be proposing to the whole bollocking restaurant ...'

It was Jimmy who eventually told the Duke about his former commanding officer's intended proposal. For some strange reason, the Admiral had been entirely unable to get his shit in one sock. It was so unlike him, that Jimmy finally decided to take matters into his own hands. Naturally he hadn't expected the Duke to give over the entire restaurant – and since the rest of the family attending had no idea Charles Shackleford had even bought a ring, the evening was likely to be a very memorable one.

Of course, Teddy Shackleford, as the Duke's plus one, was also in on the secret. But as an ex-copper, she could be relied upon to keep it to herself.

At nineteen thirty on the dot, the Admiral escorted Mabel down for pre-dinner drinks. 'This is lovely, Charlie,' she twittered excitedly, gazing around. 'It looks like the Sixteenth Chapel...'

By the time they were called through for dinner, Charles Shackleford had lost a little of his nervousness. It might have been because he was a seasoned campaigner after all said and done. It might also have been the three large gin and tonics he'd consumed on the trot.

The dinner of course was superb and by the time the cheese was served, everyone was more than a little mellow.

As the clock struck ten, Jimmy gave a small nod to Teddy, who gave a small nod to Sebastian, who gave a small nod to the head Sommelier. The champagne was brought out discreetly.

The Admiral cleared his throat and stood up. Mabel looked up at him in surprise. Putting out his hand and grabbing hold of the statue's conveniently placed fig leaf, Charles Shackleford slowly lowered himself onto one knee.

Gradually the chatter in the room faded.

'The Admiral cleared his throat again. 'The thing is, Mabel,' he began ...

'... Take hold of her hand,' hissed Jimmy.

The Admiral tossed him an ill-tempered look, but nevertheless grabbed hold of his paramour's hand. By this point Mabel was looking at him as though she suspected he'd had too much cheese.

'The thing is old girl, I reckon we've been rubbing along quite nicely since Noah took Victory off our hands. And ... well ... I think it's time we made it official ...' He hurriedly rummaged around in his jacket, casting a desperate look towards Jimmy before suddenly breathing a sigh of relief. As he brought the small box out of his pocket, the whole restaurant was watching avidly.

With a suaveness nobody would have believed him capable of, Admiral Shackleford flipped open the box, held it out to his beloved and said, 'Will you do me the honour of becoming my wife.'

The silence was absolute as everyone waited with bated breath for Mabel's answer.

After a few nail-biting seconds, the matron put on her glasses and inspected the ring in its nest. Then she gave a small nod towards Emily and regally held out her ring finger.

Seconds later the room erupted in cheers as Admiral Charles Shackleford and Mabel Pomfrey were finally, officially engaged.

Teddy looked over at Sebastian who was clapping and cheering with the rest of the room. The man she'd come to know over the last two months was nothing like the taciturn arrogant man she'd bumped into at Paddington station, and she realised she wasn't the same rude, antisocial woman. Truly she had never imagined she could ever be so happy.

She had no idea where her relationship with the Duke would go. The one thing she did know was that they hadn't even begun to tackle the hurdles that would undoubtedly stand in the way of their relationship. In less than two months she would actually be attending his fortieth birthday party as his significant other – she couldn't even begin to imagine what a bollock she'd likely make of that one ...

But those problems were for another day. Tonight was all about joy. And given that three months ago she didn't even know the meaning of the word, Teddy Shackleford was content to accept the gift, and simply enjoy it while it lasted.

THE END

The whole gang will return in Final Victory: Book 7 of The Dartmouth Diaries - to be released on 13th December 2024.

Author's Notes

Please accept my apologies for playing fast and loose with history.

HMS *Temeraire* really did exist and was immortalised in a painting by *Turner* at the end of her service.

She did indeed save HMS *Victory* from being boarded by the French ship *Redoubtable* and very much more besides - fully earning her the nickname of *The Fighting Temeraire*.

Her captain was not of course Nicholas Sinclair, but one *Eliab Harvey* – by all accounts a very colourful character and close friend of *Admiral Nelson*.

You can find out more about *The Fighting Temeraire* and *Captain Harvey* by copying and pasting the links below:

https://www.philipkallan.com/single-post/2019/09/02/the-fighting-temeraire

https://www.1805club.org/memorials/eliab-harvey#:~:text=Perhaps%20it%20is%20only%20right,great%20battle%20in%20October%201805.

As I've said in my previous books, if you ever find yourself in the Southwest of England, the beautiful yachting haven of Dartmouth in South Devon is well worth a visit. The pubs and restaurants I describe are real, and I've spent many a happy lunchtime/evening in each of them. If you'd like more information about Dartmouth and the surrounding areas, you can go to the following website for the Tourist Information Centre:

https://discoverdartmouth.com

Dartmouth Castle is also well worth a visit. The views are breath-taking, and the Castle tea rooms offer lovely snacks. The walk through the woods to Gallants Bower is truly beautiful, especially when the bluebells are in full bloom. For more information, you can either copy and paste link above, or have a look on the following websites:

https://www.english-heritage.org.uk/visit/places/dartmouth-castle/

https://www.southwestcoastpath.org.uk/walksdb/407/

And lastly, the Battle of Jutland as mentioned in the prologue really did take place on 31st May 1916. It was the largest sea battle in the First World War and there were many, many casualties. If you're interested you can read about the battle and the loss of HMS *Invincible* by copying and pasting the link below:

https://www.iwm.org.uk/history/what-was-the-battle-of-jutland

Keeping in Touch

Thank you so much for reading *A Shackleford Victory*, I really hope you enjoyed it.

As I mentioned earlier. *Book 7: Final Victory* will be released on 13th December 2024.

For any of you who'd like to connect, I'd really love to hear from you. Feel free to contact me via my facebook page: https://www.facebook.com/beverleywattsromanticcomedyauthor or my website: http://www.beverleywatts.com

For those of you who have read The Shackleford Sisters, I hope this book helps to put the family connection into context.

For those of you who haven't yet given the Shackleford Sisters a go but would like to know how the Duke of Blackmore came to marry a vicar's daughter, you can read Nicholas and Grace's story in *Grace - Book One of The Shackleford Sisters*.

Turn the page for a sneak peek...

Grace

....Reverend Augustus Shackleford's mission in life (aside from ensuring the collection box was suitably full every Sunday) was to secure advantageous marriages for each of his eight daughters. A tall order, given the fact that in the Reverend's opinion they didn't possess a single ladylike bone in the eight bodies they had between them. Quite where he would find a wealthy titled gentleman bottle headed enough to take any of them on remained a mystery and indeed was likely to test even his legendary resourcefulness.

....Grievously wounded at the Battle of Trafalgar, Nicholas Sinclair was only recently returned to Blackmore after receiving news of his estranged father's unexpected death. After an absence of twenty years, the new Duke was well aware it was his duty to marry and produce an heir as quickly as possible. However, tormented by recurring nightmares after his horrific experiences during the battle, Nicholas had no taste to brave the ton's marriage mart in search of a docile obedient wife.

.....Never in his wildest dreams did Reverend Shackleford envisage receiving an offer for his eldest daughter from the new Duke of Blackmore. Of course, the Reverend was well aware he was fudging it a bit in describing Grace as respectful, meek or dutiful, nevertheless, he could never have imagined that his eldest daughter's unruliness might end up ruining them all....

Prologue

The Reverend Augustus Shackleford rested his hands contentedly on his ample stomach and belched loudly, the stew he'd just consumed resting a trifle heavily on his stomach. It was noon at the Red Lion Pub in the village of Blackmore in Devonshire, England, and while he could have quite easily have had his luncheon back at the vicarage, the Reverend much preferred the ale and conversation the pub provided as opposed to the never-ending arguing and bickering that came with the unfortunate position of having nine females residing in his house. Though he'd never asked him, the Reverend was content that his dog Freddy was also of the same opinion. The foxhound was currently curled up under the table, happily chasing rabbits in his dreams.

Reverend Shackleford was not a man of immense wealth and fortune, and under normal circumstances would be quite content with the fact that the coin in his pocket would more than suffice the cost of the meal he had just consumed.

These were not normal circumstances, however, and the coin in his pocket – or anywhere else for that matter, would certainly not be sufficient to provide the money to set up his only son in the manner befitting a gentleman.

His only son after eight daughters. The Reverend sighed. It had taken three wives to finally produce an heir, but the cost of paying for the eight females he'd been blessed with in the first instance was sorely testing even his creativity – something he'd prided himself on up until now.

He sat morosely staring into his pint of ale next to his long-suffering curate and only friend, Percy Noon.

"You know me Percy, I've got a mind as sharp as a well-creased cravat, but I've got to admit I'm completely nonplussed as to what to do to raise the coin."

"Perhaps you can find some kind of work for your daughters,

something suitable in polite society for ladies of a gentle disposition," Percy suggested as he pushed his tin plate aside.

The Reverend snorted. "Have you seen any of my daughters lately?" he scoffed, shaking his head glumly. "Ladies of a gentle disposition? They don't possess a single ladylike bone in the eight bodies they have between 'em. They have no clue how to follow orders or how to comport themselves in any society, let alone a polite one.

"If I wish to secure even a modest fortune for Anthony, then I have no recourse but to marry 'em off. Though I can't imagine a man who'd be foolish enough to encumber himself with any of 'em. Unless he was in his cups, of course." The Reverend was silent for a while, clearly imagining a scenario where he could take advantage of a well-heeled male whilst the unfortunate victim was suitably foxed. In the end, he sighed.

"Percy, the situation is dire indeed. If I don't come up with a plan soon, there's going to be no coin left for Anthony at all. And not only that, we could well find ourselves in the workhouse." He glared at Percy as if it was somehow all his curate's fault. "If that happens, Percy my man, there'll be no more bread-and-butter pudding for you of an evening. Percy repressed a shudder. He wasn't sure if it was at the prospect of ending up in the workhouse or the thought of Mrs. Tomlinson's bread and butter pudding – the last of which could probably have been used to shut out the drafts. The curate suspected the vicarage cook was a little too fond of Blue Ruin to give much attention to her culinary skills.

"Then your only recourse, Sir, is to marry them off and marry them well," he stated decisively, settling deeper into his chair. "Somehow."

The Reverend stroked his chin, thinking about his wayward daughters. Each daughter was entirely different than the last. The only similarity they all shared was unruliness. Four of them were already at a marriageable age, with the eldest, at twenty-five, a confirmed bluestocking. What chance did he have of marrying any of them off to a wealthy gentleman bacon-brained enough to secure a fortune for his only son?

He was sure that given time, he could do it. But it would test even his legendary resourcefulness. Especially if he was going to do it without spending any coin.

"Right, we'll need a list of suitable wealthy titled gentlemen bottle-headed enough to take 'em on Percy," he decided, motioning for another mug of ale. "Then we'll let 'em know that I have, err … good, dutiful daughters who are in need of husbands."

"As you wish, Sir," Percy said doubtfully as the serving wench brought another ale for them both. The Reverend picked up his tankard and took a large gulp.

"But before we do that, we'll start by writing down all the positive attributes of the chits so that we can emphasize their good points to any prospective husbands. I mean we both know that none of them are exactly bachelor fare, but we can fudge it a bit without anyone being the wiser. At least until they have a ring on their finger.

"We'll start with Grace since she's the one most likely to end up an old maid if we don't come up with the goods pretty sharpish. Right then, Percy, you start."

Silence.

The Reverend frowned. "Come on man, surely you can find something good to say about her."

'She has nicely turned ankles," responded Percy a bit desperately.

"Steady on Percy. I certainly hope you've never had an extended opportunity to observe my eldest daughter's ankles. Otherwise, I might have to call you out."

Percy reddened, flustered. "Oh no, Sir, not at all, I just happened to notice when she was climbing into the carria…"

"Humph, well I'm not sure we can put that at the top of the list, but in Grace's case, we might have to resort to it. I mean why her mother chose to call her Grace is beyond me, considering she's distinctly lacking in any attributes remotely divine-like. And she's the least graceful person I've ever come across. If there's something to trip over, Grace will find it. Clumsy doesn't even begin to cut it," he added gloomily.

"Well, she has very nice eyes," Percy stated, thinking it best to keep any further observations about the Reverend's daughter above the neck. "And her teeth are sound."

The Reverend nodded, scribbling furiously.

"Can she cook, Sir?" The Reverend stopped writing and frowned. "I don't know that she can, Percy. At least not in the same capacity as Mrs. Tomlinson."

"Probably best not to mention it then," Percy interrupted hastily, unwillingly conjuring up the vision of Mrs. Tomlinson's bread and butter pudding again. "And anyway, marriage to a gentleman is not likely to necessitate her venturing into the kitchen." The Reverend nodded thoughtfully.

"How about her voice? Can she sing?"

"Like a strangled cat."

"Dance?"

"I don't think she's ever danced with anyone. I deuced hope not anyway. If she has, I'll have his guts for garters."

"Conversation?" Percy was getting desperate.

"Nonexistent. I don't think she's spoken more than half a dozen words to me since she was in the crib." The Reverend was becoming increasingly despondent.

"Does she cut a good mother figure to her sisters?"

The Reverend snorted. "I don't think any of 'em are without some kind of scar where she's dropped 'em at some time or another."

"How about her brain?" Percy now resorted to clutching at straws.

"Now that's something the chit has got. Every time I see her, she's got her nose in a book. Problem is, that's the one attribute any well-heeled gentleman will most definitely not be looking for…"

Grace is available in ebook and paperback from Amazon.

Books Available on Amazon

The Dartmouth Diaries:

Book 1 - Claiming Victory
Book 2 - Sweet Victory
Book 3 - All for Victory
Book 4 - Chasing Victory
Book 5 - Lasting Victory
Book 6 - A Shackleford Victory
Book 7 - Final Victory to be released on 13th December 2024

The Shackleford Sisters

Book 1 - Grace
Book 2 - Temperance
Book 3 - Faith
Book 4 - Hope
Book 5 - Patience
Book 6 - Charity
Book 7 - Chastity
Book 8 - Prudence
Book 9 - Anthony

The Shackleford Legacies

Book 1 - Jennifer to be released on 20th June 2024

The Admiral Shackleford Mysteries

Book 1 - A Murderous Valentine
Book 2 - Murderous Marriage
Book 3 - A Murderous Season

Standalone Titles

An Officer and a Gentleman Wanted

About The Author

Beverley Watts

Beverley spent 8 years teaching English as a Foreign Language to International Military Students in Britannia Royal Naval College, the Royal Navy's premier officer training establishment in the UK. She says that in the whole 8 years there was never a dull moment and many of her wonderful experiences at the College were not only memorable but were most definitely 'the stuff of fiction.' Her debut novel An Officer And A Gentleman Wanted is very loosely based on her adventures at the College.

Beverley particularly enjoys writing books that make people laugh and currently she has two series of Romantic Comedies, both contemporary and historical, as well as a humorous cosy mystery series under her belt.

She lives with her husband in an apartment overlooking the sea on the beautiful English Riviera. Between them they have 3 adult children and two gorgeous grandchildren plus a menagerie of animals including 5 dogs - 3 Romanian rescues of indeterminate breed called Florence, Trixie, and Lizzie, a neurotic 'Chorkie' named Pepé and a 'Chichon" named Dotty who was the inspiration for Dotty in The Dartmouth Diaries.

You can find out more about Beverley's books at www.beverleywatts.com

Printed in Great Britain
by Amazon